Christmas 911

by

Lori Leger

This is a work of fiction. Names, characters, places, and incidents are either the product of the author's imagination or are used fictitiously, and any resemblance to actual persons living or dead, business establishments, events, or locales, is entirely coincidental.

Christmas 911

Cover Art by *Debbie Taylor*

The Wild Rose Press, Inc.
PO Box 708
Adams Basin, NY 14410-0708
Visit us at www.thewildrosepress.com

Publishing History
First Crimson Rose Edition, 2016
Print ISBN 978-1-5092-1264-4
Digital ISBN 978-1-5092-1265-1

Published in the United States of America

Cori released a long sigh

and adjusted her position to gaze at him.

He started to fidget under her intense stare. "What?"

"Why are you here, Luke?"

He pursed his mouth, struggling to find an answer that wouldn't scare the hell out of her. How could he explain the tightness he felt in his chest every time he watched the news story about the hostage situation and shooting of the deputy? How could he justify his uneasiness when Shawn Jackson's image appeared on the television screen?

How did he clarify the feeling he had that it wasn't over yet?

He couldn't. He wouldn't lay that kind of worry on her.

"Nobody should be alone on Christmas Eve," he said.

She picked up the phone a sheriff's deputy had returned to her earlier. "Technically, it's Christmas already."

"You shouldn't be alone on Christmas, either."

Praise for Lori Leger

"When Corrine Ritter makes a Christmas Eve stop for one last purchase on her way to her family, she's in for a terrifying surprise. Christmas 911 is a juxtaposition of down-home country heart and hometown values, mixed with an edge-of-your-seat-thriller. Leger is the master of the sweet love story, creating characters that make you want to scream, 'So kiss, already!' The story delivers a touching romance that arises from the midst of terror. It's nothing short of amazing how Leger develops this love story over a trio of phone calls and a few nights of heart pounding danger. You'll have to remind yourself to breathe during this page turner until its lovely, tissue-grabbing conclusion."

~*Kimberly Hornsby, Best Selling Author of*
The Dream Jumper series

Dedication

To the "BB" Book Club of Welsh, Louisiana:
Joan, Melissa, Dolores, Tina, Margaret, Lee,
Renee, Bridget, Sherrill, and Trish.
You gals are my first line of defense
against the perils of
typos, dropped threads, and poor plots.
~*~
Also to Kim Hornsby,
who talked me into writing a novella in two weeks.

Acknowledgments

Many thanks to Blair Fontenot for the info on firearms and ammunition.

And to my soul sister Arlene Vincent, and Kim Carter for info on transportation and booking processes of prisoners in the Jefferson County Courthouse in Beaumont, Texas. What I didn't use is in a file for future reference.

Chapter 1
911: Semi-Conscious

Corrine Ritter waved good-bye to her parents and pulled out onto the street, headed for home. She blew one last kiss to her mother's shout of "Drive carefully!"

The sight of her parents waving in her rearview mirror always left her with a lump in her throat. She hated living one state over, hated having to plan ahead for weeks to see them. She'd longed to stay one more night at her old home in Richmond, Texas, but needed to get home. She'd left her husband alone all weekend at their place in Sulphur, Louisiana…an easy two and a half hour drive, but apparently too inconvenient for Jim to make the effort to visit his in-laws more than once a year.

She sighed, thinking of her husband and the mess he'd undoubtedly left for her. God forbid the man place a dirty dish in the dishwasher or pick up after himself. He hadn't answered his phone all weekend, but then, he'd told her to expect that. After the long hours he'd been putting in at the university, he'd planned on vegging out all weekend in front of the TV set, catching up on some stuffy history channel programs he'd recorded.

An hour and a half later, she'd just finished a two part harmony with Trace Adkins when the tires of the semi in front of her picked up an object on I-10 and pitched it backward with the speed of a short-range missile. The nerve-jarring *pop* that preceded the shattering of her windshield had her ducking for cover. She gave the steering wheel an involuntary jerk and swerved out of control, nearly sideswiping the car in the left lane. Its accompanying horn blast put her back into her own lane, and she somehow managed to pull her car over to the shoulder without further catastrophe. Cori waited until her Camry rolled to a complete stop before releasing the breath she'd been holding.

She wiped one hand over her face while muttering a low "Sweet Jesus!" to no one in particular. A full five minutes later, she'd stopped shaking enough to dial 911 from her wireless phone. She'd been expecting a nasally feminine East Texas twang to answer. Not so. Her breath hitched at the masculine voice, oozing with all kinds of Sam Elliott sounding sexy bass. "911...What's your emergency?"

Hell yeah. She took a moment to collect her thoughts...a moment too long, obviously.

"911...What's your emergency?" sexy voice repeated.

Double hell yeah! She cleared her throat. "Oh, I'm sorry! I'm a little rattled. An eighteen-wheeler threw an object and shattered my windshield. I'm not sure exactly what I should do."

"Can you see enough to drive the vehicle, ma'am?"

She stared at the huge spider web of broken glass, with its concentrated center directly in front of her driver's side view. "No way. Especially not on I-10 Eastbound on a Sunday afternoon." A sexy low chuckle was her reward.

"Especially after a three-day weekend, at that,

right? Are you injured in any way, ma'am?"

Ugh...again with the ma'am. "Only my pride. And only when you call me ma'am," she added in a whisper she didn't think he'd hear. He proved her wrong with a second sexy-beast chuckle.

"What's your name, *Miss...*"

"Mrs., actually. Corrine...Corrine Ritter...but everyone calls me Cori. With an i..." She winced, imagining how stupid that must have sounded. What the hell was wrong with her? She didn't simper. She didn't flirt. Not even with strange, faceless men over a phone.

"Well, hello, Cori with an i. Did you happen to get a license plate of the object-throwing semi?"

"You're kidding, right?" she snorted.

"It was worth a shot. Did you happen to notice a company name or logo on the truck's tailgate?"

She passed a hand over her face. "Of course I didn't. That would make this too easy."

"Honestly, even if you had it would have been a longshot to get them to pay. There's not much I can do other than call an emergency glass service. We have a reliable go-to in this area for just such situations. They have a mobile unit on hand and can usually get there pretty quickly. Unless you have one specifically in mind?"

"No. I do have a Triple-A membership through our auto insurance company, though. I guess I should have called them first, huh?"

"Nah, Cori. You did just fine calling me."

She grinned at the personal touch he'd added, thankful he'd dropped the "with an i" thing.

"If you give me your Triple-A info and your

3

location, I can call both them and the glass company for you. It helps for verification."

She pulled cards from her wallet and rattled off the info he'd requested. "I don't remember what mile marker I passed last." She squinted ahead, searching for the green and white I-10 milepost marker. "And I don't see any in front of me."

"That's okay. I'll find you. Have you reached Ford Park yet?"

"No."

"How about South Major Drive?"

"Nope, not that far, yet."

"Okay, do you remember passing a big plant on the south side of the road? That would be on your right if you're headed eastbound."

"Yes! The Goodyear Plant, right?"

"That is correct! See? We're narrowing it down. Do you remember the last exit you passed?"

She concentrated. "Smith Road, maybe?"

"That's good enough. I'll tell 'em you're right around mile eight forty-four. Let me call that in for you right away. Give me the make and model of your car and is it okay if I put you on hold for a minute?"

"2008 Toyota Camry, and don't put me on hold unless it's necessary, please. The sound of your voice is reassuring and I'm alone out here."

"Whatever you want, Cori. I'm here to serve."

"You know my name. Is it against some rule to give me yours?"

"You can call me Luke."

"Thanks." The name, if it was his real name, fit the voice. She tried to imagine how a guy named Luke, whose voice dripped in hot fudge syrup with a splash of bourbon, would look.

Cori winced as another semi blasted past her in the right lane, the eighteen wheels and trailer shaking her car in its wake. Her head dropped forward and she attempted to ease the strain from her shoulders and neck. The sound of fingers tapping a keyboard, accompanied by the occasional verbal update told her Luke was doing his job.

"All done," he drawled after a few minutes. "I just got a confirmation and their ETA is ten minutes."

"Awesome! Thank you so much. I wonder how long it takes to replace a windshield."

"I'd say thirty minutes to an hour, but you'll have to wait another hour before the car is drivable. Is there any place you can go to wait it out?"

"I'm only passing through on my way home to Louisiana. The only friend I have in Beaumont is on a cruise right now. I don't want to leave my car alone out here."

"Understood. How about if I stay with you until you're good to go?"

"Stay with me?" she asked, slightly confused by the offer.

"On the phone of course, and I've requested that an available police cruiser park behind you with its lights on. You'll be less of a target."

Cori studied her reflection in the review mirror, arranged a stray lock of hair, dabbed at the smudged mascara under her eyes before realizing how ridiculous she was being. "Thank you so much, but don't you have to get back to your job?"

"I'm one of many dispatchers here today. As long as you're incapacitated, you are my job."

"Oh, here's the windshield repairman." She got out of her car and approached the man, keeping the phone to her ear.

The repairman shook his head at her windshield. "Yeah, he did a number on it, all right. I'm glad you didn't try to drive with it like that, Ma'am. You'll have to wait in my truck. You can't be inside the vehicle when I'm doing my job."

She nodded and began to gather any items to place in her purse for safekeeping. Despite her insistence that it was okay for Luke to get back to the business of dispatching, he remained on the phone with her.

Cori put her phone on speaker and set it on the dash while he kept her company. In no time at all, the windshield was changed. She signed the paperwork and waved to the officer in the cruiser just pulling up behind her car.

"Is he done?" Luke asked.

She scooted into her front seat and lowered the windows. "Yes, and he did a great job from the looks of it. He even managed to get the old one off without it shattering and dropping glass all over the place. In its condition, I'm surprised he avoided that." She checked the time on her phone. "Now I only have to sit here for another hour."

"I'll try to keep you from thinking about it."

Cori pulled her electronic reader from her purse. "I suppose I could let you go and catch up on some reading."

"Are you sure? I don't mind helping you pass the time. You're my responsibility until you're on your way again."

Cori stuffed her reader back into her purse. "I have

to admit it's comforting knowing you're on the line."

"Good, it's my job to make your situation better."

Cori looked into the mirror again, caught her smiling reflection, conscious of the sweet satisfaction flowing through her at the sound of his voice. He made it better all right. *Much...much...better...*

****

By the time Luke Oliver put the call to bed a full hour later, he knew more than the usual about Corrine Ritter. He knew she was married and he strongly suspected her husband was a selfish jerk of the academic kind. He knew they were trying to have a baby, but she was beginning to worry there was a problem. He'd begun to recognize the subtle nuances of her voice, could detect when she was about to tell him something funny, or sad, or disappointing.

He also sensed that if he ever came face to face with her, he'd be sorely tempted to take a long, serious, second look. Not wanting to cross that line, he'd refrained from calling up any kind of picture I.D. on her. Luke settled back into his chair, already chastising himself. Hell, it was bad enough he'd probably dream about that sexy little laugh of hers.

Just in time, he got a call. He flipped the switch on his headpiece and focused. "911. What's your emergency?"

Chapter 2
Bad News Comes in Threes

A week after the windshield incident, Cori sat in her OB/GYN's office, still trying to digest the bitter news she'd just received. "Are you telling me I can *never* get pregnant?" She leaned forward in the chair, gripped the edge of the desk with both hands.

Dr. Lin fidgeted in the tan leather executive chair then tapped her pen upon the mahogany surface several times. "I'm saying…" She paused, took a deep breath. "With your situation being what it is—the cysts, the uterine scarring from the surgeries, combined with your age—it's highly unlikely." Her mouth drew downward in a sympathetic pout. "It's not impossible, but the odds aren't in your favor. I'm sorry, Corinne. I wish I had something more positive for you." She clasped her hands in front of her. "It might be time to explore other channels."

"You mean in vitro fertilization?"

Dr. Lin pursed her lips. "Can I be honest with you?" She continued at Cori's nod of assent. "You could try IVF, but it's very expensive and even if the procedure works there's no guarantee you'll carry long enough to deliver a viable baby. I'm not saying it's impossible, mind you—but again, your odds aren't good." She took a deep breath and released it slowly, as though weighing her words carefully. "There's always surrogate pregnancy, and even adoption."

Cori swallowed the bile rising in her throat, refused to give in to the panic. From the day she had played with her first baby doll as a child, she had looked forward to having one of her own. Having another woman carry the child for her had never been a part of the fantasy. She wanted the experience of feeling her own baby growing within her. She wanted to be the one to nurture life from the moment of conception until birth.

Her gaze flicked from the wall graphic of a woman's reproductive system to the jar of cotton swabs sitting on the white Formica-topped surface of the counter. "I won't stop trying to conceive. I want my own child. Will you help me?"

Dr. Lin smiled and reached out, giving Cori's arm a gentle pat. "Of course I will. I'm not a fertility specialist, but I can put you in touch with one of the best in this part of the country. He's located in New Orleans, but I can work with him, and do what I can to monitor you between your trips to his office."

"New Orleans?" Cori perked up at the mention of the city. She and Jim had honeymooned in the Big Easy and had returned on several occasions. It had been some of the best times of their married life. They'd toured museums, cemeteries, and nearby plantations, taken supper cruises down the Mississippi on the riverboat Natchez, visited the Aquarium, took trolleys or walked all throughout the Garden District and French Quarter. Dr. Lin spoke again, interrupting her thoughts.

"Unless you'd like to do some research and find your own doctor?"

She looked up at the woman who'd been her

gynecologist since Cori had been a college student. "No. I trust your judgement."

"I'm glad to hear it. I have another suggestion if you're open to it. I'd like you to take a leave of absence from work if it's at all stressful. I believe all forms of stress can hinder conception. The calmer you are inwardly, the better chance you have."

All the way home, she thought about what a wonderful opportunity this could be for her and Jim. A New Orleans doctor—it had to be an omen, a positive sign of good things to come. Blessings sometimes began as heartbreaks in disguise. She would carry her own child.

She would.

****

Cori lit the last grouping of candles on the mantel and hid the lighter behind a picture. She faced the front door as the key turned in the lock. "Please let this go my way," she whispered under her breath as her husband pushed open the door.

Jim stood there for a moment, his gaze searching out every candle, every grouping of flowers, and every change in the room as the subtle sounds of smooth jazz surrounded them. He dropped his brief case at the door. "What's all this?"

"I just wanted to do things a little differently tonight, and to show you how much I love you."

He lifted his nose and sniffed. "Is that shrimp fettucine I smell? I'm starving."

She sauntered over to her husband. Her black stilettos put her nearly eye level to him. "I'm sure you are, and there'll be plenty of time for food later. I'm starving for something else right now." She pushed down the straps of her little black dress and let it fall to the floor, revealing the sexiest black bra and matching barely-there panties she owned. His groan of appreciation had her smiling. "Think you can hold out for that meal a while longer?"

He reached around, placed his hands on her bare butt cheeks thanks to the piece of floss running between them, and pulled her closer. "I believe so. Are we celebrating something specific?"

Cori kissed his neck, and smiled again when he sucked in his breath at her gentle nip to his jaw. She grabbed his belt buckle and pivoted, pulling him slowly behind her toward the bedroom.

****

She lay there, sexually sated and trying to catch her breath.

He lay beside her, still breathing hard. "That was the best sex we've had in months." Finally revived, he pushed himself up to a seated position. "Now, tell me. Are we celebrating? Please tell me you're finally pregnant."

She took several more deep breaths and sat up next to him. "Well…not yet. But we will be soon, I just know it." Her stomach made a sudden lurch at the look of disappointment on his face. "No! Don't be like that. She's sending me to a fertility specialist in New Orleans. New Orleans, Jim, where we spent our honeymoon. Don't you think that's a good sign?"

"What did your doctor tell you today?" All trace of tenderness vanished from his visage as well as his voice. "I want to know, word for word. Don't make me call her myself."

The sharpness of his last words stung her. "Why

would you say that? I always tell you what she says."

"Do you?"

"Yes, I do."

"What did she say?"

"That my chances of conceiving were slim, and even if I did, I may not carry to full term. She also said it's not impossible. She suggested I even take a leave of absence from work to drop the stress level during the process."

Jim's face darkened. "Less money in our bank account will make my stress level rise considerably."

"But you're not the one trying to conceive, are you? Besides, we can live off your paycheck for a while. We have enough in savings—"

"That savings is for my trip to Europe!"

"Don't you think it's worth sacrificing *our* European trip to conceive *our* child?"

His gaze hardened. "Not unless it's a sure bet. Besides, I'm getting a new SUV in a few months."

She felt her mouth tighten in a grim line. "You know, there's no law that says you *have* to trade in your car every two years. Mine's been paid off for three years already and I'm still driving it."

"I like driving a new model every two years."

"I know. Just as you like ordering five hundred bucks worth of expensive scotch and wine every month."

"That's my reward for kicking cigarettes."

"You were supposed to quit smoking to save money for the European trip, for which you haven't contributed a dime. You spend twice the amount on alcohol as you did on tobacco. Where's your common sense, Jim?"

He pushed off from the bed and assumed his most stubborn stance, arms crossed and jaw set. "Why should I give up the things I love?"

"Oh, I don't know, honey—maybe in order to have a child with the woman you supposedly love?" Cori released a frustrated sigh. This was not at all going as planned. "Look, all I'm saying is we should be willing to sacrifice a little for a better chance to have a baby. This doctor she's sending me to—"

"Stop it, Cori."

She frowned at his abruptness. "But, she said he's the best in this ar—"

"I want a divorce."

Cori stared at her husband's mouth, positive she'd misheard. "Excuse me. What did you say?"

"I want a divorce." His voice carried a hint...no...a promise, of finality. "I've met someone else. She's much younger than you and she's already been pregnant once." He turned away from her and reached for his clothes. "I'm the only son of an only son. You know how important it is for me to have children of my own."

"She—she has a child?"

"She had an abortion, with no complications. So I know she's capable, and she knows I want children right away. I'm sorry, hon, but this is a deal breaker for me, you know that. I've done my own research, and a woman of your age with your reproductive problems has a snowball's chance in hell of giving me one child, much less a houseful. It's time to cut my losses and try to have a family with someone else."

Several different scenarios ran through her head in a flash. Her pleading with him, telling him how much she loved him, begging him not to go, insisting they could make it work. She sat there on her bed in silence, with the sheet pulled up around her, knowing damned well none of it would work. She opened her mouth to ask him who this other woman was, then closed it. It didn't matter. Nothing mattered anymore. His voice cut through the fog in her mind, and she finally looked at him, realizing he'd been trying to get her attention.

"Are you going to be all right? I mean, you won't slit your wrist or anything when I leave here, will you?"

Cori shook her head, wishing she had the energy to slap the smugness from his face, but still too dazed to move from the bed.

"I'll contact a divorce attorney tomorrow. I want to be fair, so I'll buy your share of the house and property outright."

She laughed, hearing a hint of hysteria in her own voice. "With what—*our* savings account?" She couldn't keep the bitterness from her tone.

He ignored her and continued his disassociated monologue. "After all, I can't see any reason why you'd want to stay here in Louisiana when all of your family is back in Texas."

"How young?"

He zipped his pants and faced her. "Excuse me?"

"How young is she?"

"She's twenty-two."

Her mouth fell open. "You're screwing a student?"

"She's my assistant."

"She's half your age."

"Well, yes. That's the whole point. She's young…and fertile." He reached out to chuck her gently under the chin. "It's not personal, Cori. Who knows? Maybe once I have a few kids of my own, if you're still single, maybe we could hook up again. I've always thought you'd make a wonderful mother to my children, even if it's as a step-mother."

She shook her head. "You're delusional."

He shrugged off her comment. "You never know."

"Oh, I know," she added.

"Besides, I'm being perfectly rational about this. You're the one who's delusional if you think seeing some money hungry fertility specialist will help you to have a child of your own. If it hasn't happened by now, it never will."

Her lids dropped on his hateful words. "Get the hell out of here."

"I will for now, but I expect you to take my generous buy-out for your half. I bought this place, intending to fill it with children, and I fully intend to."

"Get. Out. Now."

She sat there, her eyelids closed, until she heard the front door open and shut. Seconds after the electric garage door lifted, his car pulled out of the drive. Cori fell back upon the bed, tears seeping from her closed lids, trailing down the sides of her face onto the mattress. How the hell did it get to this? How had her marriage turned into a business contract, a deal gone badly, simply to be broken, nullified, and sold out to a new owner?

"Damn him anyway."

Refusing to give in to any more self-pity, she forced herself out of bed. A quick shower to wash the smell of him from her had her feeling better. Clean and wearing a pair of lounge shorts and a sleepshirt, she glanced at the screen of her chirping telephone. She let it ring deciding a talk with her mother was a little more than she could handle right now. Cori dropped heavily onto her sofa, making mental lists of things she needed to do. When that got too taxing she moved to the table with a pen and pad.

She sat there, with only the harmonious music of the city to keep her company. The incessant barking of someone's dog, the quiet swoosh of cars running through standing water on the street out front after this evening's shower, the clank and rumble of L & D Railroad engines and other cars six streets over. She quietly listed, planned, crossed out and added to her growing to-do list, glad to have something to occupy her mind.

Two hours later, Cori had nearly fallen asleep when the doorbell startled her.

Taking a cautious look through the peephole at the two officers standing outside, her heart set up a steady hammering in her chest. She pulled open the door, and before either of them uttered a single word, she knew in her gut her husband was dead.

****

She stared at the lump on the table, waited patiently for the coroner to unzip the body bag containing what they suspected were her husband's remains.

"How exactly did it happen?"

The officer cleared his throat. "He ran off the road and hit a tree."

Cori frowned. "Jim was an annoyingly careful driver. Was he avoiding something in the road?"

"Uh, no ma'am. Your husband wasn't alone."

She waited. "Who else was with him?" *Was this*

16

guy blushing?

The officer gave his throat a nervous clearing. "We recovered the body of a young woman in the vehicle with him."

"She died also?"

"Yes, ma'am, she did."

The slow unzipping of the bag claimed her attention as she waited to see Jim's handsome face. She gasped at the reveal, covered her mouth at the sight before her. "Oh my God, what happened to him?"

The officer cleared his throat again. "The tree, ma'am. I'm sorry, but we need a positive identification."

"But, I can't tell from…that," she sobbed into the wad of tissue the cop leaned over to hand her.

"No ma'am, we didn't think you would. We're hoping you can identify him by some other means. Are there any specific body markings you'd recognize?"

Cori looked away from the bloody mass of shredded pulp that was supposed to be her husband's face, swallowed the bile rising in her throat. She squeezed her eyes shut, tried to focus and clear her mind of anything but the information they needed from her.

"A birthmark…he has a distinctive birthmark on his inner right thigh. It looks kind of like a crescent." She faced the coroner in time to see him exchange a look with the officer—the kind of look teeming with unspoken messages and hidden meanings. The kind you send someone when words aren't appropriate. The officer followed with a grunt.

"What is it?" Her gaze jumped from one man to the other. "What is it you're not telling me?"

The officer removed his cap, used his uniform sleeve to wipe his face and grumbled something under his breath. She could have sworn she heard him say, "This is a first."

She took a deep breath to strengthen her resolve. "What is it?"

"Well ma'am. We told you he wasn't alone when he lost control of the vehicle. It seems the young woman was…uh…pleasuring him at the time of the crash."

She stared at the officer, brow furrowed, a silent plea for more information.

He developed a serious case of the fidgets. "Um…orally." The officer met the coroner's gaze. "Maybe you could check for the birthmark and take a picture of it. That way she could identify him from the picture."

Cori pivoted, faced the body on the slab. "Show me. Now. Let's get this over with."

The coroner reached for the zipper, pulled it all the way down to reveal the body's lower extremities. A square cloth pad covered the groin area, she supposed for the sake of propriety. He maneuvered the right thigh, used a sponge to wipe off dried blood from the area.

"It should be right there," she pointed to the spot, waited patiently for the man to clean the area well enough to see Jim's birthmark. "There it is." She straightened, and then took in the entire scene. "Why so much blood there?"

The cop cleared his throat again. "We told you about the girl…performing…oral…*gratification* on him."

Her gaze fixated on the square of cloth covering her husband's groin, the blood covered thighs. Suddenly it hit her. "You mean she was…at the time…when he…hit the tree?"

"Um, yes ma'am. We believe so. We have reason to believe that's what caused him to lose control."

She reached for the cloth.

The officer placed his hand on her arm to halt her progression. "You don't want to see that, ma'am. It's…it's not the kind of thing you can put out of your mind easily. God knows I won't after seeing it."

She shook her head and pushed his hand gently from her. "I have to." Cori took one corner of the cloth between her two fingers and lifted it. The blackness began as a pattern of psychedelic splotches, then waves of darkness, before her knees buckled and her world spun into a void of nothingness.

Chapter 3
Cori…Without

"Honey, are you sure you're up for this? I can make the arrangements for you if you'd prefer."

Cori's face set in determination. "No thanks, Mom. I need to do this myself."

"Do you have enough put aside to pay for everything? Was there any kind of burial policy on him? Funerals are so expensive these days."

She bit her lip. "No, I'm okay."

Financially speaking, she'd be more than okay. A quick glance at their life insurance policy the previous night had elicited a phone conference to the friend who'd sold them the policy a few years earlier. Not only had she talked Jim into the half-million dollar policy but it also included an accidental death clause, doubling its value—or would as soon as the company's adjustors deemed there was no foul play involved.

Cori wasn't worried about the results of their investigation. Although her husband's death involved healthy servings of stupidity and immorality with a side dish of bad judgement, they would find no signs of foul play.

She hadn't breathed a word about the circumstances of his death to her family, nor had she told anyone about her husband's plan to divorce her. As far as they knew, he was driving his twenty-two year old assistant home because her car was in the shop. According to police, the parents of the young woman had verified the car situation. They'd also been informed of the significance of their daughter's involvement in the accident and, obviously hoping to avoid the ensuing scandal, had chosen to keep it quiet.

Although a small part of Cori wanted to shout to the world that her husband was nothing more than an uncaring, inconsiderate asshole, another part of her didn't want this woman's family publicly humiliated any more than she wanted it for herself or the university. They'd blamed the loss of control on the possibility of him swerving to avoid an animal on the road. Cori hadn't been able to work up anything more than a begrudging agreement to play nice and go along with it.

After waiting three days for her in-laws to arrive from the Alaskan interior, the one-day, closed casket funeral for Jim finally took place. She moved through the services in robotic fashion—speaking when spoken to, shaking hands, allowing the multitude of hugs, and accepting the condolences of others—all the while wanting nothing more than to go home and crawl into her bed.

****

She'd forced herself to go back to work after one week, but her boss had been so concerned with her physical appearance, he insisted she take a month off.

That found her at home two weeks later and playing hostess to her mom for a three day visit.

Joan Granger flipped through a magazine at the breakfast table and stopped suddenly. She lifted the magazine, its page folded to an ad for a cruise ship.

"Why don't you take a trip, Cori? Go on a cruise to Mexico or better yet, the Mediterranean. Go to Greece."

Cori frowned at the suggestion. "I have no desire to be stuck on a cruise ship with hundreds of people I don't know. Besides, with my luck it'd be a ship hit by one of those awful viruses. All I need is to be stuck out in the middle of an ocean on a poop and puke fest." She shivered.

Her mother frowned. "You would think of something like that. Well, fly then. Haven't you always wanted to visit Scotland? Here's your chance. Do *something* that will get you out of this house. You've got the money to go anywhere in the world you want to go."

Yes, she did. The insurance policy had paid off, and she was a millionaire, but to what purpose? She had no husband and a slim to zero chance of ever having a child of her own. The moment her husband had insisted on a divorce, he'd smashed all her dreams to hell. It took a few moments to realize her mom was speaking to her again. "I'm sorry, Mom. What'd you say?"

"I asked if you were sleeping any better, but judging from your lack of concentration, I'd say the answer is no."

"I sleep enough." She didn't need her mother fussing and worrying over her.

"Have you been eating?"

"I eat enough."

Joan cocked her head to the side. "Is that why you have dark circles under your eyes and your jeans are hanging off of you?"

"Mom—"

"Cori, one day when you have children, you'll see

how impossible it is to watch them hurting. I understand you have to mourn, but you still need to take care of yourself."

Cori couldn't suppress the negativity oozing from her entire being. "*If* I have children, you mean."

"Don't tell me what I mean," Joan barked. "I fully believe you'll have at least one child someday, if not more."

"I'd have to have a man first. What man my age wants a woman who has little chance of having children, unless he already has kids and doesn't want anymore? I need to face the fact that I'm not a good risk when it comes to wife material." She felt more than saw her mother's gaze raking over her. "Spit it out. I know you're dying to say something."

"I'm just wondering why you aren't more torn up about losing your husband. I mean, you seem sad, but not so much over losing him as losing your chance to have a child. Was there something going on I don't know about?"

Cori's mouth tightened to a grim line. "We'd just had a disagreement before Jim died." She looked up in time to see her mother's eyes narrow to suspicious slits.

"You two never disagreed on anything. He was too…" Joan splayed her fingers, as though trying to pull a particular word out of thin air.

"Logical?" Cori volunteered, garnering a raucous hoot from her mother.

"Yes! That's it, exactly. He reminded me of Mr. Spock on Star Trek. He was always so logical and *detached.* Picking a fight with him must have been like beating an old rug."

"I didn't pick fights with Jim. Why would I want to

do that?"

"It seems like you'd need to do something to bring out a little passion in him."

"Passion through fighting is not worth it."

"Oh, honey." Her mother chuckled low in her throat. "Don't knock make up sex until you've tried it."

Cori shut her eyes and covered her mouth with one hand. "You're making me nauseous."

"Good grief, Corrine. Grow up, and stop evading the issue. What did you two argue about?" Joan rose from the table to refill her coffee cup.

Cori stood also, deciding hot tea may settle her stomach more than coffee. "I didn't say anything about an argument. He…" She took a deep breath, regretted it when the aroma of dark roasted coffee, and the cinnamon her mom sprinkled in every cup, melded with the sweet smell of the donut sitting untouched on the saucer in front of her. The combination made her stomach even queasier. "He asked me for a divorce." She spun around at the sound of breaking glass.

Her mom stood frozen in place, the empty coffee mug she'd dropped, in pieces at her feet. "He did *what*?"

Glad for a reason to keep busy, Cori pulled out her mop, dust broom and dustpan. She swept up the pieces of glass before beginning to mop away the spilled coffee. A quick glance at her mother's wide eyes and gaping mouth said the situation warranted an explanation. "When I told him my doctor suggested I see a fertility specialist, he asked for a divorce." She'd intended to say that and not a single word more. The confusion on her mother's face had her explaining further. "He wasn't willing to wait on the chance that I may get pregnant one day. As the only son of an only son, he said it was his duty to find a sure bet that would fill this house with children."

She dumped the last bits of broken mug into the garbage, and mopped the last splatters of coffee from the floor before dropping into the nearest chair. She waited for the explosion, ready to welcome a little justified anger on her behalf.

Her mom's face grew somber as she nodded. "That certainly explains it. His detachment accounts for yours."

Cori's mouth sagged. "Is that all you're going to say?"

Joan shrugged. "What do you want me to say—he was a cold-hearted SOB for hurting you? He was and he did, but the man is dead already."

"Not ten minutes after we'd had the best sex we'd had in years, he informed me he was leaving me for the twenty-two year old assistant he was already screwing."

"That son of a bitch!" her mother snarled.

Cori smiled. "That's more like it."

Arms crossed, Joan leaned against the cabinet. "So, what happened when he told you?"

"I told him to leave."

"Just like that? Didn't you blow up?"

She bit her lower lip and stared at the floor as she pondered her mother's question. "Not really."

"Have you considered why you didn't?"

It took several seconds for Cori to voice what she'd already admitted to herself. "I don't think we ever loved each other the way we should have."

Joan remained silent for a full minute before reaching for her daughter's hand. "You know, the morning you married Jim, your father told me he thought you were settling."

"He never said anything."

"We'd discussed it and I told him to keep it to himself. Besides, if he had, what would you have done?"

"I'd have denied it and married Jim anyway."

Her mom nodded. "At the reception, Charles pulled me aside. He said the hardest thing he'd ever done was to hand you over to a man he believed wasn't capable of loving his little girl the way you deserved to be loved."

The thought cut Cori, even more than losing her husband had. "Poor Daddy, I never sensed it. But he liked Jim, didn't he?"

"Honey, the point is Jim never did anything to make either of us like or dislike him—until now. He was just...*there*." She exhaled in a disgusted huff. "I'm not in the habit of hiding anything from your father, but I think we should keep this between you and me—for a while anyway."

"That's fine by me. The less humiliation heaped upon me at this point, the better."

Joan seated herself beside Cori, reached out to brush an errant lock of hair from her daughter's forehead. "You have no reason to be humiliated, Cori. Jim's actions are a testament to his lack of character, not yours."

Cori nodded, attempted to reward the woman with a half-hearted smile. She couldn't help but wonder how her mother would feel if she knew the entire, unfiltered, ugly truth.

Chapter 4
Cori...Within

Weeks turned into another month. Cori's attempt to return to life as usual fell far short of the true definition of normal living. The truth was, in the following weeks she couldn't come close to feeling any sort of normal. She imagined others pondering over the disappearance of the "old" Cori, and couldn't blame them. Every morning, she looked in the mirror and wondered the same thing. The haunted eyes staring back at her weren't her own. Those dark circles under them were new to the image, with one exception of a serious bout with the flu a few years back. She burned her personal time off at the office, barely managed to drag her sleep deprived, energy depleted body out of bed every morning. Her nausea stayed with her, and her appetite had never returned to her pre-death loss of lying, cheating husband condition.

Each new day challenged her to come up with a reason to live. She had no husband, no children, and little chance of ever having either, especially with a biological clock eating away at a body with serious reproductive challenges.

Her mom and sister urged her to sell the house, move back to Texas, insisting she'd be better off closer to family who loved and cared for her. In order to do that, she'd have to go through all the necessary steps to put the house on the market, finalize the sale, quit her job, and find another house and job in another state. Frankly, the thought of that much effort seemed an impossibly daunting task for someone living out of her bedroom. Maybe later she'd feel up to it.

Later never came. More weeks turned into two more months of avoiding calls and visits from concerned family members and friends.

Cori awoke to her alarm one particular Monday morning, consumed by depression, her chest aching and hollow with hopelessness. She turned off the alarm and dragged herself to the bathroom. Once there, she stared at the haunted, gaunt face in the mirror, tried to remember the person she'd been four short months ago. Back when she still had hope.

Pushing her wild hair aside, she got nose to nose with the image staring back at her. Who the hell was that stranger in the mirror? Where was Cori?

The simple truth was that she was gone, like everything else.

A solitary tear appeared at the outer corner of one eye and rolled down her cheek, dripped off her chin. She frowned at her image, knowing she couldn't last another day living this way. She tapped the mirrored medicine cabinet until the door popped open, and stood staring at its contents.

Her gaze landed on a nearly full bottle of prescription pills. She snatched the amber plastic bottle and studied the label—pain medication from Jim's back injury last spring. She grabbed a second bottle—muscle relaxers from the same incident, remembering his doctor's warning not to take them simultaneously.

Yeah, that should do it. Filled with determination,

she grabbed the meds and headed to the kitchen for the half bottle of wine left in the fridge. With the pill bottles in one hand and wine bottle in the other, she bypassed the glasses and headed straight for her bedroom. She maneuvered herself until she was propped up against the headboard. Cori sat there for a bit, wondering if she should leave some type of letter for her family.

"I'll have enough time for that once I've emptied these bottles." She dumped all the pills onto her mattress and uncorked the wine. One sip and she nodded, licking the taste of black currant and cherry from her lips. If she was going to use wine to swallow a crap-load of pills, it was only fitting that it should be her favorite, full-bodied burgundy.

She grabbed a handful of pills, stuffed several into her mouth, and raised the bottle in the air. A strange fluttering sensation in her lower abdomen halted the bottle's journey to her lips.

What the hell?

She waited, felt it again, stronger this time. A fluttering, like nothing she'd ever felt before. She lowered the bottle, trying to recall her last period. Had it really been since before Jim's accident? But that was four months ago.

It couldn't be. Could it?

She spit the pills into her hand and scrambled out of bed. Disposing of pills and bottle, she removed her sleepshirt, turned on her bedroom light and stood in front of her full-length mirror. The slightest pooch stood out starkly against her thinner than usual body.

Maybe.

She placed both hands over her abdomen, felt the

flutter again. Staring into her own face, her eyes grew wider. "Oh. My. God." A quick scramble to the bathroom had her scanning the cabinet for something. She found it quickly and read the instructions to refresh her foggy memory.

Less than five minutes later, with her heart pounding in her chest, she stared at the solid plus sign in the window of the test strip. She ambled to her bedroom, deep in thought, and stood once more in front of the full-length mirror. Palming the pregnancy test, she cupped both hands over her abdomen again. This could only have happened the last time she'd made love with her husband, and only minutes before he'd demanded a divorce and walked out the door forever.

She closed her eyes, summoning the child tucked away in her womb. "I'm so sorry, little one. I didn't know you were in there, but if you agree to stick out the next five months with me, I promise I'll take better care of myself from now on. Do we have a deal?" She got her answer several seconds later with another feather-soft flutter in her belly. Her lids popped open, and Cori stared at her reflection, wondering how long it had been since she'd seen a smile that wide on her own face.

Chapter 5
Sweet Child of Mine

"Jesus, Cori." Dr. Lin frowned at her chart. "What have you done to yourself? You've dropped fifteen pounds since I've last seen you, and you didn't have that much to spare."

Cori focused on where her hands fidgeted with the paper gown's tie around her waist. "My husband was killed in an accident the evening of my last visit with you. I—I haven't had much of an appetite."

Her doctor's face paled. "I'm so sorry. I hadn't heard that. When you didn't get back to me about further treatments, I assumed you'd turned to other options, like adoption. Have you been experiencing any signs of depression?"

"Yes, but if this is what I hope it is, that's over and done with, I promise you."

Dr. Lin sighed. "Are you prepared for the fact that it may not be what you're hoping?"

Cori reached for her purse. "I hadn't considered it." She removed the plastic bag containing the EPT test from home and showed it to her doctor. "What do you think of this?"

Dr. Lin's eyes widened. "Well, okay. Lay back and put your feet into these stirrups." After several adjustments, she continued. "Now, slide to the edge of the table so I can take a look."

Cori took several deep breaths in a vain attempt to relax. A difficult feat when her body was a twitching bundle of nervous energy. Thankfully, she didn't have to keep still for long.

Within seconds of her examination, Dr. Lin released a satisfied chuckle. "Oh, you've definitely got a bun in the oven." She poked her head around Cori's leg and grinned. "I'd say around four months. I'm sure you're aware that stress and depression can lead to interruptions in the menstrual cycle, but weren't you the slightest bit suspicious that you were pregnant before now?"

"To tell you the truth, I haven't thought about it once since Jim died. Not until this morning when I felt what I assume was my baby moving."

The doctor nodded, helping her to push back away from the edge and remove her feet from the stirrups. "I'll be able to tell from the ultrasound if you're far enough along for that. Do you have time for one today?"

"I've got nothing but time. I'll wait as long as it takes." Dr. Lin walked out to get the sonogram cart moved into the exam room. Within minutes Cori was jellied up and seeing an image of her baby on screen. "Is that my baby's heart?"

"Yes, it is." The doctor adjusted a nob on the machine until they could hear the embryo's rapid heartbeat over Cori's delighted gasp. "Amazing, isn't it? From what I can tell, you're between sixteen and eighteen weeks along and…" She sat back suddenly and cleared her throat.

Cori's gaze darted toward her doctor. "What's wrong? You don't see two of them in there, do you?"

"No, there's only one. I'm wondering if you'd like to know the sex of the child."

"You can already tell?"

Her doctor grinned and nodded.

It took a second for Cori to answer. "Of course I want to know. I only have, what, five more months to prepare?"

Dr. Lin leaned forward again and maneuvered the wand over Cori's belly. Eventually, she pointed toward the screen. "You see that spot there?"

Cori squinted at the monitor. "Ye-esss."

"That's a scrotum…"

The screen blurred and Cori blinked rapidly to clear her eyes. "Oh my goodness, it's a boy? I'm having a son?"

"Yes, ma'am, you are. Congratulations!"

Cori covered her face and burst into semi-hysterical sobbing, a combination of absolute joy and utter disbelief. She accepted a wad of tissues from Dr. Lin and wiped her eyes. "I can't believe it. I mean, I figured I was pregnant from the home test results, but seeing and hearing his little heartbeat…" She sniffled into the tissues.

"I know. It's overwhelming, especially since you had such a slim chance of this happening."

Cori's gaze landed on her doctor. "How high risk is this pregnancy?"

Dr. Lin sucked in her lower lip and took a moment to respond. "On a scale of one to ten, I'd say it's a solid eight. Although, this kid must be some kind of stubborn if he's survived the hostile environment you've created for him thus far." She picked up her prescription pad and began to scribble. "You have to take it easy. You're not on complete bed rest, but I want your feet elevated for thirty to sixty minute intervals at least four times a day, and even more often as your due date approaches, which is the last week in January. Get no less than eight hours of sleep each night."

"Do I have any chance of a normal delivery?" Dr. Lin gave her head an adamant shake, dashing all hope of La Maze training for a natural birth.

"I'm sorry, but there's too much scar tissue in your uterus. You have a major risk of uterine tearing during labor, which could lead to hemorrhaging. That would be extremely dangerous for both you and the baby. It's vital you should have a scheduled Caesarean section no less than two weeks earlier than your due date." She looked up at Cori, her eyes narrowed. "How stressful is your job?"

"It's not at all stressful, physically. I draw up plans on a computer, so it's ninety percent deskwork, but deadlines can get a little taxing."

"Is there any way you could take some time off? Ideally, I'd love to see you take a leave of absence for the remainder of the pregnancy if it's at all possible. I could write you a letter for medical leave."

The wheels turned in Cori's mind, and for the first time since discovering she was a million dollars wealthier, she actually welcomed her windfall from the life insurance policy. "That won't be a problem, and of course, I'd welcome a letter from you."

She never would have believed the old adage could ring true; but in reference to the well-being of their son—her lying, cheating, money-wasting, self-absorbed husband really had been worth more to her dead than alive. Cori had to wonder if his happiness over her pregnancy would have over-ridden his loss of vacation funding, as well as other necessary cutbacks to his overly indulgent lifestyle. She recalled his adamant insistence of new cars, fine Scotch, the latest tech gadgets, and expensive suits. On some level she suspected he was far too selfish to deprive himself of the material things in life. She climbed down from the table, her mind conjuring a mental image of Jim and his companion seconds before he'd plowed them both into a tree, and couldn't help but wonder what sort of indulgences, if any, he'd been granted after death.

Cori left her OB's office with a prescription for pre-natal vitamins and a smile she couldn't wipe from her face. Ensconced in her eight-year-old sedan, she pulled her phone from her purse, touched the first name in her programmed phone list, and waited. Her mother answered on the second ring.

"Hey, sweetie! Your sister's here, and we were just wondering how you've been feeling."

"Melissa's there? Excellent! Put me on speaker and it'll save me another phone call. Are you both sitting? You are not going to believe this."

Chapter 6
Coming Clean at the Baby Shower

Melissa Landry folded the last newborn onesie and placed it in a pile on the dresser. "Nice haul for a baby shower, Cori. I think you've got everything that little man will need for the first year of his life."

Cori scanned the stacks of infant clothing, blankets, and various items of baby paraphernalia scattered throughout the room. "I think you're right, little sister. Everyone has been so generous with my baby boy and me. I'm very blessed to have such good friends."

Melissa gawked at her for a moment. "What are we—chopped liver?"

Cori grinned at her sister first, and then her mom. "I'm very blessed to have such good friends *and* a fabulous family." She pulled them both to her for a group hug. "You ladies are the best and I couldn't have done all this without you."

Her mom hugged her back. "That's why we're here. To make sure you and my new grandson have everything you need for his big entrance in a little less than two months. I still think we cut it close by waiting this long to have the shower."

Cori stepped away from the two women, rested one hand on her belly and another on her lower back. "Today was perfect because so many old friends and family members were in town for Thanksgiving weekend. I asked around and the majority of them preferred it this way. They got a break from the kids and men for a bit. Aunt Sue told me it helped her to get her second wind."

She rummaged through a stack of cards. "Where's the list of who gave what? I'll need to start on those thank you notes tonight."

Joan took her elbow in a firm grip. "You need to rest with your feet up for a bit, remember? You've only done that once today. Why don't you lie down and take a nap?"

"I'm too excited for that, but I'll stretch out on the sofa if you two keep me company. I could use a cup of tea, but you ladies can finish off that wine somebody left here."

She waddled to the living room and let her mom fuss over her by propping up pillows at her back while Melissa puttered around in the kitchen.

Within minutes, her sister appeared with a tray, holding a half-full bottle of wine, two wine glasses, and one cup of tea. She placed it on the coffee table in front of the sofa. "I put one spoon of sugar and a little lemon."

Cori reached for the cup. "Perfect." She dipped the bag several times and set it on the tray before leaning back to take a sip. "Mm, it's heavenly."

Melissa filled her wine glass and sat on the opposite end of the couch before taking a sip of the fruity Chablis. She closed her eyes and nodded. "I agree. The wine, coupled with the fact that Roland and the kids are at his mom's for the night certainly qualifies as heavenly. Until ten o'clock tomorrow morning, I get to be me instead of mommy."

Joan settled in her overstuffed reading chair, her feet curled under her and cradled her glass of wine. "I adore my grandchildren, but I have to admit, it's kind of nice having both my girls here together like this."

Melissa gave Cori a cheesy grin. "Aw, *our* mommy still loves us, Sis."

Cori laughed at her sister. "I never doubted it." Using her belly as a cup rest, she turned to her mom. "Does Daddy know it's safe to come home again?"

"I told him it should be cleared out by 5:00 p.m." She checked the time. "It's five till, so he should be driving up any minute now."

Melissa's glass paused on its way to her lips. "Poor Pop. Where'd he go for the duration?"

"He went to Uncle Joey's. He's probably burnt out on College football by now and ready to come home." Joan sipped from her glass and settled deeper into her chair.

Cori dropped her head back on the arm of the couch and studied her mom's features. "That new style looks great on you, Mom. I can't wait until my hair goes all silver so I can wear it like yours."

Joan Granger fluffed the back of her short hair. "Thanks, sweetie. It's easy to keep up. My stylist calls it a "blow and go".

Cori's mouth tightened to suppress a grin at her sister's snort of laughter. "Stop it, Melissa."

Her mother shook her head in disgust. "Get your minds out of the gutter. I know I raised you girls better than that."

Melissa feigned a look of innocence. "What, Mommy?"

"Oh please." An eye roll accompanied her mom's

impatient huff. "Don't start that with me."

Cori joined her sister with an innocent flutter of lashes. "I'm sure we don't know what you're talking about."

"Yeah," Melissa agreed. "Maybe you ought to explain it to us." She joined in Cori's laughter at their mother's grunt of disapproval.

"Y'all are terrible," Joan chided.

Melissa addressed her sister. "Hmph, if we are, we come by it honestly."

Cori gave her a wink. "You must be right. The woman sounds like she knows what she's talking about—oh, my gosh." She narrowed her gaze at her mother. "Is she blushing? Mom, are you *blushing*?"

Joan reached for a magazine and fanned her face furiously. "No. I am not. It'd take a hell of a lot more than the phrase 'blow and go' to make me blush. When you *children* have *matured,* you'll learn the difference between a hot flash and a blush. It's the wine. It does it to me every time." She stopped fanning herself to savor another drink from her glass. "Mm, but it's so worth it."

Cori chuckled low in her throat as something triggered a particular memory. Eventually, the chuckle grew into hysterical, belly-shaking laughter. She held her cup of tea with one hand, trying not to spill on her tummy full of baby, and wiped the tears from her eyes with the other. "Oh, God," she gasped, attempting to catch her breath.

Melissa took the cup of tea from her. "Give me that before you burn yourself. Have you lost your mind?"

"No, but you're about to," Cori sputtered, through occasional bursts of laughter. "I can't believe I'm about to do this." She placed two hands on her belly. "I'm so sorry, baby boy, but as intelligent of a man as your biological father was, he sure pulled a stupid stunt." She intercepted the look passed between Melissa and their mom. "I guess if I can finally laugh about it, it's safe to divulge the circumstances of my husband's death."

"The circumstances?" Joan pulled her curious gaze from Cori, to Melissa, then back to Cori. "Am I missing something?"

Cori raised her hand, palm facing her mom, and swallowed one last hiccup of laughter. "Okay, you both know Jim lost control of the car that night, but neither of you know why he lost control."

Melissa's head cocked curiously. "Does anyone know why?"

"I mean, there's speculation he swerved to avoid an animal or something. But how could anyone know for sure?" Joan chimed in.

"The cops know." She snorted, cut it short. "I know." Cori took a deep breath and released it. "His girlfriend was giving my husband a little—I think the cop used the term 'oral gratification'—when he lost control and slammed into that tree."

Joan's hand flew to her mouth to cover her gasp. "Oh, my gosh!"

To her credit, Melissa tried to stop the following snort, but couldn't quite contain it. To her further credit, she managed to force her face into a masque of somberness. "You cannot be serious."

Cori pressed her lips together, nodding as laughter bubbled upward and out into a raucous cackle that crashed through her sister's barriers until Melissa finally surrendered, collapsing into a helpless pile of hysterical snorts.

Melissa shoved her finger at Cori's face. "Blow and go! Bwa-ha-ha-ha-ha!"

Joan stared at her daughters, her face stern and indignant. "Wait a minute! Two people died in that accident, so stop laughing!" Once she'd 'guilted' them both into some semblance of sobriety, she spoke again. "I'm just wondering…"

"What, Mom?" Cori bit her bottom lip. Hard.

"Well…I guess I'm wondering how they could be so sure. What proof did they have to come to that conclusion?"

Cori cleared her throat. "Um, Mom, when they found Jim, his…um…*member* was no longer *attached* to his body."

Joan's eyes widened. "Did they ever find it?"

Melissa turned in her seat to face her mother. "Does it matter?"

Tight lipped, Cori barely got the words out. "They found it." She issued a silent, but fervent prayer that her mom would not wonder about the obvious, or if she did, she wouldn't put it into question form. Someone up there was slacking on the job.

"I'm sorry, but I've got to ask. *Where* did they find it?"

Cori's jaw clamped down like a vise as she shook her head, refusing to speak the words. She didn't have to.

"Think about it, Mom," Melissa said, displaying an uncanny ability to keep a straight face. "If I were a betting woman, I'd say Jim's girlfriend left this world with a mouthful."

"Oh…" Joan's eyes widened and her hand flew to

her mouth. "Oh, no!" She shivered and gave her head a violent shake. "You mean she...oh...that's just awful!"

Cori released a shaky breath. "It's pretty bad."

"Yeah, it is," Melissa agreed. "And at this point, I find myself wondering which one of them had it worse. I mean, there they both are, leaving this world at the same exact moment and when they crossover...he's...she's..." She raised both hands in the air and let them fall to her lap.

"Well..." Joan spoke slowly, as though mulling it over. "I think it's safe to say that Jim got the *short* end of the deal." Straight faced, she picked up her wine glass and brought it to her lips. She paused reverently before adding a softly spoken "Bless his heart," which, in any state south of the Mason-Dixon line, was nothing more than a polite way of calling her son-in-law a monumental idiot.

Chapter 7
911: Fender Bender

November 27th

Cori stepped out of the baby shop in the downtown business district of Beaumont, Texas, a shopping bag looped on each arm. At her baby shower, a friend of hers had shown up with the most adorable outfit for her son. It turned out she was co-owner of a place called the Belle and Beau Baby Boutique. With several gift cards in hand she'd decided to stop by this Thursday afternoon on her way to spend a long weekend with her parents in Richmond. Thrilled with her purchases and time well spent with an old friend, she headed for the sedan parallel-parked along the sidewalk in front of the store. A particularly strong series of kicks from her unborn son had her stopping at the halfway point to suck in her breath. Once the attack on her ribcage subsided, she released a long breath and relaxed, taking another few moments to extract her keys from her purse.

Keys in hand, she took a single step toward her car when an older model Cadillac plowed into the rear end of her sedan. In less time than it took to blink, her car lost half its mass, sandwiched between a huge, black 4X4 pickup and the Caddie. With one arm extended, her thumb still on the key fob's unlock button, she stood frozen and staring at the lump of compacted metal.

"Holy moly, lady! Is that your car?"

The male voice, shouted from behind, rocked Cori from her stupor. "It used to be."

The young man called out to her, already heading for the Cadillac. "Can you call 911 while I see to the old lady driving that tank?" He stopped suddenly. "You aren't hurt are you?"

She dropped the bags on the concrete and placed both hands on her significant belly. "I don't think so."

"Lucky you weren't closer to your car, or worse, inside it. No way would you or your baby have walked away from that." He gave her a quick nod before running off to check on the driver.

In a semi-daze, she pulled her phone from her purse to call 911.

"911. What's your emergency?"

"We need an ambulance at..." Cori turned to see the numbered address on the store front. "1155 Belle Street in Beaumont. That's B-E-L-L-E Street. There's been an accident. An elderly woman in an older model Cadillac just plowed into the back of a parked vehicle."

"Okay, ma'am. I'm reporting it as we speak. Can you stay on the line please?"

"Yes sir, I'll be here." Weak kneed and teetering dangerously near the edge of some form of emotional outburst, Cori sought refuge on a bench placed in front of the store. She'd just lowered herself heavily when her friend, Ellen, ran out to check on her.

"Are you all right, Cori? Do you need me to call someone for you?"

She lifted the phone, her hand somewhat shaky.

"I'm on the phone with 911. I suppose after that, I'll have to call my insurance adjuster to rent a car for me."

Ellen dropped beside her on the bench. "That could have been so much worse had you been in it. I saw you stop and grab your stomach. I nearly followed you out to see if you were okay."

"The baby was kicking, pushing on my ribs. I kind of lost my breath for a few seconds, and had to stop until he relaxed."

"Well honey, I don't know if you could have survived what I'm looking at." She clucked her tongue. "That baby boy's kick just may have saved both your lives."

The thought had tears pooling in her eyes then spilling over onto her cheeks. Wiping the back of her hand over her eyes, she waved off Ellen's look of concern. After one last sniff, she sent her old classmate a watery smile. "I'm fine," she insisted.

And she was fine, even though Cori couldn't help recalling that fateful day three months earlier when she'd been ready to end it all. This wasn't the first time her child's kick had saved her life.

The male voice speaking in a smooth as silk bass, slightly familiar, brought her back to the present. "Ma'am, are you still there?"

"Yes, I am."

"Were you involved in the accident? Are you injured?"

"No, thank goodness. I'm pregnant and my baby kicked, so I had to stop and catch my breath. Otherwise..." She couldn't finish the thought as a soft sob escaped her. The voice came to her again.

"How far along are you, ma'am?"

Lori Leger

"I'm seven months, and all kinds of moody. So, watch that ma'am stuff."

"Understood, but are you sure you're all right? No sign of cramping or any other trauma? I can just as easily send a second ambulance for you."

"No, I'm fine. Just a little emotional, that's all." She sniffed and rolled her eyes at her friend's sympathetic smile. "This is embarrassing. I'm sure that poor old woman is in much worse shape than I am. Although..." She paused to listen as the woman in question berated the other young man for asking about her. "She doesn't act or sound as if she's hurt at all."

"Listen to her, would you?" Ellen said.

"What's going on?" deep sexy voice asked in Cori's ear.

"Well, I'd say she's tearing the young man who's trying to help her, a new one."

The voice chuckled. "Some people handle stress differently from others. Can you tell the year model of that Cadillac?"

"Old. Very old. The guy talking to her called it a tank." Cori turned to Ellen. "The 911 guy wants to know—"

"Luke...my name is Luke," sexy voice replied.

"Luke..." Suddenly it all came back to her. "Luke...Luke! This is Corrine...Cori—"

"Cori...with an I?"

"Yes!"

"I remember you. I thought your voice sounded familiar. How are you?"

"I'm great." She turned back to Ellen. "*Luke* is asking what model the Cadillac is. You got any idea?"

Ellen shrugged. "It looks just like my

46

grandmother's old car. My dad keeps it covered with a tarp in his garage. I know that one is a 1979 Cadillac Fleetwood."

"Did you catch that, Luke?"

His immediate answer was a low chuckle followed by, "No wonder she doesn't seem hurt. That thing *is* a tank."

"There doesn't seem to be much damage to her car at all." Her gaze wandered to what used to be her Camry. "Can't say the same for the car she plowed into, though."

"Is the owner of that car around?" Luke asked.

"You're talking to her."

"Sorry to hear that. If memory serves, you drove a Toyota, right?"

"Right, or I used to. It was a 2008 Toyota Camry. Now it looks more like something you'd see at a museum of modern art."

"Ouch! That bad?"

"Worse. Much, much worse."

"Well, it's a good thing your baby kicked when he did. Otherwise you may have been in that glob of twisted metal. And congratulations on the baby, by the way. I'm glad that all worked out for you."

She recalled how she'd opened up to him months ago about the struggle to conceive. They'd had an hour-long conversation filled with playful, entertaining banter. It had ended with a friendly goodbye, best wishes, and her driving off to meet her husband. "And here comes the ambulance, so I guess I have to let you get back to your job assisting other callers in need."

"Only if you're absolutely sure there is nothing else I can do for you," he said.

"No, I'm good. And as much as I've enjoyed chatting with you...*again*...it's time to say goodbye...*again*." His laughter filtered through the phone, making her smile.

"All right then, I see the ambulance has indeed made it to the location. Thank you for calling 911. Goodbye again, Cori."

"Goodbye Luke." Cori ended the call and exhaled slowly. "And thank *you,* Mr. Sexy Voice, for that extremely pleasant exchange." She winked at her friend.

"Oh, really? You should have gotten more information. Maybe he's single."

Cori snorted with laughter. "I've spoken to him before, and if I remember correctly, he is single. Not that it matters."

"What do you mean by that? And when did you speak to him?"

"My windshield got busted on I-10 in Beaumont a week before Jim's wreck. Luke was my phone buddy while I waited an hour for the adhesive on the replacement windshield to dry. Oh and sure. He'd be all over this, right?" She waved a hand vertically across her body. "But, it is strange how my libido has seemed to go into overdrive since I've discovered the pregnancy."

"I remember!" Ellen exclaimed. "When I was pregnant I couldn't get enough of it. Travis thought he'd died and gone to heaven. And now, with two kids under the age of five and this business to keep me busy, we barely have time for a 'How was your day?' much less sex."

"That does kind of suck." Cori sighed and arched

her aching back. "I'll probably go home and fantasize about a mysterious 911 operator named Luke, whose sexy, deep voice triggers my overactive imagination, as well as my unfulfilled sexual urges."

"You won't be pregnant forever, sweetie."

"Are you certain? Some days I feel as though I'll always walk with this waddle."

Ellen laughed and placed an arm around her shoulder. "I know it feels that way sometimes, but you'll be back to your hot little size two body in no time."

"Hmph, I'm doubting that more and more."

"Oh, bull. You don't even look pregnant from behind."

Cori struggled to her slightly swollen feet. "Well, even if I do get back into shape, I don't expect many men will be interested in a widow with a newborn."

Ellen gave her a wink and a mysterious smile. "You never know what fate has in store for you, Cori. You just. Never. Know."

Chapter 8
911: Third Time…No Charm

December 23rd, 8:00 p.m.

"Houston, we have a problem of catastrophic proportions."

Corrine Ritter smiled at the sound of pure panic in her sister's tone. If Melissa wasn't freaking out over something, she wasn't breathing. "What's wrong?"

"That stupid talking puppy toy is a dud. We put batteries in it and the damn thing just sits there. It's the only thing Lilly asked the mall Santa to bring her, even when he made other suggestions to go along with it. When she doesn't find it under the tree in the morning there may not be blood, but there will mostly likely be tears to go along with that tiny little broken heart. I'm just calling to warn you ahead of time."

"Will she even notice? I mean, between my gifts and Mom and Dad's, she'll have plenty to keep her occupied."

"We can only hope, Sis. It's all she's been talking about for weeks. Neither Roland nor I have time to exchange it by tomorrow morning. With Christmas Eve at our place and Christmas Day at his folks, we're swamped."

"How about if I leave early tomorrow morning and try to find a replacement?"

"Unnecessary. I just called to vent. I'm not about to ask my almost eight and a half month preggo sister to hit the toy stores for me on Christmas Eve. Lilly will have to get over it. I think I'll wrap it anyway and let her open it."

"You're going to let her open a broken toy?"

"Uh, yeah. At least this way we can blame it on Santa. I'll tell her it must have fallen from his sleigh or something and we'll make sure she gets a replacement."

"No, I'll stop on the way in tomorrow. I feel fine and I don't mind doing it for my adorable niece. Besides, no way can I sit for two hours without needing to walk around and take a restroom break. All I need is the name of the toy. I'll find a store that has it in stock along my route."

"I don't know, Cori. Your C-section is scheduled for one week from now. You're already pushing it by making this trip."

"I'm fine, and I insist." She smiled when her sister's protests finally turned to acceptance.

"If you could manage that, you'd be sister of the century, but are you sure you're okay? No cramping or lower back pains?"

"No cramping and no more than the usual back pains since the sixth month. I got this, Sis. Don't worry."

****

December 24th, 3:45 a.m.

"In one thousand feet, your destination will be on your right."

Cori beamed when she saw the brightly lit storefront. "And there it is. Thank you Google Map app. You are a genius." She steered her Explorer into a mini mall on the outskirts of Beaumont, Texas. Viv's Toy Emporium was a family-owned business that promised to keep its doors opened from midnight Christmas Eve morning until noon—perfect shopping hours for a pregnant woman with a backache and insomnia. The store boasted a convenient location; right next to an open all night fast food restaurant, also perfect for someone who needed to pee at least once an hour.

She chose a parking spot between the two businesses, thinking it would give her a chance to stretch her legs and get the kinks out of her lower back. Walking with a pronounced waddle, she headed for the restaurant, in hopes of finding clean restrooms with an abundance of toilet paper. Cori bypassed the food counter, and headed to the back of the restaurant first. She met the gaze of a man seated alone in a booth near the back. The "Good morning" she'd been prepared to give him froze in her throat. He had creamy skin the color of café au lait, but hard, angry eyes seemed to cut right through her—eyes that shade of green common in people with equal parts white and black. His scruffy beard matched the shaggy, light brown hair on his head. She shivered and hurried into the bathroom, making sure to lock the door behind her. Some people were just plain evil, and that guy had the look.

She took her time in the restroom, hoping he'd be gone by the time she left. No such luck. Not only was he still there, but a second man had joined him, this one thin, his arms covered with tattoos, his head shaved bald, but with a trimmed goatee, and possessing much kinder eyes. The first man's voice reached her, deep and disturbing, and sent a feeling of absolute horror and dread throughout her body.

"You ever do a big, pregnant bitch, man?"

"Hell no," the second man replied.

"Me either, dog. Might have to give that a try."

Cori hit the door as fast as she could waddle, her heart thumping in terror as all thoughts of grabbing a quick bite to eat dissipated with the need to put as much distance as possible between her unborn child and that animal.

She covered her heart with one hand, looked around to make sure she hadn't been followed, even considered getting in her car to find another store. Unfortunately, this was the only one she'd found along her route that was open and still had the toy in stock. Throwing occasional furtive glances behind her, she pushed through the entrance of the toy store and searched the area for a salesclerk.

A shuffling sound toward the back of the store got her attention and she headed in that direction. A tall, athletically built woman with skin the color of dark toffee faced away from her, stocking a shelf. The wire of one earbud hung from her ear, a possible explanation for why she hadn't heard Cori come in.

She'd nearly called out to the woman when her gaze landed on a display of talking robot puppies. The exact one she needed as a replacement for her niece, and ten bucks cheaper than what Melissa had paid, too. *Score!* Head bent, she picked up one box, then another, struggling to remember if Melissa had specified a color. She resorted to *eeny, meeny, miny, moe*, and her finger landed on the pink puppy. Lilly loves pink. No problem there.

Tucking the pink one under her arm, she re-stacked

the other boxes as she'd found them and grabbed a large pack of double A batteries, enough to keep the pink pup yipping, barking, and speaking long after the Christmas holidays ended. She looked up, her mouth open and ready to ask if they gift-wrapped. She snapped it shut when she realized the clerk had disappeared.

A commotion at the front of the store accompanied a woman's shriek. Cori took a cautious peek around a huge wire container filled with multicolored balls, slapped a hand over her mouth to stifle a scream. That man…that same man from the fast food joint, stood behind the woman, one arm around her neck, the other hand holding a pistol to her head.

Cori ducked back behind the ball-filled container, situated herself where she could observe without being seen and kept quiet.

The thug jerked the woman by the neck, his voice deep and gravelly. "Anyone else in here?"

The store employee didn't answer, got slapped for her silence.

"No. I'm here alone!" she cried out.

"No customers?"

"No!"

Cori sucked in her breath. The clerk hadn't seen her after all. She checked for mirrors, cameras, or anything that would reveal her location to the robbers. One convex mirror hung from the ceiling on her aisle, but her current location was out of range of the mirror.

"Open both registers for me. I want all the cash in the drawers!" the thug demanded.

Cori stood frozen. *Just give them the cash so they can be on their merry way.* What kinds of assholes rob a toy store on Christmas Eve? She recalled the man's angry, terrifying gaze, along with the tasteless, threatening question he'd asked his buddy. It sent a shiver of fear up her spine. Yeah, *that* kind of asshole. She placed a protective hand around her belly. She had to protect her baby—she *must* do whatever possible to stay away from them.

"Where's the rest of it, bitch?"

Cori's stomach turned at the sound of a fist hitting flesh, followed by the clerk's cry of pain. She bit back tears. *That poor woman! What could she do to help her?*

"The owner left with the bulk of it just after midnight, I swear!" the clerk cried. "There's another two hundred in smaller bills and coins in a desk drawer in the manager's office at the back of the store. We don't keep a lot of cash here. Most people use debit or credit cards now."

He shoved her toward the back of the store. "Show me."

"Get the damn money and let's go," the second guy called out to his partner.

Hurried footsteps headed in Cori's direction. Overwhelmed by panic, she slipped around the opposite side of the basket of balls, in case they turned in her direction. They entered one of two doorways against the back wall.

It got quiet for a moment, and Cori took a chance and peeked around the corner. The second man stayed upfront, his foot tapping in a rapid cadence, as though waiting for the starting gun of a fifty-yard dash. A scream from the sales clerk and sounds of a struggle had him rushing to the back of the store.

"Aw, hell no! I ain't here so you can satisfy your

need for brown sugar, man. Get the damn money and let's get the hell out of here. I *told* you cops patrol this place a couple times a night."

The would-be rapist laughed, his evil cackle rang out. "Brown sugar's just as good as any other, bro."

Cori's gaze wasn't on the gun-waving thugs, but on the lights from a car pulling into the parking lot. Her concern turned to panic as the vehicle parked in front of the full-length glass door. The overhead canopy lights revealed the distinctive markings of a Jefferson county cruiser. A tall, burly black man wearing a Deputy Sheriff's uniform stepped out of the car. Cori stifled a groan, certain the shit was about to hit the proverbial fan. *Why didn't they just take the money and get out? What kind of idiots waste this kind of time robbing a store on Christmas Eve?*

The officer jerked on the door, seemed surprised to find it locked, pulled out his phone and put it to his ear. In seconds, "All I Want for Christmas is You," sounded from the phone vibrating on the sales counter.

"Shit! There's a cop at the door," the second thug hissed.

"It's my husband," the clerk whimpered. "Please, just let me talk to him. I'll tell him I'm doing paperwork and had to lock the door. I'll convince him to go so I can finish. No one has to get hurt."

"Your husband's a deputy?" Thug two groaned in frustration. "That shit ain't gonna work, man! Not with her split lip and swollen jaw, and all because you can't stand to have a bitch around without using her as a punching bag. I *told* you, Shawn! Get the damn money and get out. Now we're stuck in a situation we got no choice but to shoot our way out of."

"Do I look like I want to hear your shit right now? And didn't I tell you not to use names?" Shawn sneered. *At least she could put a name to the face.* "Keep it up and your ass is goin' down first, *T-Bone!* Now, how you like that?" Both men let a steady flow of profanity fly as the cop started tapping on the door. "Is there another way out?"

"There's a set of double doors in the stock room for truck deliveries, but it's locked up tight." She pointed to a pegboard hanging from the wall. "The spare key usually hangs right there, but the owner must have forgotten to put it back. We had a truck come in late yesterday evening."

"Show him."

The woman indicated a second door.

The one called T-Bone yanked open the squeaky door and lights illuminated the room. He came out, seconds later. "We ain't gettin' out through there. That latch is welded onto the door with a heavy duty padlock."

More door banging, followed by more profanity from both men. His face hard with look of resolution, Shawn walked out in plain sight of the cop, his arm around the clerk's neck and the gun pointed to her temple.

The Deputy's face froze in absolute horror as he drew his gun and pointed it at the man.

"Yo, put it down or she's dead!" Shawn yelled to the cop.

Seconds later, the cop's partner joined him at the door, his pistol gripped in one hand and his radio in the other.

A shot rang out and a large shatter pattern appeared

in the upper half of the tempered glass door, but the glass remained in place. The clerk screamed as the second cop went down, Cori assumed before he'd had a chance to radio in the situation. The first cop dove to safety.

"Oh my God. Oh my God. Oh. My. God!" Cori repeated in a low whisper. A back and forth screaming match between the cop and the two thugs escalated as Cori eyed the entrance of the stockroom. Making a mad dash for the door, she managed to squeeze through the half-opened portal without making it squeak. She found the farthest, darkest corner behind the tallest stack of boxes and hid herself. She felt exposed in the brightly lit room. T-Bone had turned on the lights, and it would be too risky to turn them off now. She looked down, realizing she still clutched the toy and batteries in a white-knuckled death grip. She set them on a box and started digging in her purse for her phone. Everything had shot out of control so quickly she could barely think straight. She dialed 911 and waited.

In seconds she was connected to a dispatcher, but the feminine twang was a far cry from the deep sexy drawl she'd hoped would answer her call.

****

Luke Oliver rubbed his left hand over his face, ready to get the hell out of this place. It had been the typical craziness of a holiday shift, with everything from drunken partygoers, car wrecks, stolen farm animals from a local church nativity scene, stolen lawn decorations, crazy ex-girlfriends, obnoxious neighbors, and parental custody disagreements, with enough action in between to keep him awake during the twelve-hour shift. So far, only a couple of injuries, but nothing life threatening had occurred, for a pleasant change of pace.

He checked the time…3:58 a.m. Christmas Eve. He'd have just enough time to throw some things into a carry-on duffle-bag, take a two hour nap, and drive his butt to the George Bush Intercontinental Airport in Houston for his flight to a much needed tropical vacation to Cozumel.

Byron entered the room, his face a mask of discomfort.

"What's up, buddy?"

Byron's hand moved to his belly and he let out a low, miserable groan. "Sorry, man. I know you need to go, but can you spare me a few more minutes?" His eyes widened as an ugly below-the-belt rumble carried over into the otherwise silence of their personal space.

Luke shuddered at the foul sound. "Dude! Have you been eating burritos from your neighborhood street vendor again? Didn't I tell you to stay away from that?"

"No, man—you remember when I had an early Christmas at my folks last weekend?"

"Yeah, I covered for you."

"My sister waited until after my toddler niece kissed on me to tell me she'd just recuperated from some kind of intestinal virus. I think she gave it to me, man." He made a face as his stomach gave another rendition of some creature that could have co-starred in a "Men in Black" movie.

Luke pointed at the door. "Get the hell away from me before something explodes out of your belly. I'll hang on until you're done."

Byron took off at a run to the nearest bathroom. "I'll be back!"

Luke settled back into the chair his ass had

practically worn a hole in during the last week of long hours and little sleep. He reached into the drawer and pulled out the can of disinfectant spray he kept on hand, and gave his air space a liberal dousing. He coughed and waved it away as Lucy called out to him from the other side of the room.

"Hey Oliver, I've got a panicked pregnant lady here requesting to speak to a "Luke" if he's available. Want me to tell her you left already?"

"No! Send her on over." His phone rang and he resettled his headgear before hitting the answer button.

"911, what's your emergency?"

"I hope you can hear me because I can't speak above a whisper."

Luke straightened to attention, every nerve-ending alert, and ready for an emergency situation. A whisperer was never a good sign. "Yes, I can hear you. What's your situation, ma'am?"

"Is this Luke?"

"Yes, ma'am, it is. Do I know you?" he said, struggling to recognize the feminine whisper.

"It's Corinne Ritter."

His adrenaline shot through the roof at the familiar name. "What's going on, Cori?"

"I'm at Viv's Toy Emporium on highway 90 in Beaumont. Two men with guns came in to rob the place. They're holding the sales clerk at gunpoint but none of them know I'm here. The clerk was wearing earbuds and I don't think she saw or heard me when I came into the store. I'm hiding out in the stockroom. I'm thirty-five weeks pregnant. One of the men...he...he already tried to rape the female clerk here, but his partner stopped him. Then two sheriff's deputies showed up at the store. I heard the clerk say one of the deputies was her husband. And…"

She stopped, attempted to stifle a sob. "One of the deputies got shot when he tried to radio for help. I don't know if he's dead or not, but the other deputy, the clerk's husband, is still outside the building. When I hid in the stock room, they still had the woman at gunpoint but I don't know what's going on out there now. The stock room is at the back of the store and I'm hiding behind stacks of boxes."

"Okay, Cori. I'm going to stay on the phone with you until this is over, do you understand?"

"Yes."

"I've already dispatched units to Viv's Toy Emporium at the intersection of 90 and Sebring. They're on the way already. They'll also have a CNT, a Crises Negotiation Team. I've also alerted the SWAT unit, but until they can get here from Austin, the Special Response Team will be on site." As he spoke, he typed out the dispatch codes and information.

Officer down, hostage situation with one female, second female (caller) thirty-five weeks pregnant and hiding out in stockroom at back of the store, her presence unknown to the perps, proceed with caution.

"Oh God, I'm so scared for the sales clerk, and for my baby. Those two men, I saw them at the fast food joint next door before I walked over to this place to shop for something. That one man…Shawn, his partner called him, looks mixed race and has green eyes…he said something to his buddy when I passed by him. He's…he's a monster. That poor woman out there must be so terrified. Shawn called the other one T-Bone."

If he could snap his fingers, he'd have been in that

room with her in a second. His training at his former career had prepared him to handle situations like that with little or no effort. "It'll be okay, Corinne. You said you're in the stock room. Is there a back exit?"

"Yes, but it's locked. I heard her say her boss left with the key a few hours ago."

"What kind of door is it?"

"Double steel doors—heavy duty."

"Is it padlocked? Do you see chains or anything like that?"

"No chains, but it's got a padlock on a heavy duty hasp lock."

Luke's fingers flew over the keyboard as he asked more questions, gleaning every bit of information he could about the situation from the terrified woman—anything that would help the officers already en route to the location. It was possible she'd give them something they could use to diffuse the situation before anyone else was hurt—or worse.

"So, Cori, you'll be a mom in a few weeks."

"Yes, I'm scheduled for a C-section December thirtieth. I hope you don't mind that I asked for you, but when I dialed 911, I was a little shocked you didn't answer. I know that sounds ridiculous when the odds of catching you the second time were practically non-existent."

"In this city, with our current shortage of workers and considering as many hours as I've put in the last couple of months, I'm surprised I didn't. You know, I saw a picture of your accident after that call ended. You were so lucky not to be anywhere near your Toyota."

"Yeah, but I'm not so lucky today, am I?"

"Lucky enough not to have anyone in that building

know you're there."

"I guess you're right."

"So, do you know if your baby is a boy or a girl?"

"It's a boy."

"That's awesome, Cori. Man, I can't wait to have a kid one day." *Keep her distracted and calm.* "You know, you don't have to talk. I can keep talking to you if you're worried about them overhearing you."

"I hear them yelling and cussing at each other out there, so I know I'm okay as long as I whisper."

"Can you hear any of their conversation?"

"It sounds like they're blaming each other. Do you want me to go to the door to hear more?"

"No. Just stay where you are. Do you have plenty of battery left on your phone?" He waited patiently while she checked.

"Shoot, I've only got about twenty-five percent left."

"No charger with you?"

"Hang on," she hissed.

After a minute of shuffling around, she came back on the phone. "I remembered to put it in my purse, thank goodness."

"Okay, here's what I want you to do. Look around for an outlet, preferably one you can plug into and keep talking to me." After another minute she came back on.

"I found one, Luke."

"Can you plug into it and remain hidden?" He heard more shuffling.

"There are several lightweight boxes I can stack to keep out of sight. I'm going to do that now. Don't hang up on me, okay? You promise you'll wait?"

"Of course I'll wait, but first make sure your phone

is set to silent. We don't want any notification noises to alert them to your location."

"Done, now hang on."

****

Cori moved around the room without making a sound, even though she still heard the two thieves throwing insults at each other. She checked every large box she found, careful not to choose anything too heavy. One particularly heavy box was already in place but needed a slight adjustment to its position. She finally managed to push it, using her knees for advantage. It took several minutes of huffing and puffing but she eventually built a fortress of boxes, a barrier to give her some semblance of security. Before hiding away, Cori peeked through the hinged side of the doorway to check out the situation at the front of the store. After a minute of catching glimpses and bits of conversation from the others in the building, she returned to her spot behind the façade.

"Okay, I'm done. Luke? Are you there?"

"I'm here. I told you I wouldn't go anywhere. Is it safe to talk?"

"Yes, they're still blaming each other and they've shoved a large display case in front of the door. I guess so no one can see what's going on inside the store."

"You checked it out again?"

"Yes, but I was careful. I keep thinking how terrified that poor woman must be. Shawn keeps threatening to shoot his partner. T-Bone wants them to give themselves up, but he didn't shoot the cop, so he doesn't have as much to lose. Shawn shot him."

"You said you saw them earlier and he spoke to you?"

Her blood chilled at the thought. "Not to me, but about me." She related what the man had said to his buddy. "I don't know, it's like he hated me just for existing. And the way he laughed afterwards…" She shivered, remembering how the sound had chilled her blood.

"You were right to hide. Do whatever you can to stay away from him."

"You don't have to tell me twice."

"So, is your husband excited about the baby? I remember you saying you'd been trying for a while."

She listened to make sure she still heard their voices up front. Satisfied, she returned to her lifeline. "My husband died before I discovered I was pregnant."

"Oh, Cori, I'm so sorry. That must have been awful for you."

"In some ways, it was really awful, but in others, not nearly as bad as you'd think."

"How long after he passed away did you discover the pregnancy?"

"Four months and by then I was four months along. I know, I know. You must be thinking 'how could she not know', right?"

"Not at all. That kind of emotional trauma can wreak havoc on a woman's nervous system."

"I thought it was stress. My doctor had just told me I couldn't get pregnant." She smiled to herself, thinking about one particular visit to her gynecologist. "From the moment I saw that little life kicking and squirming on the ultrasound, heard his heartbeat, I went from having this deep, dark, void in my soul to a feeling of total fulfillment. I couldn't believe it." She rubbed her aching back and sat on a sturdy plastic storage container labeled "Christmas Decorations" in neat, black print.

"How did it happen, if you don't mind me asking?"

"The usual way. You know, one sperm out of millions courting a single egg." She smiled at his laughter. "You have such a great laugh."

"And *you* have a wicked sense of humor, but I meant your husband's death."

"I know you did. I find it helps to see the humor in a situation or at least the irony, which in some cases, ends up being humorous whether you like it or not."

"Care to elaborate?"

She hesitated at what she was about to divulge but decided she had nothing to lose at this point. "My husband wrapped his car around a tree. His college student girlfriend was with him." Something about the faceless "voice" had her confessing things she would normally keep to herself.

"Oh. Wow."

"It gets better. He'd left me because our fertility specialist said my chances of getting pregnant were slim to none. Jim said he needed to raise his odds of having a son, so he cut me loose and moved on to more fertile ground."

"Was he a farmer or a gambler?"

"My grandfather farmed and he claimed it was almost the same thing. But no, Jim was a college math teacher. As the only son of an only son, having a male heir was important to him."

"Yeah. There's your irony."

"Oh. You have no idea."

"Enlighten me."

She bit her lip, wondering how much to tell him.

Considering her situation, she decided this confession may be necessary. "He lost control of his car while his girlfriend was performing oral sex on him."

"Are you serious?"

"Oh yeah."

"Son of a…"

She smiled at his obvious attempt not to curse. "You can say it."

"Son of a bitch."

"Yeah. Here's a tad more irony for you. There he was, wanting to procreate, but his last DNA ends up…well, one can only assume where it ended up, I guess." She grinned as Luke's chuckle rumbled in her ear.

"I'm sorry," he said, choking back his laughter. "I know it's callous to laugh."

"Go ahead. I sure as hell did once I got over my initial anger. It took several months, but it happened."

"Are you always this funny, or is it a trait that pops up during intense situations?"

Cori passed a hand over her belly. "Always, I guess; enough to be voted wittiest girl by my peers in high school. I figure that's about the only senior superlative with any kind of stick-to-it-iveness. You should see our handsomest boy."

"Early balding?"

"Much worse. Guys can't help from going bald, that's just genetics. Besides, I know lots of sexy bald guys. No, old Jerry got hooked on crack and rotted all his teeth out of his head. The dude could pass for sixty at thirty-two."

"Bummer."

"I know, right? And the most spirited girl walks

around in an anti-depressant induced state of semi-zombie-ism. Did you catch that? I think I just made up a new word there…semi-zombie-ism."

"I'll expect to see it in Funk & Wagnall's by the end of next year."

She snorted. "Wikipedia, at best."

"It may be your second of the evening. I think stick-to-it-iveness is your first."

"Nah, somebody beat me to it. Google it, you'll see."

He was one-step ahead of her. "I'll be damned. There it is, right there in Merriam-Webster's dictionary."

"Told ya. How the hell did we get on this subject anyway?"

"I believe you were commenting on your husband's wasted DNA."

"Oh, yeah." She turned her head, listening for two male voices in the store section. The thug's foul responses to the Crises Negotiations Team's spokesperson set her teeth on edge. "I got the best of my husband." *Along with the one million dollar life insurance policy.* Of course, the money hadn't meant a thing to her until she'd discovered the pregnancy. Now, it ensured a good future for her son.

"What about your son's paternal grandparents? Are they still alive?"

"I've only seen them a handful of times, the last time at the funeral. From the way they talked, they wouldn't be making any return trips to see me. They're homesteading in Alaska, believe it or not."

"You're kidding."

"I kid about lots of things, but not when it comes to

my in-laws—both doctors and lovely people, by the way. I admire them for doing what they did. They love to travel and have been all over the world. They spent a month in Alaska about six years ago and called Jim to let him know they weren't coming home. Said they were tired of the big house, fancy cars, and keeping up with the Joneses. They live a simple life over there."

"Do they live along the coast around Anchorage or Juneau?"

"Heck no. They're closer to the interior where it gets really cold, like thirty below cold."

"Damn!"

"I know, right? I don't think they'll be the "doting grandparents" type. They're too worried about reducing their carbon footprint, and trying not to starve or freeze to death." She released a long sigh. "It's just as well. I don't want to share my son with them, anyway. My parents are both still around and I'm very close to my sister, so I'm good for family."

"You seem like you're a strong, capable person, Cori."

She paused a moment. What is it about life-threatening situations that made a girl want to bare her soul to a semi-complete stranger? "I nearly wasn't."

"What do you mean?"

"Is this conversation being recorded?" She hadn't told anyone what she'd almost done the day she discovered her pregnancy. Figured she'd go to her grave without telling another person.

"No, not for a while, now."

"Before I knew I was pregnant, I nearly killed myself. I propped myself up in my bed, with two bottles of pills in one hand and a bottle of wine in the other. I was going to write my family a letter after taking the pills. An old friend was supposed to come by the next day, so I knew I'd be found. I didn't want anyone in my family to find me."

"But you didn't do it."

"No, I didn't. I popped some of the pills into my mouth and before I could swallow, I felt this fluttering inside me. The quickening, they call it. I knew it wasn't gas because I hadn't had anything to eat or drink in two days. It was strong enough to make me wonder if my lack of appetite, nausea, and missed periods were more than depression or trauma. Turned out I was already seventeen weeks pregnant."

"That's amazing. God is good."

"Are you a believer?"

"I am. Are you?"

"I admit I've been skeptical over the years. I'd been married since I was twenty-five, and trying to get pregnant for six years. I prayed so hard for it to happen but it never did. It was easier to start thinking he didn't exist than to think he'd purposely deny me a child."

"The magic is in the timing."

"So it is, but I believe He definitely had a hand in making me feel life when I did."

"That's a good story."

"That I've never shared with another living soul, until you."

"Your secret is safe with me, Cori. I promise."

She had no way of knowing for sure if he meant it, of course. Something in his voice told her she could trust him. "Thanks." She shifted on the container, trying to get comfortable. "Oh, God…"

"Is something wrong, other than the obvious, of

course?"

"I've got some serious lower back pain."

****

Luke sat up in his chair, his senses sharpening. "More than usual?"

"The backaches have gotten increasingly worse since the sixth month or so, but this is the worst. Of course, I'm sitting in a cold stock room with bare concrete walls and floors, with nothing but storage containers and boxes of toys for furniture. I guess that's to be expected, right?"

"Understandably." He notified EMT's to be on standby, just in case. "Look for something you can use to support your back. Maybe open up a box of stuffed animals or something like that." Another groan from Cori and her horrified gasp had his fingers hovering in frozen animation over the keyboard. "What?"

"Luke. I think my water just broke."

He made a face as Byron re-entered the room. "You *think* or you're sure your water broke?"

"I'm sure. That's what happened all right. Oh my God. This can't happen here. I'm scheduled for a C-section for a reason. I have severe uterine scarring from previous surgeries. My OB worried my uterus could tear during normal labor."

Luke's training went into overdrive as her whispers turned to panicked hysteria. "Shhh…hush, now. You don't want to get anyone's attention. You're going to stay calm. Remember, I'll be here for you every step of the way, and I've already alerted the paramedics to your condition. They'll be there to help at the earliest possibility." He looked up at Byron.

"Sorry, Luke." Byron gave him an apologetic

smile. "I think I'll be okay for a while. Catch me up and I'll take over for you. You need to get out of here."

"What?" Cori hissed on the other end of the phone. "You're leaving?"

"I'm not going anywhere." Luke shook his head at Byron as he muted his mic. "Not possible, I've got a thirty-five week pregnant woman hiding out in a hostage situation, with one deputy down and another whose wife is the hostage. The pregnant woman's water just broke and she's experiencing severe back pains. Early labor but she's scheduled for a necessary C-section in a week."

With Byron looking on, Luke continued to type, steadily updating the situation to the EMT's and members of law enforcement agencies gathered around the building.

"Holy Moses! This is the kind of call you live for, man."

Luke grinned at his co-worker. "You know me well, buddy. I'm not leaving until I've seen her through this. Now get the hell out of here before you get me sick with whatever it is you've got."

"Are you sure? What about your flight?"

"There'll be other flights. Get your ass in one of those cots in the break room. Quit contaminating my airspace, dammit." He picked up the can of sanitizer and gave the air another liberal spritzing.

Byron backed out of the room, holding his arm over his mouth as he coughed and choked on the spray. "Just keep me posted on the situation."

"Are you there, Luke?" Cori's panicked voice reached his headset.

"I told you, I'm not going anywhere. Now, listen to

me. I want you to start looking around for anything that could possibly help your situation. Tarps or anything you can put on the floor to cushion it or create some kind of insulation."

"Shh…"

He held his breath at her whispered command, wishing he could do more for this poor woman. The two minutes he sat there waiting felt more like fifteen. When she finally spoke again, he released his breath.

"Okay they're at the front of the store again. I can talk."

"Start looking around for items you can use, Cori. Anything at all you think would make your situation more comfortable."

"You won't hang up?"

"Nope, I'll be here when you get back."

Several minutes later, she came back on the phone, out of breath, but her voice carried a note of success. "I hit the jackpot. I found kiddie sleeping bags, a case of those blankets that fold into pets, and I found a box cutter."

"Hang on to that." *And I'll pray you don't need to use it.*

"I found something else."

"What's that?"

"One of them set a backpack down by the door. I checked it out and it was full of ammo. No guns, just ammo."

"No kidding?"

"I have it. I hid it from them."

"You took the entire backpack or just the ammo?"

"I removed the ammo out of it. There still a few other items left in it to give it some weight.

Hopefully, the guy will probably think he just forgot to put the ammo in it."

"I'm sure you're right." *God, if you're listening, please don't let them go looking for that ammo.* "Are you sure you're hidden well? I'd hate for them to get suspicious and go snooping around your hiding place."

"I'm well hidden. From the door or even the center of the room you can't see the nest I've made for myself."

"Can you tell me what kind of ammo?" She read off the descriptions, and Luke entered the data into the computer system. The multiple units outside the building would be glad to get this particular information. He'd bet anything they were carrying Hi-point 9 mm pistols—most likely 8 shot. "How many shots were fired?"

"Just the one that injured the deputy. Do you...do you know if he's alive?"

Fifteen left between the two of them, that's assuming the guns were fully loaded. Here's hoping they didn't have any more on them. "I'm sorry, I don't. I know he was picked up and brought to the hospital for emergency surgery, but I have no way of knowing how that turned out."

"Oh, I was just wond—oh...oooh..."

"What's wrong?"

"Oh, God...I'm no expert on labor and delivery but I think I may be experiencing my first contraction."

Well, hell. Of course she is. No way will this go easy for her. "I'd say it's possible since your water broke. On a scale of one to ten, how bad was it?"

"Mm, a point-five maybe."

He smiled as he wrote down the time and her pain

rating. Her answer told him she more than likely had a background in some kind of math or engineering field. "We didn't talk about your job before, did we? What do you do for a living, Cori?"

"I'm a drafting technician for a civil engineering firm in Sulphur, Louisiana."

"I thought so. Most women would have said one-half rather than point five."

"Yeah, I guess it is second nature, now. That and using tenths of a mile," she whispered. "Shhh…"

He sat with his eyes squeezed shut, whispering a silent prayer for this to have a good outcome. The chances of her remaining undiscovered in a building the size of Viv's would get slimmer by the hour. He'd looked it up, and the store had a footprint of approximately eight thousand square feet. The storage area where she'd hidden herself made up less than one tenth of that.

"I can talk now," she said.

"Do you live in Sulphur?"

"Yes."

He opened another tab and typed in the info he had on her. In seconds, he'd accessed her driver's license. "Are you still living at 1026 Montferro?"

"Y-y-es. God, please tell me you didn't pull up my driver's license. That picture is awful."

He stifled a chuckle as he stared at the adorable face looking back at him from his monitor. Pixie cut blond hair, big blue eyes, and full lips. "No, it's not. You're five-five, a hundred and fifteen pounds—"

She cut him off with a low groan. "Not anymore, I'm not."

"You can't count baby weight. That'll be off in no

time." He frowned as he focused on her DOB. "You've got a birthday tomorrow."

"Yep."

"What was that like? Being a Christmas baby, I mean?"

"Not as great as you'd think. Try planning a birthday party when all your friends are out of town for the holidays."

"Yeah. That would kind of suck."

"I can't believe I'll be thirty-two years old already. Yesterday I was still in high-school, you know?"

"Tell me about it. I just had my fifteen-year class reunion. I'll be thirty-three on Valentine's Day."

"Go figure," she whispered. "A Valentine's Day baby talking a Christmas baby through her labor from a 911 call during a Christmas Eve toy store robbery. This has got to be a first."

He chuckled at her description. "Can't make this stuff up, can you?"

"You can, but nobody would believe it. Now you know what I look like, but I know nothing about you. This situation is one huge bucket of suck."

"Ask whatever you want and I'll answer to the best of my ability."

"Height and weight."

"Six-one, two-twenty-five, and I don't want to brag, but it's all muscle."

"No doubt," she snorted. "Hair?"

"Existence, or color?"

"Both, I guess."

"Then yes, I have hair." He paused to pass his fingers through his short-cropped hair. "No sign of thinning yet and it's light brown, kind of wavy if it gets too long, so I keep it cut short. I have one green eye and one blue."

"No kidding?"

"No kidding."

"Can you ride ponies backwards and flip pancakes in the air, too?"

"Excuse me?"

"Like Aiden Quinn's character in the movie "Practical Magic"…"

"Don't know that I've seen that one."

"It's only the best chick flick ever…"

"Could explain why I haven't seen it."

"It's so good—one of those I have to watch anytime it pops up on a movie channel. It used to annoy the hell out of my husband. I'd always have to go watch it in another room."

"So how do the two different color eyes fit into the plot?"

"Sandra Bullock's character, Sallie, is Wiccan. The women in her family are cursed and any men they love die. When Sallie is just a little girl, she casts a spell so she'll never fall in love and get hurt. Her true love would be able to ride a pony backwards, flip pancakes in the air, have a kind heart, his favorite symbol would be a star, and he'd have one blue eye and one green eye. As an adult, she meets a cop with all those qualities and falls in love with him."

"So that's good?"

"Well, not at first. She cast the spell so she *wouldn't* fall in love. A guy with all of those qualities wasn't supposed to exist, so she'd never fall in love and she'd never lose him and get hurt."

"That sounds complicated to me."

"You'd have to see the movie to understand." After a pause, she whispered her next question. "Do you have something against longer hair?"

"What? No."

"You said you keep it cut short."

"It's the waves I don't like."

"Why not? Wavy hair on a guy is so sexy. Like cover model sexy."

"You think?"

"Mm…I know," she sighed. "Aidan Quinn's hair is wavy in the movie. He's a cop, and it's *extremely* sexy."

"I guess I got used to having it short in the military."

"What branch?"

"Marines. Twelve years."

"Wow…I guess you've been everywhere, haven't you?"

He laughed into the phone. "Maybe, if you consider the middle-east everywhere. Places I've been are not exactly tourist destinations."

"Twelve years. Why'd you stay so long? Did you plan to make a lifetime career of it and change your mind?"

"Not at all. I was a sniper, set up to protect squadrons. They'd put us where our guys were feeling the heat. I kept a lot of men and women safe, and…I don't know. I just felt like I couldn't leave. And then one day I had enough and walked away."

The silence grew heavy and ominous between them.

"Are you okay?" she finally asked.

"I'm fine."

"I mean no lingering effects? No PTSD or anything?"

"Civilian life took some getting used to again, I'll admit. But no, I haven't had any of the episodes some servicemen experience. I'm lucky."

"Well…good. I'm glad to hear that."

The lull in their conversation had him thinking about the bag full of ammo she'd found. "So, have they searched the bag for the missing ammo, yet?" He found himself whispering, and then cleared his throat to repeat the question.

"No, they didn't come inside the room. They just stood outside trading insults. I'm okay for now, but I have to wonder how long I can stay hidden. If this turns into a prolonged stand-off, I may have to make myself known—"

"We'll get you out of there before that becomes necessary." he said. Her silence had him struggling to find something to keep her hopeful. "What's your son's name? I guess you've had one picked out for months."

"I have not. I don't know what I'm going to name him."

"That surprises me. Haven't you been pouring over a book of one thousand baby names or scouring the internet?"

"No. I'm holding out for something that moves me, something that has some kind of meaning. They'll be building snowmen in hell before I name him after his father."

"I can't blame you for that. Is your place all set up and ready for the baby?"

"Not at the moment. I haven't even put the crib together. I'm missing the patience gene when it comes to reading directions and constructing things."

"I think it shows patience that you didn't jump on it right away. Some friends of mine had their entire nursery furnished and ready before she started her fifth month."

"That was my sister. I've always found first time expectant parents to be annoying as hell so I was determined not to be one of *those* moms. But...I can see now that I should have tackled that crib sooner. And I guess I'll have to scratch to find a name sooner than I expected."

Another thirty minutes dragged by with no headway on the hostage situation.

Luke cocked his head at the sound of voices in the background. "What's going on over there?"

"They're arguing again...oh, shhhh..."

****

Cori craned her neck to peek between two large boxes facing the room's entrance.

Shawn shoved T-Bone up against the wall, one hand around his neck. "Where's the ammo? What'd you do with it?"

T-Bone pointed to the bag. "Man, I coulda sworn I put it in here."

"You about a damn zero, man." Shawn raised his gun to T-Bone's head. "You just said yours is empty and I only got two shots left. You know, I woulda had more, but some dumbass had to go shooting at stray cats." He slapped T-Bone upside the head. "You got shit for brains, dude! I shoulda known better than to plan any damn thing with you."

"I'm sorry, man. But you saw me put the ammo in that bag, didn't you?"

"I saw you put it in a bag, but you musta put the wrong damn bag in the car."

"I didn't, Shawn. I swear I didn't!"

Cori held her breath, kept the phone tucked close to block out the screen's glare as the men argued with each other, drifting closer to her and her baby belly.

Shawn pointed the gun at T-Bone's head again and bared his teeth. "I oughta shoot your worthless ass right now and be done with it. You ain't good for nothin' but gettin' my ass killed."

"Please, man, don't do that! We'll find a way outta this!"

A ruckus at the front of the store had both men running toward the noise.

"Something's happening," she hissed into her phone.

"I sent word the perps were in the stock room at the back of the store. The department may have taken the opportunity to try to clear the doorway."

She gasped as the female hostage let loose a blood-curdling scream.

"Stop or she's dead, man. I ain't foolin' around, and I ain't goin' back to jail!" Shawn bellowed.

"Oh God, they have to stop whatever they're doing! Shawn, the really mean one, is threatening to kill the sales clerk if they don't." She sucked in her breath as sharp pain sliced across her abdomen. "Oh. My. God."

"Cori? What's happening?"

"Something's wrong, Luke. This can't be normal. It's too soon in the labor process for the pain to be this bad."

"Rate it for me—one to te—"

"Eleven!" She panted through the pain, gritting her teeth. It finally eased up enough so that she could catch her breath. A new kind of wet seeped through her maternity jeans. She stared at the dark stains. "And I'm bleeding. What do I do?"

"You're going to stay calm and get through this. Does it feel like heavy spotting?"

She didn't have to undress to know this was more than an episode of spotting, heavy or otherwise. "Not spotting—much heavier—more like hemorrhaging. Oh, my God. I can't lose my baby!" In all the scenarios she'd played out in her mind since discovering her pregnancy, this had never come up. Not once, in all her stages of shock and disbelief had she imagined she would lose this child. She could hear the rapid tapping of Luke's fingers on his keyboard.

"You won't. I'm getting you some help. Where are they?"

"I don't know, but they aren't in here. Luke, I need you to do something for me."

"Anything."

"I need you to call my family if I don't make it out of here…" She stopped just short of adding the word 'alive'.

"You'll make it."

"But if I don't, or if I'm not capable of communicating with them, or if my baby makes it but I don't. My parents are Joan and Charles Granger. They live in Richmond, Texas. My sister, Melissa Landry lives south of Houston with her husband, Roland Landry. If my parents aren't there already, they will be soon."

She gave him their phone numbers, heard his

fingers hitting the keyboard before he called them back to her for verification.

"That's it." She exhaled, relief rushing through her. "It's important they hear from someone soon because they'll be waiting for me."

"I've got it and someone will let them know immediately, I promise."

"Thank you, Luke. It means a lot to me."

"They're going to make some noise at the front of the store, but it's a diversionary tactic. They finally have a key to the padlock on those doors. They'll be using some kind of laser torch to cut out the lock, and pass you the key. The perps only have one gun with ammo and they can't be in two places at once."

"Will it be loud?"

"No, but there'll be sparks flying, so stand clear of it until they're done."

She rolled up one of the smaller blankets and stuffed it between her legs to staunch her bleeding, then eased her way out of her self-made hide-a-way. As soon as she saw the first sparks flying, her gaze flew to the opened door leading into the shopping area. She waddled to the door, held her breath and waited. The sudden blast of the firetruck's air horn gave her the cover she needed to close the squeaky door several inches. She waited off to the side until they'd cut out the door's locking mechanism. A couple of taps and thuds later, a hole appeared in the steel door as the lock disappeared from sight.

"Are you there?" A masculine voice cut through the silence of the room.

She peeked through the circular opening where someone shined a flashlight. "I'm here. Where's the key?"

Seconds later, someone used a pair of pliers to pass the key through the still smoldering hole in the door. She grabbed at it and immediately went for the padlock. Lightheaded and shaking, it felt like forever before the lock released. She had to keep herself from crying out when she freed it from the heavy-duty hasp. A steady flow of banter from someone in charge on the law enforcement's PA system gave the team the cover needed to push the doors open.

A swarm of officers entered silently, all of their weapons trained on the door. One turned, focusing on her. "We're going to get you to the hospital right away. We've got an ambulance wait..."

Cori gazed at the man's mouth. His lips moved but the humming in her ears drowned out his words. She raised the phone she'd been clutching in one hand. "Luke? I can't..." She paused, struggling to hear her own words over the deafening hum in her ears. "Tell my family—my baby—I love them."

Her hand dropped to her side as though it were made of lead. She watched as her phone skidded along the floor in front of her, wondered if the impact resistant case kept it from shattering. She felt a gush of something warm and wet between her legs a second before a sea of blackness engulfed her.

****

"Cori? Are you there? Is anyone there?" An icy chill settled over Luke's heart as he heard the pop of gunshots and shouting in the distance. He waited several more minutes until the line went dead. His fingers flew over the keys, making a swift inquiry as to the hostages' conditions. It took several tense minutes to get a response.

Pregnant woman en route to Christus St. Elizabeth Hospital on Calder Avenue.

He released his breath at the news he'd been hoping to hear. "Condition?" he typed.

Critical due to severe blood loss from hemorrhaging. Patient was unconscious.

"Oh...shit." He wiped one hand over his face. "Condition of hostage?"

Sales clerk safe and unharmed.

"Thank God."

One perp down, the other in custody.

"Whatever." As far as he was concerned, those two could live with the consequences of their choices, or not.

He typed one last question. "Any news on the officer shot earlier?"

Negative.

Byron entered the room, his gaze curious.

Luke gave his co-worker a brief nod. "It's all yours, buddy."

His co-worker took his place and logged-in. "What happened to the hostage and the pregnant chick?"

"Hostage is free and unharmed. The pregnant lady is on her way to the hospital, but she hemorrhaged and passed out."

Byron grunted. "Man, that's rough. Hope she makes it, and the kid, too."

Luke headed for his locker to get his bag and coat. "Yeah, me too. Merry Christmas, bro."

"Merry Christmas, Luke. I'll be sitting here all week, waiting to hear all about your conquests of the fairer sex."

"Man, I just want to chillax, you know? Do some diving, some snorkeling, explore the Mayan ruins for a day, and get in some deep-sea fishing. Between this job and my class load last semester, I'm burnt out."

"Well, if anyone deserves a break, it's you, man."

Luke gave Byron a two-fingered salute. "Later."

Chapter 9
Facing Facts

Luke had just enough time to take a quick shower at his place and slip into some fresh travelling clothes. He'd arrive at his friend's place in Humble by 6:00 a.m., leave his truck there to keep from paying for parking, and take a ten minute cab ride over to the airport.

His mind should have been free from thinking about work, but all he could think about was Cori and whether or not she was all right.

Two calls to 911 in a different state, and twice she got him. Not only that, but got to know him enough to ask for him a third time…and he was dispatching, when he actually shouldn't have been. *What were the odds?* When he couldn't stand wondering what happened to her any longer he called a friend of his, an old high school fling who worked as an ER nurse at St. Elizabeth's.

"Lucas Oliver! To what do I owe this immense pleasure?"

"I need a favor, Janie. I need some information on a caller I had earlier. She was brought to St. E's, but I know from experience they won't give me any information on her. I'm just concerned, is all."

It took all of ten minutes for her to call him back. "Hey, Luke, I found the pregnant lady. By any chance, is the kid yours?"

"No, hon. I've only spoken to her over the phone. Sounded like she's had some tough breaks and I wondered how she's doing. End of story."

"Well, she's out of it."

"What?"

"In a coma."

"Oh, hell. What about the baby?"

"Delivered. All his signs are good."

"Any of her family members there, yet?"

"Her parents have been contacted but they're still waiting on them. Not sure about the father of the baby."

"Her husband died several months ago."

"Oh wow. That's got to suck for her. Sure hope she makes it."

"She will."

"You're sure about that?"

"She has to."

"Are you sure you don't have some kind of history with this woman?"

"Nope."

"Oh…it's just…you sound determined, like your mind's made up."

Did he? Was it? She'd know if he was. They had been close once. Extremely close.

"Like I said, she's had a rough time of it in the past, and her kid needs a momma, right?" That's all there was to it. "Thanks for the info, Janie. I appreciate it."

He drove on, tapping an old drum cadence from high school onto his steering wheel. The idea of spending the next week wondering about Cori's condition sucked all the fun out of this vacation for him. How could he feel zero interest in something he'd looked forward to only a few hours ago?

Luke fought the strongest urge to turn his truck around and head back to Beaumont—or to be more precise, head straight for St. Elizabeth's hospital. He didn't, because, well…that would have been insanity, right? He'd be crazy to cancel this trip for someone he didn't know. He'd paid for everything already, planned for months in advance. Surely, it was non-refundable.

He kept driving, but called the twenty-four hour hotline for his travel agency. Fifteen minutes later, he turned his truck around, satisfied that he hadn't thrown thousands completely out the window. While they couldn't refund the money, they could reschedule the vacation at a later date, adjusting the package as necessary. The agency had also taken care of his flight—note to self: always, always, *always* pay for the flight cancellation insurance. He remembered grumbling about it after his travel agent had talked him into it, but damn if it hadn't paid off.

With every mile closer to Beaumont, the heaviness on his chest lessened by degrees. Instead of heading back to his empty apartment, he took the Calder exit and drove to the hospital.

He maneuvered his truck into the parking garage, marveling at the vast choice of available spots at this early hour on Christmas Eve.

Minutes later, he approached the information desk and got the info he needed from the sweet senior citizen volunteer, a porcelain-skinned elderly woman with light blue eyes, thinning white hair, and a bright smile that reminded him of his own grandmother. A short elevator trip later, Luke stepped out into the ICU ward. He approached a woman in lavender scrubs standing behind the desk.

"Excuse me, but can you give me any information on Cori Ritter? She was brought in as one of the toy store hostages, eight and a half months pregnant."

"Are you a family member, sir?"

"No, I'm the 911 operator she contacted during the hostage situation. I stayed on the phone with her through her entire ordeal and I was concerned."

The nurse's face wilted in sympathy. "I'm sorry, sir. Unless you're a family member—"

He raised one hand. "I understand. Are any of her family members here yet? I believe she was on her way to her sister's place in Houston for a family gathering."

"It shows they've been contacted but no one has come in claiming to be family members, yet."

He reached into his shirt pocket and pulled out a slip of paper. "She gave these numbers when I was on the phone with her. Are these the numbers that were called?"

The nurse took the slip of paper and compared it to the numbers listed as contacts. "Yes, sir. These are the same numbers."

He nodded and started to turn away then doubled back. "Excuse me, but I heard the baby was delivered successfully. Where would I find the nursery?"

She smiled. "That would be on the third floor."

"Is he in the NICU?"

"I don't think so. Reports are that he's a big, healthy, baby boy."

He grinned. "He's just waitin' for his mama to wake up, so she can hold him."

The nurse lifted her chin and looked down her nose

at him. "Sounds like you've got an informant on the inside."

"I'll never tell." He touched his forehead. "Thank you, ma'am." He headed for the elevators and the third floor. Within minutes, he found himself standing in front of a large plate-glass window with the curtains drawn. He saw movement inside and tapped on the glass. A middle-aged woman peeked around the curtain. "Ritter…a boy?" he asked, hoping she'd show some sympathy for him.

She nodded, lifting one finger in a silent plea for patience.

Luke stood there, waiting, one toe tapping a rapid sequence against the glossy tile beneath it. Finally, a nurse pulled the curtain aside. She rolled a portable bassinet in front of the window. The bassinet boasted a blue tag labeled *Corrine Ritter*. He'd nearly forgotten her name was Corrine rather than Cori. Both hands shoved deep in his pockets, he stared at the infant. This child of a complete stranger…a woman he felt inexplicably drawn to for some reason.

"Hey there, little dude. I wonder what your mom's going to call you." No one else was around to hear his one-sided murmurings to the newborn infant on the opposite side of the glass. The kid was cute, for sure. Light brown hair and a small, straight nose, with full, rosy cheeks. No doubt, his seven pounds, twelve ounces contributed some to that adorably chubby face. He raised one hand, placed it on the window glass, a poor substitution for a living, breathing miniature human. "You would have been an eight-pounder; at least, if she'd carried you full term. You're a good looking little man, and I hope you have your mom's strength, sense of humor, and character. Sorry, but I hear your dad was kind of a jerk, kid. You ended up with the best parent, and boy are you ever gonna have a story to tell your buddies about how you came into this world."

He stood there a few more minutes, until another nurse rolled a bassinet out of a patient's room. Swaddled in pink, the baby girl must have spent some time in her mom's room. Nursing, maybe? The thought brought to mind his sister's embarrassing displays while she'd nursed his niece and nephew. She'd whipped that boob out like there was nobody else in the room. Sure, breast-feeding was natural, wonderful, and all that, but jeeze Louise, would it hurt to cover it up with a blanket or something?

The nurse peeled Cori's son out of his blanket, Luke presumed to change his diaper. He had to laugh when, as soon as the baby was exposed to the open air, he peed straight up. The nurse covered him then used wipes to clean the area before putting a clean, dry diaper on him. Through it all, the closest Baby Ritter came to crying was a slight pooch and trembling of his lower lip.

His caretaker swaddled him in the blue and white striped blanket again and lifted him. She brought him closer to the window for Luke to get a good look at him then mouthed the words "Good baby".

Luke smiled and gave her a thumbs-up, hoping he stayed that way. His mama could use all the help she could get right now.

When the nurse placed baby Ritter back in his bassinet, Luke took a few minutes more to admire the kid's handsome little face. He could understand how parents went all gaga over their newborns. It must be an awesome feeling to hold a child of your own the first time. Something you created with a person you loved, hopefully. But then again, his own parents both said they felt the same way the first time they held him and his sister, Lee, and they'd been adopted. He figured there were all kinds of prospective parents waiting to dole out the love, and all kinds of babies who needed good parents.

He headed back to the elevator thinking about something his mom had said to soothe him when he was in first grade. Some insensitive kid at school had teased him, said he didn't have a *real family* because he was adopted. She'd hugged him tightly and whispered in his ear. "Out of all the little boys we could have adopted in the whole, wide world, we chose you. That makes you special."

Luke entered the elevator thinking Baby Ritter had half that battle won already with a mom like Cori.

****

His belly satisfied with a breakfast of bacon, eggs, and grits from the cafeteria, Luke stepped out of the elevator carrying a large cup of coffee and a bottle of water. He'd already decided he wasn't leaving until he'd spoken to at least one of Cori's family members. Maybe the coffee would hold him over until they arrived. He'd only taken a few steps when the second elevator door opened with a quiet whoosh. A couple looking to be in their mid-fifties or so exited the elevator followed by a younger couple with a toddler and a little girl around four or five.

Luke paused, suspecting he'd hit pay dirt when they approached the nurses' station.

The older man spoke up. "Excuse me, but we're

93

here for Corrine Ritter. We're her parents and this is her sister and brother-in-law. What can you tell us about our daughter?"

"And when can we see her?" her mother interjected.

"Dr. Tina Reed is in with her right now. I'll let her know you're here. I'm sure she'll speak to you as soon as she's finished. The ICU waiting area is right through those doors."

"Is there anything you can tell us right now?"

"I'm sorry sir, but it'll just be a few minutes longer." She pointed to the doors. "Right through there."

Luke entered the room and waited until the other group made their entrance to approach them. "Excuse me, sir, I overheard you speaking to the nurse and I believe I can give you some information on Cori."

The man gave him a look brimming with equal measures of desperation and suspicion. "And you are?"

"Luke Oliver. I was on the phone with your daughter during the entire episode."

The younger woman stepped forward. "You're the 911 operator?"

"Yes. Has anyone told you about the baby? I just saw him in the nursery and he's fine."

The older woman clasped hands with her daughter. "Oh, thank God! Now, if someone would just tell us what's going on with Cori."

"We got a few details from the Beaumont police, but they were sketchy," Charles admitted.

Luke sat with them, told them everything that had gone down before, in the fast food restaurant and during the hostage situation. His voice faltered when he told them how Cori had begun to hemorrhage toward the end.

Cori's father stood, obviously too upset to keep still. "I can't believe this." He stopped. "And you said you saw the baby?"

Luke grinned. "Yes sir. He's a healthy baby boy in the third floor nursery. He weighed seven pounds and twelve ounces."

The man nodded and wiped his eyes as he faced his wife. "Well, hon. He's too big to throw back, so I guess we'll have to keep the little booger." He faced Luke again and offered his hand. "I'm Charles Granger, and this is my wife, Joan, our daughter, Melissa, and her husband, Roland Landry."

"It's a pleasure to meet you all." He shook hands with all of them and felt a tug on his jeans. He looked down at the diminutive blond beauty with big blue eyes. "And who are you?"

"I'm Lilly!" She pointed at the baby, fast asleep in her father's arms. "And that's my brother, Eli."

Luke got down on one knee and extended his hand. "I'm Luke, and it's nice to meet you, Lilly."

"My brother is still little. He can't even run yet. When he tries to walk fast, he falls on his butt and cries."

Luke chuckled at the precocious child's animated speech. "Yeah, that happens sometimes. But, I bet it won't be long before he can run as fast as you."

"I hope so. Then I can play with him and not get fussed at for being too rough." She gave a dramatic sigh. "I get so tired of hearing 'He's just a baby!'" She cocked her head to the side, placed her hands on her face. "You just don't know how *hard* it is…all this *waiting* for him to grow up."

"Well, now that I've met you, I can understand what a hardship that is for you." Luke stood and quirked one eyebrow at the child's parents.

Roland raised both hands. "You don't have to say anything. We know. She gets it from her mother."

"Well, of course she does," Melissa agreed. "We all know you're the strong, silent type." She gave her husband a loving pat on the face. "Maybe our son will take after you, sweetie."

"Hmph...We can only hope."

All heads turned as the door opened and a woman entered the room.

"Corrine Ritter family?"

Joan reached her first. "Yes, she's our daughter. How is she?"

"I'm Doctor Reed. She's still in a coma."

"A coma?"

"Yes, ma'am. By the time she was transported to our ER, she'd already lost so much blood due to a tear in the lining of the uterus, which I repaired. We gave her four pints during the C-section to deliver the baby. The coma is the body's defense against brain damage from severe blood loss. I suspect it's temporary since all her tests detected normal brain activity. I expect her to wake up within the next few hours, but it could take longer, so if it doesn't happen right away, try not to panic."

Melissa reached out to stop the doctor as she turned to leave. "Doctor Reed, about her uterus—this pregnancy was kind of a miracle—should she be able to have more children?"

The woman smiled. "I see no indication that she

couldn't have another child, but if it happens it should definitely be another C-section delivery. It's not visiting hours but under the circumstances, I'll allow two family members at a time to go in and see her. The stimulation may help wake her from her coma sooner."

Her parents followed the doctor through the doors first. Melissa turned to Roland for a hug, and Luke looked away to give them a moment of privacy.

"I'm sorry, Luke." Melissa pulled away from her husband, still sniffling as she wiped her tears away. "It's just that nothing about this entire pregnancy has been 'ordinary' since the beginning. She wasn't supposed—"

"To get pregnant, I know. Cori did a lot of talking during the hostage situation. I know about her husband leaving her because she supposedly couldn't give him a child and how he…" He stopped there, thinking they may not know her husband was with another woman at the time of his death.

Melissa sobered instantly. "How he was in a car with his *girlfriend* when they wrecked."

He nodded. "And I even know what they were doing when they wrecked."

Her eyebrows inched upward. "She told you about the…"

He nodded again, but kept his silence.

Roland's low snort sounded from beside his wife. "Man, I can't believe she told you that. She didn't tell us until six months after it happened."

"We find that it tends to calm the callers if we keep them talking during situations. I found it amazing that she kept her sense of humor about it during the crisis. Of course, she had to do all her talking in a whisper so she wouldn't be heard. I've gotta admit, I've handled thousands of calls over the past three years, but that particular situation…that was a new one for me."

"What did you do before becoming a 911 dispatcher?"

"The Marines had me for twelve years, and dispatching is temporary for me. A buddy of mine had been a dispatcher for five years and complained that they hardly ever worked with a full staff. I took some training and applied. I figured I'd do that until I decided what to do with the rest of my life. After I started, I enrolled in Lamar University. I'm getting my Bachelor's degree in Construction Management. As a matter of fact, I'll be starting my final semester in a couple of weeks."

Roland took his son from Melissa. "Were you in construction as a Marine?"

"No, I was a sniper."

"Kind of like Chris Kyle?" Melissa added.

"He was a Navy Seal, but yes, exactly like Chris Kyle. If you saw the movie…that was my life for ten of the twelve years I served."

"Afghanistan?"

He nodded. "And Iraq, as well as a few places in Africa."

Roland switched his sleeping son from one shoulder to the other. "A friend of mine was stationed in Somalia for a while. He said it was the worst."

"Your friend is right. Without getting into it, because I just ate, Somalia was deplorable, I kid you not."

Roland gave his head a thoughtful nod. "Yeah, that's what my old buddy Tex said too."

"I know a Tex. He's a Broussard from an area just east of Beaumont."

"Matthew?"

"Yep, he's a big ol' boy, six foot six if he's an inch, kind of dirty blond hair, and solid as a brick wall. He gave the Corp twenty years and retired about a year after I did."

Roland's mouth widened as his grin lit up his face. "That's him. He bought a small cattle ranch in Blanco several months ago."

"I know. I went up there to help him renovate that old cabin a couple of months after he moved into it. He's got a real nice place now and I'm happy for him. Tex is a good man, and a heck of a Marine."

Roland's grin grew wider. "It's some kind of coincidence that we both know him, isn't it?"

Luke answered with a low chuckle. "Speaking of coincidences, I answered two previous 911 calls from Cori. The first one when her windshield got smashed along I-10 several months ago and then again about a month ago when some old lady rammed her parked car. This time she actually requested me."

Melissa straightened. "Holy crap! You're that Luke?"

He gave her a nod. "Sure am."

"That is absolutely bizarre that she's gotten hold of you three times when she doesn't even live in this area."

"That's what she said earlier. Sometimes I'm amazed at how small this world is." He wiped his face and yawned.

Roland placed his sleeping son on one of several couches in the waiting room and turned to face him again. "You look like you could use a little of what Eli's doing. How long was your shift?"

"About fourteen hours of non-stop calls, but I've been pulling sixteen hour shifts for the last week. I'm hittin' bottom on my reserve tank."

Melissa placed a hand on his shoulder. "If you give me your number I'll call you as soon as she wakes. That way you can go on home to get some rest. Unless you want to go in to see her?"

Luke only considered it for a split-second. "Nah, this is the family's time. Besides, I don't want to see her until she can see me." That was the honest truth but damned if he could figure out why he felt that way. "I'll go home and hit the rack once I hear what your folks have to say about her condition."

He watched the couple interact with their children. The ever-entertaining Lilly finally succeeded in waking her little brother from his slumber. Eli was a good-looking young man with huge brown eyes like his dad. Sleepy-eyed, but smiling, he let his big sister plaster kisses all over his face. Luke looked up from watching the children and stood as the Grangers re-entered the room, both sporting smiles.

"She's pale, but the nurse said she's showing signs of waking up. The staff expects it'll happen in the next hour or so." Joan passed the back of her hand against her forehead. "Poor thing, she's going to be so disappointed she missed the whole birth experience."

"Considering the alternative, she'll get over it," Charles added as Melissa and Roland headed out to take their turn with Cori. "We need to find out where the nursery is. I want to see my new grandson."

"I can show y'all. It's on the third floor." Luke

pointed toward the door. He looked at the little girl. "What do you think, Lilly? You ready to go see your new cousin?"

"Yeah! What's my new cousin's name, Grammy?"

Joan grabbed her granddaughter's hand and led her down the hall toward the elevators. "We don't know, yet, Sweetie Pie. We'll have to wait until Aunt Cori wakes up so she can give him a name."

Lilly's face twisted with confusion. "But we knew Eli's name for a long time before he came out of mommy's belly."

"Well, yes, but Aunt Cori's situation is different than your mommy and daddy's."

"Because of Uncle Jim dying?"

"Well, yes, among other things…" Charles grunted.

Joan's indignant "Hmph!" was just loud enough for Luke to catch.

They entered the elevator and Luke hit the button for the third floor. When it opened, they piled out and he led them to the window, now fully visible with the curtains opened. He pointed to the right. "There he is, over in that corner." He tapped on the window, and caught the same nurse's attention. She smiled and immediately rolled baby Ritter closer to the window.

"Oh, he's beautiful! He looks just like Cori, thank goodness!" Joan's voice filled with pride.

"He sure does," Charles agreed. "He has *his* cleft chin, though."

"Yes, I see that now. I wonder if that's all he gets from his…from him."

From the older couple's comments, Luke got the feeling they were somewhat at a loss as to how to feel about their dead son-in-law. "Cori told me about the situation with her husband. Was he a decent kind of guy toward her before he died?"

"James was the academic type," Joan replied. "You know the kind—book smart, but not a lot of common sense?"

Charles' grunt was in obvious agreement with his wife's opinion. He hefted his grandson higher on his hip. "He was snooty to people without a college education."

Joan's face twisted in a grimace. "Well, not so much snooty as…"

"The man was a snob, hon. You know it and I know it. Hell, everybody knows it. I'm not about to pretend I was crazy about him just because he's dead." He turned to Luke. "I never liked the SOB. I only put up with him for Cori's sake."

"Jim was…difficult to get along with at times."

Charles gave up trying to control the active toddler in his arms and lowered him to the floor. "Oh come on, hon. Tell the truth."

"I was taught it wasn't nice to speak ill of the dead, Charles. Now leave me be, damn it. *Darn* it!" She added the last after giving her granddaughter a cautious glance.

"Grammy cursed!" Lilly chirped.

"Yes, Grammy did. I'm sorry."

"Just the mention of that man's name makes me want to curse," Charles added.

Joan gave her head a slow shake while gazing at Luke. "When a man hurts your little girl that way, it doesn't matter if she's three or over thirty. It's still a hard thing to swallow."

"Well…" Charles sent his wife a one-sided smirk. "Maybe his passenger that night swallowed enough for all of us."

Luke coughed into his hand as Joan swung around to meet her husband's gaze, her face flushed with embarrassment. "Charles Granger, you did *not* just say that!" Her agitated hiss accompanied a frantic search for Lilly's whereabouts.

He shrugged. "I guess I did."

She wilted with semi-relief, seeing their granddaughter busy playing peek-a-boo with her baby brother. "I hope she didn't hear you. You know that child repeats anything she hears, whether it's fit for mixed company, or not. You should be more careful what you say around her."

He waved off his wife's concern. "I knew she was occupied, or I wouldn't have said it."

"Sometimes she seems occupied, but she hears everything, I'm telling you."

"Oh, stop being paranoid, hon. She didn't hear a thing." Charles crossed his arms and grinned. "As far as I'm concerned, your son-in-law got exactly what he deserved."

Joan tightened her lips. Despite her disapproval and shaking head, she couldn't keep the spark of amusement from her eyes. "You're a terrible man." She left them to keep her grandson from escaping his big sister's desperate hold on him.

Charles grinned at Luke. "I guess I should explain—"

Luke stopped him mid-sentence. "No sir. I know the story."

"She told you what happened the night he died?"

"I guess your daughter figured a little comic relief was needed during a tense situation."

Charles grunted in agreement. "That girl has always had a wicked sense of humor. I can see how she'd rely on it for backup, but did she tell you everything?" He leaned closer and lowered his voice. "Like how he died with part of his genitalia missing?"

Luke rubbed at his two-day beard growth. "She never came out and said it, and I didn't want to press my luck by asking."

"So she left out that tidbit of information?"

"Obviously. It did have me wondering if someone reattached it—you know, afterwards." Luke wiped his mouth and cleared his throat to stave off a threatening burst of laughter.

Charles nudged him with his elbow. "Man, can you think of a worse way to die?"

Luke covered a laugh with coughing. Once he'd managed to control himself he cast a glance in Charles' direction. "Live by the sword...die by the sword."

The older man chuckled and rested a hand on Luke's shoulder. "You're okay, man."

Joan had returned in enough time to hear the last few comments from the men. She turned her back on both of them, grumbling something about all men being heartless heathens. She pressed her nose close to the window. "Oh, but isn't he beautiful? I can't wait for Cori to wake up so she can hold him. Everything will be so much better for her when she does."

Luke turned his attention back to the baby. "He is a handsome little guy. Guess I'll have to take your word that he looks like his mom. The only picture I've seen of her was from her driver's license, and it was taken six years ago."

Cori's mother faced him again. "Oh, that's right. I keep forgetting that you and our daughter have never met." She seemed to study him. "Do you have some kind of identification?"

"I do." He reached for his wallet, waving off her husband's protest. "She's right to ask." He pulled out his driver's license and handed it to her. As an afterthought he reached into his coat pocket and pulled out his dispatcher badge as further proof that he was who he said he was.

After a moment, she handed them back. "I'm sorry. I just needed to be sure."

"Don't apologize. It's not possible to be too concerned or too careful. Believe me; I know what I'm talking about." He tried to suppress a yawn, but failed.

"You look tired. Why don't you go home and get some rest?"

He rubbed his aching neck with one hand. "I guess I should." He returned his license to his wallet and pulled out a business card. "I already gave my number to Melissa, but you take it also. I'd appreciate a call when she wakes. I'll turn the ringer off while I'm sleeping, but go ahead and leave me a voice message or a text, and I'll check it first thing after I wake."

Joan took the card. "I'll do that. Now you go get some sleep. If she wakes up before you get here, we'll tell her you came to check on her. Do you have another shift later tonight?"

"Thank you, and no ma'am. I started my one-week vacation this morning. I'll be back later." He waved before stepping into the elevator.

He was home in ten minutes, shaved, and showered

in another fifteen, and fell into his bed. He yawned and rolled over, his last conscious thought about Cori and whether she'd met her son yet.

****

Luke woke up six hours later, without the benefit of an alarm, but still feeling fully rested. He checked his phone, released a Texas size whoop of excitement when he read a text from Melissa.

—Hey Luke, Cori's awake! We told her you came by and she's really sorry she missed you. She's looking forward to meeting you. Mother and baby are fine. Call before you come. They're talking about moving her to a private room soon. Melissa Landry—

"Thank you, God. That little man needed his mama to hold him." The second text message was from his mom, asking how his flight had been. "Uh, try non-existent." He rolled over on his back and hit the number to call her. She answered with her usual exuberance, even though she hadn't been thrilled with his decision to spend Christmas and New Year's in Mexico rather than with his family.

"Well, hello there, baby boy. Are you lounging in the sun with an ice cold beer in your hand?"

"Not quite. I didn't go."

"You didn't? What happened?"

He paused, wondering how to answer. He couldn't use work as an excuse. He'd left the call center in plenty enough time to make the flight. "I—I don't know, Mom. I guess I wasn't as into it as I thought I was. I'll reschedule for a later date."

"Does this mean you'll be here this evening for our family Christmas?"

"Yes, ma'am. I will. What time do the festivities

start?"

"The neighbor will be by in his Santa costume around 6:30 to pass out the gifts. If you want your photo taken sitting on his lap, I wouldn't get here any later than 7:00."

He laughed into the phone. "I don't think your neighbor would be thrilled to have my two hundred twenty-five pounds resting on his lap."

She snorted. "I think he'd rather enjoy that."

"Wait, which neighbor? Old Mr. Miller or the gay guy on the opposite side of you?"

"The second and his name is David. He is the sweetest thing."

"Then I definitely won't be sitting on his lap. I wouldn't want to give him false hope."

"My, but aren't we full of ourselves today?"

He couldn't help but laugh at her snarky attitude. His mom was a trip.

"So when can we expect your bodacious presence?"

"I've got to run a couple of errands first then make a trip to the hospital." He spared her the panic of jumping to the wrong conclusion. "And no, it's not for me. I'm going to visit a…an acquaintance."

"Anyone we know?"

"No ma'am. I'll explain when I make it to your place. Has my sister made it in yet?"

"Do you hear bickering adults or a whiny child in the background yet?"

"No, it's rather quiet."

"Then, no." Her light-hearted laughter rang in his ear. "I'm expecting them in an hour or so. I'm sitting here, enjoying a cinnamon laced cappuccino before the chaos ensues."

"And speaking to your favorite child."

"I'm speaking to my favorite son."

"I'm your only son."

"Yes, you are, and so bright, too! Later, my little prince."

"Later, Mom."

"Luke?"

"Yeah?"

"All jokes aside, Son. You've made my day. I love you."

He smiled, knowing she spoke the truth. "I love you too, Mom."

Luke rolled out of bed and dropped for a quick fifty push-ups, finishing up with ten one-arms on each arm. A quick shower to wash the sleep from his eyes and a protein shake for breakfast would have him ready to face the day. He started his coffee and flipped on the tube, switched it to a local station, hoping to catch a weather forecast. He reached for the remote to turn off the TV when the local anchor's next words had him freezing in his tracks.

"I'm Bridget Leger. Around 4:00 a.m. this morning, two men, Shawn Jackson and Theodore "T-Bone" Jefferson, entered Viv's Toy Emporium in Beaumont and attempted to rob the store. The store's salesclerk, Simone Davis, wife of Sheriff's Deputy Shemar Davis, was being held by Jackson and Jefferson when her on-duty husband, Deputy Davis, and his partner, Deputy Michael Lawson, stopped by for a routine security check, thereby interrupting the robbery. When Lawson picked up his radio to call for backup, Jackson shot him in the chest. Deputy Lawson was taken in immediately for emergency surgery. Sadly, he has since lost his life, a direct result of the wound. Our hearts and prayers go out to Deputy Lawson's family, including his wife, Jaqueline, and two young sons, Michael, Jr. and James, ages five and three.

Jackson had been released earlier this week from the Jefferson County Correctional Facility when the star witness for the prosecution failed to appear to testify against him in court. Mrs. Denita Lewis alleged she'd been beaten, raped repeatedly, and held hostage by Jackson for several hours back in October before her husband came home unexpectedly and overpowered Jackson, then held him at gunpoint until authorities arrived. Jackson, who denied the allegations and pled not guilty, has a long list of priors, many connected to gang activity in the Port Arthur area. But hold up, there's an unexpected twist to this story. Stay tuned, and we'll tell you more when we return."

"Well, how can I resist when you make it sound so intriguing?" Luke used the time to blend his breakfast protein shake. He'd nearly finished it by the time the anchor returned to the screen.

"We promised you more on the sad story of the officer shooting and hostage situation in Viv's Toy Emporium. Here's Renee Bertrand, on location at Christus St. Elizabeth's Hospital, here in Beaumont."

A different woman appeared on the screen, standing in front of the hospital.

"When eight and a half month pregnant Corrine Ritter entered Viv's Toy Emporium early Christmas Eve, she had no idea things were about to turn ugly. She approached the back of the store to find the clerk, but before she could speak to her, two men entered with guns. When she realized what was happening, she slipped into the stockroom situated at the rear of the store and hid herself before calling 911 to report the incident. The dispatcher worked with her to coordinate police activity. At some point, Jefferson deposited a bag loaded with ammunition for the two guns in his and Jackson's possession. Mrs. Ritter snuck out of her hiding place long enough to empty the bag of its ammunition and hide it from the robbers, thereby hindering them from reloading their weapons. Even after going into labor she aided law enforcement. After they obtained a key to the back door from the store manager, they cut out the door lock with a laser torch and passed the key to Ritter through the hole. She used the key to remove the heavy duty padlock on the loading area doors, enabling officers to enter the store from the rear and control the situation. Police credit Mrs. Ritter's quick thinking, as well as her collaboration with the 911 dispatcher for helping to end the situation before the clerk, Simone Davis, was hurt, or worse. Late in the situation, Mrs. Ritter began to hemorrhage, collapsing as soon as the officers gained entry to the store. I spoke to Doctor Tina Reed earlier about Mrs. Ritter's condition."

The camera broke to video of a woman wearing green scrubs, covered by a white lab coat, and with a microphone stuck in her face.

"Doctor Reed, what can you tell our viewers about Mrs. Ritter's condition?"

"The patient arrived here comatose from severe blood loss due to hemorrhaging. We performed an emergency Caesarian section to deliver the child, a healthy little boy, while giving his mother multiple units of blood. After a six-hour coma, the patient has since awakened. She's in an extremely weakened state, but she's healthy, and will no doubt make a quick recovery."

Renee spoke into the mic. "And can you tell us if she's seen her new son yet?"

The doctor beamed into the camera. "Yes, she has. The baby boy is in the room with his mother as we speak, along with several of Mrs. Ritter's family members. It's our own little Christmas miracle here at St. Elizabeth's."

"Has she named the baby yet?"

"Not that I'm aware of."

"Thank you, doctor." The anchor pulled the mic back and stepped in front of the camera. "A sad note to the story is that Mrs. Ritter became a widow several months ago after her husband was killed in a car accident. Although Baby Ritter is meeting his mother right now, he'll never have the opportunity to meet his father. I'm Renee Bertrand, reporting live. Back to you, Bridget."

Luke hit the power button on his remote, cutting off any further comment. "Not as sad a note as you might think, Renee." He downed the rest of his shake and grabbed his coat. In minutes, he was on his way.

After making a quick trip to the nearest Walmart, Luke stepped out of the hospital elevator, loaded down with a two-foot-tall stuffed bear, and a Christmas flower arrangement. A second text from Melissa had provided him with Cori's new room number. He approached room 325 and paused at the chatter coming from inside the room. He took one deep breath to calm a rare case of nerves, and raised one hand to knock on the door. Roland opened it and grinned as he waved him inside.

Luke took one hesitant step, then another into the room.

"How is she?"

The crowd quieted perceptibly as three adults stepped aside, leaving a clear path to the woman lying in bed holding a bundle of blue. Her big, blue-eyed gaze locked onto him, wide and curious. Her full lips parted, with just a hint of a smile. Gone was the blond, pixie-cut hairstyle, replaced with shoulder length waves, soft, golden-brown, and framing her beautiful, heart-shaped face.

"Luke?"

He nodded. "It's me. How are you, Cori?"

Her face broke into a smile, even as her eyes flooded with tears. "We're fine, thanks to you."

"I didn't do anything special." He jutted his chin forward. "Looks like you did all the difficult work." He remembered the gifts he carried, held up the arrangement. "These are for you. I figured since you'd be spending your Christmas in the hospital, you'd need something festive in your room."

"Thank you, they're beautiful." One silent glance at her sister had Melissa moving to take the flowers from his hands.

He approached the bed and lifted the stuffed bear. "And this is for the big guy, there. I hear he's nearly eight pounds. That's pretty good for being almost three weeks early. You did good, Cori."

She stared at her baby, wiped at a tear that had trailed down her face and threatened to drip from her chin. "Thank you. For…for…" Her face crumbled and her shoulders shook as she broke into soft sobbing. "I'm sorry."

He placed the bear at the foot of her bed and fought the strongest urge to wrap his arms around her—struggled for some comforting words. "Don't apologize. You're allowed to fall apart after what you've been through, especially when you were so strong for the duration." He leaned in closer, so that his face was nearer to hers. "If anyone in this room knows how strong you were, I do." Unable to resist touching her any longer, he extended his hand. "Luke Oliver—it's a real pleasure to meet you face to face."

She adjusted her hold on the baby and reached out to grasp his hand. "Corrine Ritter, and it's a pleasure to meet you also."

Luke held her hand an instant longer than necessary, hating to break the contact. He couldn't say why, since he barely knew the woman. Although, he did know something about her that no one else did, if she'd spoken the truth about her planned suicide. The thought of this beautiful young woman coming so damn close to taking her own life sent a chill through him. His gaze landed on the infant, the baby boy with so many of his mother's traits, and he couldn't help but smile.

This child had saved his mother's life by revealing his existence when it mattered most, and that made him special in Luke's opinion.

"Would you like to hold him?"

"I would." He reached out and took the infant in his arms. Adjusting the bundle to see him better, he pulled back the blanket to see baby Ritter's face better.

"Hey, little man. You're an armful already, you

know that? Has your mom given you a name yet?"
****

The room grew even quieter as Cori cleared her throat. "Well, I wanted to talk to you about that first." She studied Luke's handsome face, the strong jawline, straight nose, and just-full-enough lips.

"Why's that?" He lifted his gaze to meet hers.

She'd noticed his eyes as soon as she'd seen him—one blue, one green—just like Officer Gary Hallet's eyes in "Practical Magic". A condition called heterochromia—complete heterochromia iridis in his case, since each iris was a different color. *Striking—and in that handsome face—even more so.* He hadn't lied about that, or his height or hair color. She could see he was over six feet tall, and judging from the fit of his clothes on that buff body, the weight he carried was indeed, all muscle. His light brown hair, just a tad longer than a military cut, its texture indicating it would curl if he let it grow. She caught herself thinking she'd love to see that. Her fingers would itch to run through those curls, no doubt. She pushed all those sex-starved thoughts aside and returned to her present condition of post-baby delivery with a patched up uterus and stitches in her lower abdomen.

How the hell was it possible to even think about a man in her current physical condition? She glanced at the IV going into her arm. *Oh, yeah…good drugs.* Well, that and the fact that his voice had fed her sex-starved fantasies since her first contact with the dispatcher. She'd fictionalized countless scenarios of meeting this mysterious sexy-voiced man face to face, but no one else knew that and she planned to keep it that way.

"Well, I thought I'd call him Luke. If you don't

mind, that is." She watched his face as he absorbed the information.

His brow lifted, his breathing hitched as his dual colored gaze moved from her, to the baby, and then back to her. His mouth opened, closed, then opened again as he finally spoke. "Are you serious?"

She used her knuckle to wipe the tears from the corner of her eyes. "If it's okay with you, I am."

"I'd be honored, as long as you don't give him my middle name, too."

"What is it?"

"Harrison, and for no other reason than George was my mom's favorite Beatle." He adjusted his armload. "I guess I should count my blessings she didn't go with George or Ringo, huh, little man?"

"Hmm…are you sure? Luke Harrison sure goes well together." Cori sent him a playful wink.

He cringed. "Please, no. I've always hated it. I'm sure you can come up with something better. What about your dad's name?" He looked up, as though to ask her father. "Where'd they go?"

She looked around, surprised to find that at some point during their conversation the others had slipped out of her room. "Huh. Maybe the cafeteria?"

"So, what's your dad's middle name?"

"James, but I think it should be at least two syllables. Is your name Luke or Lucas?"

"It's Lucas, but everyone calls me Luke."

"I prefer Luke, but it should be paired with something like Fitzgerald, or Madison, or…" She stopped to laugh at the face he made.

"Good grief, don't do that to the poor kid. I know you can do better than that."

"Well, I do love the singer Luke Bryan."

He nodded. "Now you're talking. Luke Bryan Ritter."

"I'm considering giving him my maiden name. Luke Bryan Granger."

He shrugged. "It's understandable in your situation, but you might want to sleep on it before you decide. He may have questions when he's older. However, it is your decision." He lifted her baby to eye level. "How do you like that, huh, buddy? Luke Bryan Granger."

She sighed, her shoulders sagging in relief. "Now someone can finally fill out the form for this child's birth certificate."

"Yeah," he snorted. "It's no fun being called 'Baby Ritter'." He swayed from side to side when Luke started to fuss.

"I know, but I think I told you before, his name had to have meaning to me."

"I'm honored you chose my name and I hope Luke finds his middle name equally inoffensive." He lifted the baby and stared into his face. "Even though no one will remember who the hell Luke Bryan, the singer, is by the time you're an adult."

"Hey now, do you remember George Strait?"

"He's King George, the King of country music, and he's still recording after forty years."

"But when he became popular, people in the music industry called George Jones the king of country music."

"And people still love his music."

"Yes, they do. I'm just saying, music changes with the times but people will always remember their favorites. Besides, I love both King Georges, but neither one of 'em can fill out a pair of tight jeans like Luke Bryan can."

"Oh, please. It doesn't take a lot of effort when his jeans are custom made a size or two tighter than they should be, and let's not forget that roll of quarters placed strategically in his front pocket."

She closed her eyes, remembering Luke Bryan's performance at Bayou Superfest the two consecutive years she'd seen him. "Sorry, but I've gotten close enough during two live performances to know, and that's no roll of quarters."

"Oh, please!"

Luke's amused snort got her attention. She opened her eyes. "What?"

He yanked a tissue from the generic box on her bedside table and dabbed at the corner of her mouth. "Drool much?"

She grabbed the tissue from his hands. "Jealous much?"

He flexed his right arm. "Hell, no. Maybe I can't sing for shit, but I can hold my own, physically."

She pursed her lips at the ripped arm, bulging with muscles. "Nice, but just so you know, every time I hear a guy say he 'holds his own' I'm tempted to ask him if he does that in the shower with a bar of soap."

Luke's stare turned blank for the second it took him to get her meaning. He shook his head as laughter rumbled through his broad chest. "I'm glad to hear your recent brush with a life-threatening situation hasn't stifled your sense of humor, even if it does curve slightly toward the dirty-minded. You truly deserved that 'Wittiest' superlative title."

She shrugged. "It's the one thing I could always count on, even when I looked like a beached whale." She pressed her hand to her middle. "Speaking of which, I hope I can lose this baby weight."

"What baby weight?" He pointed to her thin frame under the blanket. "That swelling will all go down in a couple of weeks. And if you keep a few pounds, who cares? Personally, I've always preferred women with some meat on their bones."

Her grin came out twisted, telling him without words, that they'd spent too much time on this subject matter.

He got the memo, cleared his throat before speaking. "Did you or anyone in your family happen to see the special bulletin they did on the local news?"

"No. If my family did, none of them said anything to me."

"They filmed the story outside the hospital this morning and even interviewed your surgeon. She kept it general, and said you were awake and would make a full recovery. I suspect someone has a source with the local PD or Sheriff's Department."

She sobered. "Luke, the deputy who was shot—what's his condition?"

He paused before answering. "He didn't make it."

"Oh no...Did he have a family?"

"Deputy Lawson has a wife and two little boys, ages three and five."

"How awful! And on Christmas Eve, too. How truly awful for them." Tears flooded her vision. She lowered her head and used the tissue he'd given her to wipe her eyes.

Melissa chose that moment to re-enter the room

carrying a gift bag. "Hey, sweetie. Look what the owner of the store had delivered."

Cori stared into the bag and pulled out the robot puppy and large pack of batteries. "Fabulous! No Lilly tantrum tomorrow morning!"

"And that's not all. You're somewhat of a local celebrity all of a sudden. People are dropping off gifts and donations for you and the baby, thanks to a reporter for a local news station. She's outside and wondering if she could get an interview with you. We told her how weak you are and she promised to make it quick." She held a hand to her chest. "Personally, I'd pass, but I told her I'd ask."

Cori thought of the young mother and two small boys who'd be facing Christmas without their husband and father, and decided to do what she could for them now. "Tell her I'll speak to her."

Melissa blinked twice and stared at her sister. "Are you sure?"

She nodded. "Yes, but ask her to give me a few minutes, and someone get me a mirror, please."

Melissa swung the bedside table around and over Cori's lap then opened one of the trays to reveal a mirror.

Cori gasped at her red-rimmed eyes and puffy nose. "Oh my Gosh. Why didn't anyone tell me I looked like crap?"

"Because you don't." Melissa glanced up at Luke. "You know, when I told the reporter that the 911 dispatcher was in here visiting with Cori, she was so excited she nearly peed herself. She's dying to interview the two of you together."

Luke frowned. "You think?"

"I'm telling you, the woman is salivating over the prospect," Melissa said.

Cori snorted. "Salivating and peeing herself." She pointed to the box of tissue. "Give that to her, along with a roll of toilet paper from the bathroom. It sounds like she may need it more than I do."

Luke's laughter rang out. "You're still funny."

"Sis, do you happen to have any make-up with you?" Cori wiped at her eyes.

Melissa grabbed her purse and opened it. "Honey, I was so rushed after we got that phone call, I brought my make-up with me. I put my face on while Roland drove." She extracted a pouch from her purse and handed it to her. "I'll go tell Ms. Bertrand and then I'll come back to help you."

True to her word, Melissa was gone for only a few seconds when she popped back into the room. With a few well-placed finger fluffs to Cori's hair, a little concealer, and some fine-tuned re-applications of Cori's barely-existing make-up, she proclaimed her sister camera-ready.

Melissa turned to Luke and gave him a head to toe perusal. "Good googly-moogly, Mr. McStud Muffin! I think you're fine just as you are."

Luke frowned. "Thanks, but please don't say that in front of your husband."

She waved off his concern. "Roland is the *original* Mr. McStud Muffin. He can handle the competition." She exited the room.

"Here, I think you should be holding your own child for the interview." Luke placed his namesake back in her arms. "Are you sure you're up to this? And are you comfortable knowing Shawn Jackson may see this at some point? He's bound to recognize you."

The man's name had her pausing to consider his comment. "He's in prison, right?"

"Oh yeah, and he killed a sheriff's deputy, with two eye-witnesses. He'll be put away for a long, long time."

"Then, I want to do this. Besides, it's not like he'll have a TV in his cell, right?"

"No, but prisons generally have a dayroom where the inmates can gather to watch one television. I'm sure they have to earn watching privileges, though. I'm not sure if they're allowed to watch the news, either. But, I think you'd be surprised at what gets through to them."

She gave her head a final nod, making her decision. "I want to do this." She looked up as the door opened, and Melissa led in a woman with a camera operator in tow. With all introductions behind them, they got down to the interview.

It was over in less than ten minutes and her guests left the hospital satisfied with the results.

"You did good, Cori." Luke leaned over to pass a finger along the side of his namesake's face. "And so did this little man."

"Until he started screaming for his supper," she added.

His shoulders shook with laughter. "The nurse said he was a good baby, and only cries when he's hungry. When a man's gotta eat, a man's gotta eat, huh dude." He checked his watch and grunted. "Speaking of, I better get to my mom's for supper."

"I understand. I hope you have a wonderful Christmas, Luke."

"Thanks, I will. Do you have any idea how long

you'll be here?"

"Dr. Reed said it should be a couple of days. She wants to make sure there are no complications with the uterine repair. My family has decided to stick around here for the duration."

His face lit up. "That's great! I'm glad you won't be alone for the holidays. Would you mind if I came by tomorrow?"

She smiled shyly, excited at the chance to see him again. "I'd like that…a lot."

Chapter 10
Mess With Me?

"Hey, dog. You're famous. I just saw a story about you on the TV in the common room."

Shawn looked at the trustee through the bars of his cell. "You mean, I'm famous *again*, don't you, Jug? This ain't my first time on the tube."

"Man, they interviewed a bitch who hid out in the back of that store you hit. She's the reason the cops got in through the back door. They showed a video of a white chick sitting in a hospital bed holding a newborn baby. There was a dude standing next to her bed during the interview."

"Her old man?"

"Nah. Turns out her old man died several months ago. The dude next to her was the 911 operator she called while she was hidin' out. She said she'd seen you next door at some fast food joint just 'fore she went in."

Shawn's gaze narrowed. "Yeah, I remember that pregnant bitch."

"Said she started havin' pains while y'all were in there, then she started bleedin'. She found y'alls bag of ammo and took out all the rounds—put 'em where she was hidin' out in the store room so you couldn't reload. She's the one that unlocked the back doors so the cops got to you and Jefferson, man. Lame-ass bitch got on there and asked everyone to stop sending gifts and donations to her and her kid…said to send 'em to the family of the *slain officer* instead. Asked everyone to pray for his family, too. You believe that shit?" He looked around to make sure no one else could hear. "And you know what else she did?"

"What's that, Juggy?"

"She named her kid after the 911 dispatcher, man. They're *friends* now. Ain't that some shit?"

"You know their names?"

"Cain't remember 'em right now, but I can find out."

Shawn nodded. "Yeah man, you do that." His insides churned with hatred for the woman. He had to get outta here. He had to make her pay for landing him in here. He'd been prepared to die. He'd brought along plenty of ammo to make sure that happened. But that shit grew legs and walked away. Last time he was sent up, he'd done okay for himself. But cop killers didn't get any special privileges.

"Thanks man. I needed to hear that today." He turned his back on the bars and dropped onto his cot, his hatred for the bitch multiplying by a hundred.

He lay in his cot and smiled. *It's all good. Once word got out to the right people—he knew damn well he wouldn't be locked up in this place for long. Soon as he got out, he'd find that bitch.* He rolled over on his side and faced the wall.

He couldn't wait to shut her up. And her friend with 911, too.

Chapter 11
Fifteen Minutes of Fame

Christmas Eve, 6:00 p.m.

Luke sat with his parents in front of the flat screen he'd given them a few weeks ago as an early Christmas gift.

"Okay, here we are." His chest filled with unaccustomed warmth when the screen switched from the reporter to Cori, holding the baby in her arms.

They listened as she told her story. How she'd recognized Shawn from the food joint, and hid in the back of the store to call 911. She described emptying the ammo from the robbers' bag. Luke described how he and Cori had worked together to keep law enforcement updated and how Cori eventually helped the officers to enter through the building's back door.

"I've been told that people have been making donations to me and my child. I thank those of you who've done so, but I'm asking everyone to please consider making donations to the family of the slain officer, instead. It's true I'm a widow, but I'm financially stable, and I've been blessed with a new child..." She paused to place a hand on Luke's arm, before continuing. "As well as a new friend in Luke, here—while Officer Lawson's wife and sons face a lonely, heart-breaking Christmas without their husband and father. My heart goes out to them as well as the rest of his family. We should all be generous with them and keep them in our prayers. I also hope Mrs. Simone Davis, the sales clerk for the toy store, isn't too traumatized by what she went through. It had to be a terrifying experience for her. Please keep her in your prayers, as well."

"Thank you, Ms. Ritter, but we're all curious back at the station. Since your baby is a Christmas Eve miracle, did you happen to name your son Jesus?"

Cori laughed. "No, but his name means something wonderful, just the same. I named him after a man who was my lifeline for nearly two hours." She moved her hand over the baby's head, in a protective motion. "I named him Luke."

The camera shifted to Luke's face. "How do you feel about that, Mr. Oliver?"

He grinned at the baby, who'd taken that opportunity to start making some noise. "I couldn't be prouder."

The reporter stepped in front of the camera. "There you have it, folks. Our own little Christmas Eve miracle. A story of birth and renewal after a tragic death…" She stepped out of the way so that the camera was on Cori and Little Luke again. The camera zoomed in on the baby, starting to fuss for his supper. "Straight from the baby's mouth! I'm Renee Bertrand, reporting for KPBT in Beaumont. Back to you, Bridget."

"Oh, my gosh." Dolores Walker Oliver sat staring at the TV set. "Arthur, our son is a celebrity."

"What's that?"

She leaned closer to yell at him. "I *said* Luke is a

126

celebrity."

Arthur Oliver sat there wearing a look of confusion. "What was that we just watched with Luke on TV? I couldn't hear a damn thing."

"Oh, good grief. Are you wearing your hearing-aids?"

"Don't need 'em. I can hear just fine."

She threw up her hands. "Of course you can. That's why you don't know what the heck I'm talking about or what we just watched." She turned to Luke, keeping up a steady diatribe of grumbling. "I do believe your father is one of the most hard-headed men in the whole wide world. You know, even if he has his hearing aids in he pretends he doesn't so he won't have to do anything I ask him to do. He just sits in his recliner and watches me do all the work around here, with that TV blaring loud enough to wake the dead."

Luke followed his mom into the kitchen, snickering into his hand. He stopped short when she turned on him, her eyes flashing with anger.

"It's not funny! That stubborn old fart makes me crazy. I wish you'd talk to him."

"Yeah, sure, like he'd listen to me any more than he'd listen to you?"

"He always listens to you kids before he listens to me. I swear you'll be getting a 911 call from *him* one day. He'll be running from me or hiding in a closet while I'm chasing him down with a fireplace poker. Hmph!"

"I doubt that." Luke attempted to placate his mom with a hug. "You move a lot faster than he does. The call will probably come from you telling us you've murdered your husband and want someone to remove the body because it's bleeding on your rug." He smiled when his mom burst into laughter. "When can we expect Lee and Joe?"

She checked the digital clock on her microwave. "It should be anytime, now. Before they get here and suck up all the quiet, tell me about this Cori Ritter woman."

"There's nothing much to tell. She was my last call before I left work this morning."

"Uh huh, I know that. What I want to know is why you cancelled your trip for a veritable stranger?"

"I didn't cancel my trip. I postponed it for later rescheduling. And I didn't do it because of her." He reached over to steal a taste of crunchy topping from the sweet potato casserole.

Dolores used the spoon in her hand to rap his knuckles. "Do you want to lose that thing, boy? You know better than to dig in my casseroles with your fingers."

"Ow!" He jerked his hand back and nursed his throbbing knuckles. "Dammit Mom!"

She clucked her tongue. "That is so sad. Call that reporter woman back so I can talk to her. I can see the headlines tomorrow...Big, bad, ex-Marine taken down by an old woman with cooking utensil."

He frowned. "If you do, make sure you let her know that's a solid, stainless steel spoon, not one of those cheapie wooden or plastic ones."

The slam of car doors had him heading outside to meet his sister and her family.

Joe's mouth fell open when his gaze landed on him. "Why are you here, brother-in-law? You miss your flight or something?"

"Nah. I'm not going."

"Dude! I live vicariously through your single man sex-capades, don't you know that? I count on your stories to get me through the long, dry years of domestic torture ahead of me."

Luke's sister, Lee, turned on her husband. "Excuse me?"

"Shi—"

"Joseph!"

"Shoot." Joe looked down at the tiny woman who ruled with equal parts love and firmness. "Sorry, babe."

"Give him a break, Sis."

She pointed a finger at her brother. "Don't you dare! He can apologize to me now, or apologize to someone else later, when our six-year-old starts punctuating his dialogue with all the four letter words he hears from his daddy."

He thought about it before giving his sister an abrupt nod. "You're right."

His sister did a double take. "What?"

"Whaaat?" Joe cloned his wife's shocked response.

"That's what you do when you have kids, right? Act responsibly, clean up your act..." Luke poked a finger in Joe's chest. "Strive to set better examples for them."

Leona, or Lee, as everyone called her, stared at him. "Hold the darn phone! Who are you, and what have you done with my brother?" She raised one hand. "On second thought, I don't want to know. Whoever you are, you're an improvement and I'm keeping you. So tell whatever pod people you came here with to fire up the mother ship and leave without you." She wrapped her arms around his waist for a hug.

"Welcome, brother. You're an earthling now."

He hugged her back then placed his large hand on the top of her head, giving it a gentle shove away from him. "It always amazes me how the smallest of people can be the most obnoxious. Merry Christmas, you tiny little pain in the ass."

"Merry Christmas to you too, big brother. But why the sudden change of attitude? Has something happened to turn you into an adult?"

Luke cocked one eyebrow playfully at his sister. "I have no idea to what you are referring."

After things had settled down inside, it didn't take long for his mom to bring the subject to light. She grabbed her satellite remote and pulled up the DVR list. "Just watch, Lee. Your brother's a celebrity."

"Good God, you recorded it?" he said, somewhat shocked she even knew how.

"Of course. Now we can watch you all the time. I suppose Arthur could learn to read lips so he'll know what's going on." She turned toward him and raised her voice. "Since he doesn't *need* his hearing aids."

Lee leaned closer to the forty-two inch screen. "Who is this woman?"

"Watch the interview and you'll see."

When it ended, Lee turned on her brother. "She's the reason you canceled your trip."

"Absolutely not. I'd just been on the edge about going." He scratched around, turned to humor to downplay the situation. "I mean, considering their ages, this could be mom and dad's last Christmas with us."

His dad chuckled, proving once more that his old man had selective hearing. His mom, however, turned on him like a rabid dog.

"That's a nice thing to say about the woman who's been laboring over a hot stove for you all day."

He pointed at his mother. "You were slaving anyway. You had no idea I'd be here."

Hands on hips, she nailed him with a hard glare. "If that's the case, I'll go pick up a couple of burgers and some cardboard fries from the Mickey D's down the road, just for you."

Six-year-old Christopher piped up at her words. "I want a Happy Meal!"

Lee slapped a hand over her son's mouth. "No you don't, Chris. Maw Maw has delicious food in her kitchen that she worked hard preparing for us. And we brought a spiral cut ham and green bean casserole, remember? Now, go play in the toy room."

Luke watched his nephew run off and turned to find his sister's gaze on him. "What?"

Leona shook her head then hugged her mom. "Relax, Mom. That little act of his is only a distraction to keep us off the scent." She threw back a glance at her brother. "It won't work, by the way, because I won't forget. I want to hear all about it by the end of tonight." She used two fingers to alternate pointing between his eyes and hers. "I'm watching you, boy."

Chapter 12
A Lick and a Promise

After the meal, Lee kept Chris busy in the back room while the men transferred hidden, wrapped packages from various cars and hiding spots to the neighbor Santa's large, red velvet bag. Santa entered via the front door, his sack stuffed to the brim with gifts, thoroughly surprising Luke's nephew.

Santa, with his jovial personality, made a good impression on Christopher, one factor that kept the kid from tugging on the fake white beard covering the man's face. The boy sat on Santa's lap while Lee and Dolores snapped pictures. Lee took her turn on Santa's lap for a picture, as did Dolores. Once she'd vacated his knee, the over-stuffed Santa slapped it and sent the remaining three men looks laced with amusement.

"Who's next?"

Luke exchanged a look of warning with Joe, before they declined in unison. He stared, shocked when his dad stood from his recliner and approached the Santa.

Arthur's tone dropped to an ominous growl. "Santa, I'm telling you now. If you try anything funny with me," he pointed to the empty bag hung over the fat man's shoulder, "you'll have more than one red sack to haul around."

"Ho, Ho! Heck No, my friend! You are far too old for my tastes, grandpa." Melissa snapped her picture and Arthur walked away. Santa rubbed his knee and pointed at Luke. "How about you, young man? Wouldn't you like a prime photo opportunity with Santa?"

Chris tugged at his hand. "Do it, Uncle Luke! Sit on Santa's lap…for me? Please? Mama can even take a picture."

Lee waved her phone and snickered. "Yeah, mama's dying to take a picture of that…and post it all over social media."

Luke didn't want to disappoint his nephew, but he wasn't quite ready to relinquish his "man card" just yet. He glanced over at Joe. His brother-in-law had doubled over with laughter at the situation. "I will if your daddy goes first."

Joe sobered immediately, frowned at Luke's barely concealed dare. "That's just wrong, man."

"Daddy, please!"

Luke chuckled, thinking he'd found the perfect way of getting out from the humiliating situation. His stomach fell when Joe spoke up.

"I'll do it for you, son."

Joe sat on Santa's knee and grinned for the camera." After a quick whisper in Santa's ear, he slipped something into the man's palm before standing with arms crossed. "Your turn."

His mouth twisted with regret, Luke approached the neighbor Santa, thinking his best course of action was to get it over.

"Don't worry, I'll be gentle with you," Santa purred.

Luke's jaw tightened as he sat gingerly on the man's knee.

Lee's taunt of "Smile for the camera, sweetie!" had Luke growling under his breath.

"One, two, say cheese!" his mother chortled.

He pulled his cautious gaze from Santa and bared his teeth in a "cheesy" grin. With his attention focused on the two cameras aimed at him, Santa's lick to his face caught him completely off guard.

Too shocked to move, other than a slow turn of his head to stare at the man, Luke's eyes widened at the fifty-dollar bill Santa waved in front of his face.

Joe guffawed from the sideline. "And it was worth every penny."

Luke stood; his glare of accusation narrowed dangerously at Joe, and then snatched the fifty from Santa as he leaned close to speak to him. "Consider this your 'I won't whip your ass' card. You're donating it to the worthy cause of the officer shot this morning. His family can use this."

Santa nodded. "I'd planned to donate, anyway."

Luke turned to the man who'd set him up. "It's on. Pay back and revenge is hell, man. When you least expect it." The look on Joe's face told him his threat was worth more than the actual payback. If he knew anything about his brother-in-law, he knew how paranoid the son of a bitch got when he *expected* something to happen. The waiting alone would drive him crazy.

"Come on man, don't be like that." Joe's voice took on an annoying whine.

He stepped into the half bath to soap up a washcloth in order to clean his face. As he dried it, the glare he sent the man turned into a shit-eating grin. "Too late, bro. PB and R is on the table. I can promise one thing; you will *never* see it coming."

Joe's face fell like the stock market on Black Monday. He turned away. Any attempt by Joe to talk his way out of the shit storm he'd gotten himself into would be futile.

Later, with every trace of wrapping paper collected, and Christopher playing with his toys, the adults sat around the table, drinking his mom's homemade eggnog recipe.

Lee pointed to the TV. "Look, they're talking about the hostage situation again. Turn it up, Mom."

Luke's gut clenched as the image of Shawn Jackson appeared before them. The man looked hard, as though whatever experiences he'd gone through previously had tainted him, permanently turned him from someone capable of compassion, to what he was today…someone who lived only to hate others and take advantage of anyone weaker than himself. Of the two men involved, he couldn't help but wish Jackson had been the one who'd lost his life. He got the feeling the other man had been a family man at one time who'd fallen on hard times, without much of a previous record. If either man had a shot at reform, it would have been Jefferson.

He listened as the evening anchorperson rehashed Jackson's ugly record, last year's home break-in, his incarceration, and eventual release when the homeowners went into hiding, refusing to testify against him for brutally attacking the woman. He heard, again, how the Sheriff's Department suspected recent gang-related activity had something to do with it. It seemed Jackson had many friends—dangerous friends—and all in extremely low places.

If the nagging feeling in his gut hadn't convinced him Cori's situation wasn't over, this latest newscast certainly did the trick. Somehow, some way, that son of a bitch would find a way to get to her. And maybe even Mrs. Davis, as well.

Lee snapped her fingers in front of his eyes, jerking him from his disturbing thoughts. She faced him, her face plastered with determination. "Okay, so tell me what it is about this girl that made you cancel your trip to Cozumel."

"I told you, it's not cancelled. It's postponed."

"Whatever, Lucas. Why are you *here*, and not *there?*"

He considered her question. "Honestly? I don't know," he admitted, unable to come up with a solid answer for her. "I was on my way to Bucky's place, and couldn't get rid of this uneasiness, this heavy feeling in my chest. I called my travel agent, and discovered I could postpone the entire package and not lose all my money." He dragged his hand through his hair until it rested on the back of his neck. "All I can say is, once I turned my truck around, a tremendous weight lifted off my chest. I just…" He faltered, struggling for the right words. "I feel like it's not over yet."

Lee's eyes widened. "But the guy's in prison, right?"

"That's right," Joe added. "He killed a cop, man. He's not getting out."

"I know all that." Luke lowered his voice. "But, things happen, you know? I can't explain it. I just know it's not over." He pointed to the screen. "You heard that, right? How they suspect gang related activity in the disappearance of that couple set to testify against him? He's obviously got a long reach."

"Does she have anyone else around to take care of her? From what you told me, she'll need help afterwards, and she lives in Louisiana, right?"

"She does, but her parents live in Richmond, and her sister's family is near Houston. I think her family rented hotel rooms and they're planning to camp out at the hospital all day for the duration. I met them all this morning, and they seem to be good people. Her parents are in their early to mid-fifties, I'd guess. Her sister is two years younger than Cori, so that would put her at twenty-eight or twenty-nine. She and her husband have a four-year-old daughter and a baby boy around a year or so."

His mother's face registered her distress. "We cannot let those poor people spend Christmas in a hotel, especially with babies."

"Well, they don't want her to be alone."

Dolores slapped her hand on the table. "Well, by golly we can do something to make their stay more pleasant over the holidays. I think we should invite them here when they need a break. No one should have to eat hospital food for Christmas. As a matter of fact, we've got another spare bedroom here with a comfortable queen mattress. They are more than welcome to stay here."

"I've got a spare room too, for that matter," Luke added, thinking his mom might be on to something.

"Why don't Joe, Christopher, and I stay at your place with you, and we can offer mom and dad's two rooms to them?" Lee suggested. "I think they'd be more comfortable if they stayed together, don't you?"

"I think that's a good idea," his mom added.

Luke surveyed his parents' home, all decked out for Christmas. "Are you sure you want to open your home to them, Mom? This sounds inconvenient for you."

Arthur harrumphed. "Inconvenient or not, it's the Christian thing to do, Son."

All gazes landed on Arthur, whose rare utterance took everyone by surprise.

"There you have it!" Dolores said. "Even Arthur agrees. Why don't you call them right now? Ask them over tonight. Of course, one of them may choose to stay with their daughter. Even if they chose to keep the hotel rooms, they could still relax here and eat a few meals. Call them, Luke."

****

All eyes landed on Melissa as she re-entered the room from the hospital corridor. "That was Luke. He's at his parents' place and his mom suggested we stay over there rather than a hotel. He let me speak to her, and she sounds so sweet. She said nobody should have to stay in a hotel over the holidays."

Joan frowned. "Oh, I don't think we should impose on them like that."

"But she's insisting. Her house is decorated for Christmas and she's been cooking all day. What do y'all think? Luke's sister and brother-in-law are there now with their six-year-old son, but they'll be staying at Luke's place tonight. His parents have two big guest rooms, each with their own full bath. He said, at the very least, they'd like us to go for a home cooked supper."

Cori checked out her mom's doubtful expression. "What do you think, Mom? I hate the thought of y'all camping out in hotel rooms for the holidays."

"Oh, I'm not sure. I don't know if your father can take staying with complete strangers."

Cori settled her gaze on her father. "Dad?"

"I'm not leaving you alone here, sweetie." Her dad's mouth drew downward in distaste. "Y'all go and I'll stay here and sleep on the sofa."

"Luke has already caught up on his sleep for today and he knows we've all had a long day. He said he'd be glad to stay here with Cori." Melissa gave her sister a cheesy grin. "I guess that's up to you, sis."

Cori couldn't deny wanting to see more of Luke. "He'd be more comfortable sleeping on the couch than you would, Dad. He was a Marine for twelve years and deployed all over the Middle East. Besides, I'm sure I'll be asleep most of the night."

Charles looked hopefully at his wife. "What do you think, Joan?"

"I hate the thought of being in a hotel for Christmas," Joan admitted. "I think we should at least go meet them and stay for supper since his mom was gracious enough to offer. We can decide once we're there whether to stay or get hotel rooms." She faced Cori. "Are you sure you wouldn't mind being here with Luke?"

Melissa snorted. "I think she'd prefer it."

Cori rolled her eyes at her sister and waved off her mother's concern. "Go, please go. Just be sure to take her with you." She cocked her head toward Melissa.

****

Luke stayed long enough to make all the introductions and get his parents' guests settled before giving his sister the keys to his place and heading back to the hospital. Cori answered his soft knock on her door with a quiet "Come in." He felt like a king when her eyes lit up as he entered the room.

"Hey, they didn't give you any trouble coming back after visiting hours, did they? I didn't think about it until after my family left."

"No, they said during holidays they leave it open for family visiting from out of town." He pointed at the baby in her lap. "Has he been here the entire time?"

"No, they just brought him to me. He's been in the nursery for the past couple of hours. What did my family decide to do?"

He settled into the chair beside her bed. "From the looks of it, they may stay the night. I gave them the option to stay there or at my place where they'd have the house to themselves. But my folks' house is a lot bigger and nicer. I'm a bare necessity kind of guy, other than the 60 inch flat screen with surround sound."

"Man's gotta have his priorities."

"That's right. When you don't have a life, you live for ball games and boxing. Between school and work, it's my one luxury."

"Dad said something about you being in your last semester of college for Construction Management? It's a great field to go into in this area—in my neck of the woods, too."

He leaned forward in his chair. "Can I ask why you're still in Louisiana when the rest of your family is in Texas?"

"My husband was from a place between Sulphur and Lake Coburn. He got a job teaching at the university near there so that's where we settled. It's a great area. I finally got around to putting my house on the market. When it sells, I plan to move closer to my parents. Other than my former co-workers and a handful of good friends, I have no reason to stay."

"*Former* co-workers?"

"I quit my drafting job once I discovered I was pregnant. As long as it took me to conceive, I didn't want any other factors like stress from work getting in the way. Jim's life insurance policy provided well after the accident so I'm okay through the move to Texas, but as soon as I'm settled I plan to find work in my field."

"Would you be interested in working for an up and coming contractor just starting his own business? He's trust-worthy, a hard-worker, and promises to be a fair and generous boss."

"Hm…maybe so. Is it anyone I know?"

He gave her a one-shouldered shrug. "Just some ex-Marine, slash, nine-one-one dispatcher, slash, college graduate hopeful wanting to make something of himself."

Her eyes softened with the tiniest hint of a smile. "Well, that sounds like something I might seriously consider."

He raised both hands. "It may be rough for the first couple of years, until I build up my reputation, but I'd try to keep your salary competitive. I've met some influential people in that field over the past couple of years."

She nodded while adjusting her son's position. "Fair enough."

Luke stood to get a better look at the baby. "Can I hold him again, Cori?"

"Sure you can." She lifted her baby boy so Luke

could take him from her. "Sherrill should be bringing a bottle soon. It's getting close to his feeding time. I have to say, the nurses here are fantastic."

Luke put the snorting, snuffling baby up to his shoulder. "That's why he's getting so impatient. Poor little guy's getting hungry."

After a brief knock at the door, a tall brunette entered, carrying a bottle. "Hello. I'm Trish Leger, your night-shift nurse. Is that little one anxious for his supper?"

Luke lowered the fussy baby from his shoulder to the crook of his left arm. "I believe he is. He's sucking on his fist."

"Aw. Are you feeding him, Daddy?"

"Oh, I'm—I'm not the father." He looked at Cori for help.

"He's a friend," she smiled.

"I'm sorry. You looked so natural holding him, I just assumed." She held out the bottle. "Who's going to feed him?"

He puffed with pride at her assumption. "Is it okay if I feed him?"

Cori nodded. "Go for it."

Luke grabbed the bottle and a small towel from the nurse and thanked her.

"Call if you need anything at all."

He waited until she left to lift the towel. "What am I supposed to do with this?"

"It's his burp rag. Tuck it under his chin while you're feeding him then put it over your shoulder when you burp him."

He nodded. "I got this."

"Are you sure?"

"No problem."

Five minutes later, he reneged on his previous comment. "How do you burp him when he's all rolled up in a ball?"

She giggled and held out her hands. "Give him here. I'll show you a different way."

He watched as she sat her son up, lifting his chin with one hand to support him and patted his back with the other until he burped several seconds later.

"That way seems to work better. You're good with him, especially considering he's your first."

"I did a lot of babysitting as a teenager and learned even more after Lilly and Eli were born." She handed him back to Luke. "Here you go. You can finish feeding him and burp him the next go round."

He cradled the infant's tiny head in the palm of his hand as he fed him. "I can't wait to be a dad."

"You generally need to find a girl first."

He grinned without looking at her. "I realize that."

"Unless you're one of those guys who's just out looking for a 'baby mama'."

His jaw tightened. "Nope, I don't plan on having one without the other. When I settle down, I reckon it'll be for life."

"You reckon so?"

Luke glanced at Cori, and found her mouth twisted in a suppressed grin. He laid on a thick Texas drawl. "I sure do, little lady."

A yawn cut off her giggle. "Oh, oh…the meds are kicking in. They gave me my painkiller just before you arrived. As soon as you're finished, I'll call for the nurse to take him back to the nursery."

Luke remained quiet, assuming her closed eyes

meant she'd fallen asleep. When the baby finished, Luke positioned him as Cori had done then started patting his back. Within seconds, Little Luke let out a good burp. Luke wiped the baby's mouth then settled him back into the crook of his arm.

He sat there, staring at the child who looked so much like his mother, except for the slight indentation in his chin. He had to admit it looked good on the kid, though. Luke sucked in his breath as his namesake opened his dark blue eyes and stared at him. The tiny brow furrowed, and Luke reached up to smooth the lines away. "What are you so worried about, huh, little guy?"

The infant blinked and his lower lip pooched out in an adorable pout. Luke slid his finger down the side of the infant's downy soft skin, stopping when five tiny fingers wrapped around it with a remarkably strong grip.

There they sat, each of them sizing up the other, until the infant's eyelids grew heavy.

Luke rocked back and forth, and within a minute, the baby had fallen asleep. He stared at the sleeping infant, wondering at the miracle of life, unable to tear his gaze from him.

"You seem to be good with babies, yourself."

He looked up, found Cori watching him. "Not babies, in general. Just him, I guess. I think we have an understanding. It must be the name thing."

She smiled. "That must be it." She let a few more moments pass before speaking again. "Are you ready for him to go back to the nursery? I'm fading fast."

He stood slowly and placed the baby in the bassinet at the foot of Cori's bed, tucking the blanket around him. A glance up at Cori showed her eyes closed again. Rather than calling the nurse to remove Little Luke, he decided to leave him in the room.

Luke returned to the couch, pulled out the end that turned it into a sleeper, and arranged the extra pillows. He kicked off his shoes and settled back, thinking about the day's events. Twenty-four hours ago, he'd been counting down the hours until he could steal away to the white sands and soothing surf of Cozumel. Now, nothing could be further from his mind.

Amazing how much difference a single day could make in a man's life.

****

A muffled groan cut through to his dreamless sleep and he opened his eyes, immediately alert, He blinked twice to clear his sight and sat up straight. "Cori? What's wrong?"

"Oh, just trying to get to the bathroom without passing out."

He jumped up and met her on the opposite side of the bed, careful not to disturb the baby in his bassinet. Using his arm as support, he helped her to the door at one end of her private room. "Do you need me to get a nurse for you?"

"No, I can handle it. It's just that the pressure on my bladder is painful. I'll be fine in a few minutes."

Luke checked on the baby while waiting for her to finish. Little Luke squirmed in his bed and made funny snuffling noises. He checked his watch, surprised to discover six hours had already passed. He stepped outside to ask a nurse if it was time for a bottle. Nurse Trish followed him into the room.

"We don't normally leave them in here all night,

but when I came in to get him all three of you were sound asleep. Rather than wake anyone by making noise, I just left him. If you could hold the door for me, I'll roll him back to the nursery. How's the patient doing? She okay for pain meds?"

"I know she had some trouble getting to the restroom."

She nodded. "As soon as I get this little one back to the nursery I'll come back and check on his mom." By the time she reentered, Luke had helped Cori back into bed. "Are you ready for your pain meds?"

Cori shook her head. "I think I'm okay for a couple of hours, but I wondered how long before I could try breast-feeding."

"Because of the hemorrhaging, Doctor Reed wanted to give you twenty-four hours to recuperate."

"I can't help but feel like I'm missing out on bonding time with him."

The nurse smiled. "How about you let the pediatric nurse feed him once more and we'll let you try for the next one? He's starting to squawk for it right now, and it's 1:30 a.m., so I'll bring him to you first thing in the morning. I'll make sure to send the lactation specialist around to talk to you as soon as she arrives." She placed a hand on her shoulder. "Don't worry, you've got plenty of bonding time yet to come."

Luke approached the bed once they were alone. "Do you need anything? A glass of water or something?"

"I'm fine." She yawned and lowered the head of her bed. "You know. You could have stayed home. I've never had a problem staying in the hospital alone."

"Had many stays, have you?"

"More than a few. I've had surgeries to correct some problems, conditions that kept me from conceiving."

"And they obviously worked."

"Not until I'd given up all hope. But, none of it matters now, does it?"

"Nope. You've got a good looking baby boy as proof." He returned to his spot on the sofa and stretched as much as he could in the space allowed.

Cori released a long sigh and adjusted her position to gaze at him.

He started to fidget under her intense stare. "What?"

"Why are you here, Luke?"

He pursed his mouth, struggling to find an answer that wouldn't scare the hell out of her. How could he explain the tightness he felt in his chest every time he watched the news story about the hostage situation and shooting of the deputy? How could he justify his uneasiness when Shawn Jackson's image appeared on the television screen?

How did he clarify the feeling he had that it wasn't over yet?

He couldn't. He wouldn't lay that kind of worry on her.

"Nobody should be alone on Christmas Eve," he said.

She picked up the phone a sheriff's deputy had returned to her earlier. "Technically, it's Christmas already."

"You shouldn't be alone on Christmas, either."

"But dad would have stayed with me."

"I've got a better chance of walking away from this

couch without a hitch in my giddy-up than your dad. He should be with the rest of his family."

"I could say the same for you."

Well, hell, it didn't look like she planned to let this go anytime soon. Maybe he needed to explain his situation. "I wasn't supposed to be home anyway. I was supposed to be in Cozumel this week. I postponed my trip."

"You did? All that white sand, wind and surf, tanned beach babes in bikinis, and all the Mexican beer you can drink? Why the hell are you here?"

He shrugged. "It's no big deal for me. Hell, compared to spending Christmas with a bunch of Jarheads in Afghanistan, this is a walk in the park."

"I suppose it is." Cori settled into her bed. She sighed and turned her head.

He waited until her breathing evened out before readjusting the pillow under his head. Only when he knew for sure she was sound asleep, did he closed his eyes. A few short minutes later, he'd joined her.

Chapter 13
Fame and Misfortune

Christmas Morning, 9:00 a.m.

Luke dumped and stacked his food tray before heading from the hospital's cafeteria back to Cori's room. Several women smiled as he passed them in the hallway. God, it would be damned easy to pick up a date here if he wasn't so preoccupied with more important things. He hit the button for the elevator and waited for its arrival.

A tall brunette with a gorgeous rack and legs stretching to heaven joined him, as well as an older couple, both wrinkled and gray, the man holding the woman's elbow. A strange combination of smells assaulted Luke…menthol and talcum powder…sending him back in time, to weekends spent with the grandparents he'd adored as a kid. A bitter-sweet memory, since they'd both passed away while he was deployed. What he wouldn't give for one final lazy afternoon sitting on their porch, shucking corn and snapping beans while his great grandpa Tom before he passed away and his Paw Paw Garrett told him stories of being young boys in rural Texas during the early and mid-twentieth century.

The brunette coughed softly, pulling him from his reveries.

She caught his gaze and smiled at him, looked away, then did a double take. "You're the guy from the news interview…about the toy store hostage situation. The mother and child are both patients here."

The woman was a solid nine-and-a-half for sure. If he was the slightest bit interested, which he wasn't, he'd strike up a conversation. Instead he gave her a barely there smile, neither denying nor confirming her conclusion.

"Happy holidays," she said.

He sent her a half-nod, smiled, and replied pleasantly, despite his annoyance at her greeting. "Merry Christmas."

"Ugh!" She rolled her eyes and gave a low snort of disdain. "Not for me. I don't believe in the fairy tale of Jesus Christ."

Luke shrugged, but remained silent. *Everyone's got a right to their own opinion, right?*

"Oh, then Happy Hanukkah," the older woman added.

The brunette shook her head adamantly and sent the woman an indignant huff in her direction. "I don't believe in God, either. It's all nothing but foolishness."

There'd been a time when Luke would have let it go, clamped down on his jaw and kept his mouth shut.

Not today. Not when she'd gone out of her way to stir that particular kettle.

"If you'd spent time in some of the Godless places I have in the military, and seen some of the things those people do to each other, you'd want nothing more than to believe."

"There are plenty of people here in our own country who do awful things to each other," she said.

"Yes, and most of them are Godless as well," he shot back.

"Well, I'm an educated person, and I'm offended when someone tells me Merry Christmas."

He turned to face her. "I am also educated, and I guess that makes us even, because I'm offended when someone doesn't." He lifted one finger when she faced him, her mouth already opened. *"Normally,* I'd recognize your right to believe whatever the hell you want and keep my mouth shut—"

"Then why don't you?" she cut him off, her eyes narrowed.

"You mean like you did?" He crossed his arms. "Sorry lady, but I'm not feeling that today. Especially when you've made it clear how superior you think you are to the rest of us poor imbeciles."

She took a deep breath, her shoulders stiff. "You people make that so easy."

The older woman's laughter rang out around them. "Excuse me, young lady. Are you insinuating that my husband and I, along with this nice young man are imbeciles for being Christians?"

The brunette lifted one bony shoulder. "If the shoe fits. There is plenty of scientific evidence to prove there is no God."

"Really?" The older woman spoke in a quiet voice. "Do you have first-hand knowledge of that, dear? In what field of the sciences do you work?"

"Well, no…and I'm Dr. Haywood's assistant here in the hospital." The brunette seemed to deflate a bit.

The old man cleared his voice, obviously ready to throw his fedora into the ring. "His assistant…do you 'assist' him in surgery?"

"No. I'm his administrative assistant," she said, coloring slightly under the old man's scrutiny.

"So you're his secretary," the older woman said.

The brunette looked as though someone Gorilla-glued a two-by-four to her spine. "I'm not a *secretary*...I'm an administrative assistant."

The old woman's light chuckle reverberated over the *ding* of the arriving elevator. "Yes. Po-ta-to, po-tah-to...it's all the same, dear." The doors opened, revealing a middle aged woman holding a toddler.

After the four of them piled on board, the old man pointed a thumb in his wife's direction. "She should know...she was a secretary for ten years while we both worked our way through college. She got her Master's and a PHD in higher education."

"And *he* became a Pediatrician," his wife said, obviously proud of her husband's accomplishments.

"You don't say," Luke said.

The old man nodded. "That's right. Even after delivering thousands of babies, I've never stopped being awed by the miracle of birth." His mouth widened in a broad grin as he leaned closer to Luke. "You don't have to convince me of God's existence. I saw proof of it every day for forty years."

"Amen to that!" the woman with the toddler added. "If I wouldn't have believed in him two years ago today, I sure as heck would have afterwards. Not a scratch on this baby girl from an accident that took the lives of both her parents."

The brunette seemed to catch her second wind. "I'm sorry for your loss, but you must realize that scientific technology created the car seat she was no doubt buckled into."

The woman holding the child ran the fingers of one hand through the toddler's golden curls. "Her car seat malfunctioned. Isabelle was thrown thirty feet and the car caught fire. The rescue unit couldn't explain how or why she survived with no injuries." She blinked back her tears. "But I know. God knew I couldn't take losing my only child and my grandchild, too. Not a day goes by that I don't thank him for sparing her." She pressed a kiss on the child's forehead.

Luke smiled as the Shirley Temple look alike patted her grandmother's cheeks with both hands. "My MeeMee!" she said, giving Luke a toothy grin.

He reached out to touch a silky-soft ringlet. "Hey there, beautiful."

"Hi!" she said, waving her chubby hand.

The doors opened and Luke stepped out of the elevator onto the maternity ward. He turned back to acknowledge the older couple and the woman and child. "Merry Christmas, everyone."

The toddler answered with a bubbly "Mewwy Kwis-mas!" before blowing him a kiss he pretended to catch.

The old woman's eyes lit up, as her husband chuckled and nodded. "Merry Christmas to you also, young man, and you have a blessed day."

"You too, Ma'am. Thank you."

He threw a glare at the brunette, wishing for simpler times, when people didn't have their heads so far up their own self-important asses. He was still fuming over her attitude when he answered a call from his mom.

"Good morning."

"Hey son, I wanted to let you know we're about to

walk out of the house. I made a fresh batch of my caramel sticky buns this morning and I'm bringing some over for the new mama."

"Sounds good, Mom. I'm sure she'll love them. See y'all in a few minutes."

By the time he reached the nurses station he remembered it was Cori's birthday, as well as Christmas. He stopped at the desk and two women dressed in scrubs gave him their full attention. He turned on the charm, hoping for the best results.

"Hi, I was wondering if I could bother you two lovely ladies with a small request..."

****

Luke got to Cori's room a few minutes later, still wearing a grin. He knocked before opening the door a crack. "Is it safe to come in?"

"Sure."

He pushed it wide, poked his head around the edge. "What's going on? Oh..." He paused, seeing her seated on the sofa, nursing the baby, a receiving blanket covering little Luke's head. "I can come back later."

"You don't have to leave, Luke." She waved him inside the room. "I'll keep myself covered."

"If you're sure."

She nodded. "Sit. I needed a change of scenery while my son enjoys his breakfast. How was yours?"

"It was okay. They were working short-handed so I grabbed a packaged ham and egg biscuit and nuked it."

A frown tugged at the corners of her mouth. "You should go home. Mom called while you were gone. Your mom had a huge spread ready for them when they woke up this morning. I'm getting glowing reports from *my* family about *yours*."

"Yeah, Mom loves cooking for a lot of people. She says it makes her feel useful."

"They're coming over later."

He waved his phone. "She just called to tell me they're on their way."

Cori's smile brightened at the news. "I can't wait to meet everyone."

"I know mom's coming, but my old man is, too?"

"I think they all are. I hear your dad and mine get along well."

He made a face at the idea of both their families crowded into the small room. "The whole bunch, huh? Aren't you a glutton for punishment this morning?"

She grinned. "Someone's bringing you a change of clothes. You can shower in my bathroom when they get here, or go home and get some real rest. You had to be miserable on that tiny couch."

"I slept like a prince. Even hospital pillows covered in crinkling vinyl beat using a discarded water jug or my helmet as a headrest."

She grew somber, as though trying to picture it. "Bless all members of the military, far and near."

"I can't speak for all of 'em out there, but he sure blessed me. I came home with all my limbs and my sanity. Or at least as much sanity as I possessed the day I enlisted."

"Thank God for that."

He looked away while she separated Little Luke from his meal source to switch him to the opposite breast, grinning as his namesake's impatient cries pierced the air.

"Now piglet," she cooed. "This'll only take a few seconds."

"Someone doesn't have a lot of patience. Does he get that from you or his da..." He closed his eyes and sucked in air through his teeth. "I'm sorry, I shouldn't have said that."

"Nah, it's okay, and you can turn around now."

He faced her, thinking he'd see a trace of sadness, found only the most beautiful sight in the world. Luke drank in the image before him—Cori's content and sweetly smiling profile as she watched her son take nourishment from her body. He tuned in to what was becoming one of his favorite sounds, the whisper soft suckling of the infant on Cori's breast.

Inhaling deeply, he was strangely comforted by the mild aroma of mother's milk, combined with that distinctive new-baby scent he'd become accustomed to in a short period of time. Did all babies smell the same, or were each born with their own unique scent? The latter wouldn't surprise him. He had the distinct feeling that if Cori were sent blindfolded into a room full of newborn infants she'd surely be able to sniff out her own child.

Hell, at this point, I may be capable of doing the same thing.

"I'm long over any anger about my son's father. I just focus on the fact that, no matter what happened or how it happened, he gave me the chance to have this child. I'll always be grateful to him for that"—she looked up to meet his gaze headlong—"no matter how much of an ass he was."

He nodded in response, soaking in the peace and solitude of bonding time between mother and child for several more minutes, until the approach of animated chattering had him rushing to block the door. "I'll hold 'em off for your dignity, as well as my old man's sense of propriety."

Cori lifted Little Luke from her breast. "It's okay, he's done."

Luke pivoted to look back at her, couldn't turn away at the flash of creamy breast when the blanket fell away. He swallowed as she pulled her robe closed, covering herself. "Are you ready?"

She met his gaze and nodded. "All set."

He pulled open the door at the first knock and let Cori's parents walk in first. "Good morning and Merry Christmas!"

"Same to you, Luke." Charles shook his hand before following his wife to their daughter and grandson on the couch.

His own parents followed them into the room. "Merry Christmas, Son!" His parents both gave him hugs. Melissa and his sister trailed in last and Cori's parents made all the appropriate introductions.

Joan fawned over her newest grandchild. "Oh, he's even more beautiful today; look at those full cheeks!"

"He's so handsome." Dolores elbowed her son. "How does it feel to have a child named after you?"

He puffed up, grinning. "I've got to admit, it feels pretty damned good."

His mom leaned closer to the baby. "He's every bit as good-looking as you were as a baby, Luke." She turned to wink at him. "Are you sure you two haven't met before? Say, around nine months ago?"

Cori laughed at his mom's insinuation. "No ma'am. Before yesterday, I'd never laid eyes on Luke Oliver. I sure am glad the man upstairs saw fit to remedy that situation. I don't know what I'd have done without him."

The wink she sent him warmed his heart as he shrugged off her compliment. "It was nothing."

His sister poked him in the ribs. "Look at you, all 'Why shucks, ma'am. I was just doing my job.' I think I see a blush starting up."

He gave her a playful shove. "Shut up, Lee, and where's Joe, anyway? If he was here you'd be too busy nagging at him to bother picking on me."

"Oh, grow up, you big baby. Speaking of big babies, we decided to leave the guys home with the kids," Lee said. "They were playing with their toys so well together."

"I take it Christopher liked the Indy racetrack and car I got him?"

Melissa laughed. "Oh, we're not talking about our *little* children. We're talking about the *big* ones. When we left, Roland and Joe were crashing Christopher's cars on the racetrack so they could send them to the garage set he got from your parents. I'm just glad Lilly is into dolls, or else there'd be a fight."

Lee leaned against the wall. "But she sure is sharing her robot puppy with Chris. Those two were playing so good together. Chris asked this morning if he could send his toys back and have Santa bring him a little sister, instead."

"That's so sweet. So the puppy is a success?" Cori asked.

Her mom snorted. "It better be for what you went through to get it."

Melissa's facial expression turned to a mixture of embarrassment and regret. "I feel bad enough having called you to vent the night before last. If I wouldn't have said anything, you'd have driven straight through and none of this would have happened."

"Don't go there, Sis. I figure I was supposed to show up exactly when I did."

"If she hadn't, those guys still would have robbed the store. The sales clerk's deputy husband still would have shown up when he did. Chances are, if she hadn't been there to hide their ammo and help me to keep law enforcement informed, that cop would have lost his wife, along with his partner, and who knows how many others. Jackson seems sadistic enough to take down as many as he could before he went down, just for the pleasure of it."

Cori chewed her lower lip, deep in concentration. "He's right. You may have saved lives by calling me when you did."

Luke thought about the obvious. *Not to mention if Cori hadn't stopped when she did, if she'd had no reason to call 911, I never would have met her…and that would be unacceptable.*

"And if I hadn't been there at that time, on that day, to share this experience with Luke…"

Luke waited for her to finish; looked up to find her gaze on him—his heart sputtered in his chest.

The corners of her mouth turned up in an impish grin. "I may have named my son something totally lame like Ian or Blanket."

"Or something that would have gotten him beaten up all his life, like Gaylord or Seaman," Luke added.

Cori's mouth fell open. "I would never name my son Gaylord, and excuse me, but *why* would anyone name a kid after…" She lowered her voice to a hiss. "You know—that's just nasty."

Luke smiled at the slight blush in her cheeks. "It's not spelled the same. It's S-E-A-M-A-N, like a sailor-seaman."

She frowned, her distaste on full display. "Still, no. Just no." Her brow furrowed suddenly as she scanned the area, her nose sniffing the air. "And what smells so good? I keep getting a whiff of something sweet, like pastry."

Dolores straightened. "I nearly forgot! I brought you a treat." She pulled a plastic container from a bag.

Luke sidled up to his mother, groaning when she removed the container's lid. "You are in for a real treat, Cori. Mom makes the best caramel sticky buns in the world."

Cori lifted her son, as though offering him up as a sacrifice. "Trade ya, Ms. Dolores!"

Dolores laughed and set the container on Cori's lap before taking the baby. "Sounds like a worthy trade to me."

Luke spoke to the infant in his mother's arms. "How do you like that, little man? You've been sold out for a handful of sticky-buns." Before Cori could reach for one of the treats, he ripped the container out of her hands. "Hold on, it's not quite ready, yet." He pulled a birthday candle from his pocket and stuck it in the center of the biggest bun. Cori's delighted laughter warmed his heart.

"You always walk around with one of those in your pocket?"

"Always prepared." He'd leave off how he'd charmed the nurses into scrambling to find it for him on the way to her room. He waited for Lee to light it before turning around to lead the group in a round of the birthday song.

"Thank y'all! With everything that happened I almost forgot it was my birthday." Cori blew out the candle, lifted a gooey, caramel covered pastry from the container, and took a bite. "Oh-ma-gosh, this is so good." Her eyes rolled in ecstasy as she released a muted groan. "It's only temporary, baby boy. Mama will steal you back as soon as I've licked the last bit of caramel from this container."

Luke reached for a roll but paused. "You plan to wolf those down alone, or share them with me?"

She held the container out to him. "You've earned your share."

He lifted one and bit into it, savoring the sticky goodness. "I missed these so much I tried to bake a batch when I was stationed back stateside. They were decent, but not nearly as good as these." Luke leaned closer to Cori. "I'm convinced my mom left something out of her recipe on purpose, so they wouldn't be as good as hers."

"I heard that!" Dolores said. "I'll have you know I gave you the same recipe I've used for twenty years. Don't blame me for your failure to execute."

Cori laughed. "Well, I'd love to try it, if you don't mind, Ms. Dolores. Or better yet, give it to my mom."

Joan gave her head an adamant shake and crossed her arms. "I don't want any part of that. She started making those at 5:00 a.m. You know my rule. I don't cook anything that takes longer than thirty minutes. Just call Charles and me over. We'll do the babysitting while you work on your technique."

"You've got a deal." Cori licked a blob of gooey caramel from her finger, accepted the damp napkin

Luke handed her. "Mm...now all I need is a good cup of coffee."

Dolores reached inside her bag and pulled out a thermos. "I brought some. Hospital coffee is never as good as mine. It's already got a little sugar and cream in it." She filled a disposable cup and passed it to the new mom.

Cori took a sip and closed her eyes. "Thank you, Ms. Dolores. This is a great birthday gift."

Her sister sighed. "Your gift from us is at home though, along with the Christmas gifts Roland and I were too freaked out to remember to bring after that early morning phone call yesterday."

"No problem, Sis. I got the only gift I needed this year."

Melissa smiled at her new nephew. "Yeah, you had to one up the rest of us." She cocked her head. "Does that mean I get to keep what I got you? I like it...a lot."

Cori chuckled. "I'll let you know after I open it."

Halfway through his second cup of dark roasted coffee, Luke nudged Cori's mom. "So, how'd it go last night, Ms. Joan?"

"We had a wonderful evening. Your parents have opened their home and made us feel welcome and comfortable." She faced Cori. "Dolores enjoys sewing as much as I do, and she quilts, too. She's offered to teach me some things."

"So, Dad's not uncomfortable being there?" Cori's gaze landed on her father and Luke's dad, deep in a conversation about which NFL team had the best chance of winning the Super Bowl this year.

"Not at all. He and Arthur take turns sitting in the recliner."

"We're glad to have you all in our home," Dolores added. "I swear to you, Arthur hasn't talked this much without dozing off in years. I don't know what it is, but we all seem to 'click'."

Joan responded with a nod. "I know exactly what you mean, Dolores."

Luke's gaze landed on Cori, thinking he sensed some definite clicking going on between the two of them. But was it wishful thinking on his part, or did she feel it too?

****

An hour later, the two young mothers grew antsy at being away from their little ones on Christmas day and Dolores wanted to start on lunch preparations for her guests. Within seconds of their farewells, the room had cleared out, leaving Cori alone with Luke.

He helped her back to bed and stood looking down at her. "Is there anything I can get for you? Do you need the nurse?"

She smoothed the covers over her lap. "I'm fine, thanks. You should go home and get some rest."

"I told you I don't require that much sleep." He paused and lifted his gaze to hers. "I'll go if you feel you need some time alone, though."

She swallowed the panic building in her chest at the thought of losing her connection with him, tried to play it as if it wouldn't matter one way or the other if he walked out. "I'm not saying that at all, but if you have things you need to do I'd be okay for a while."

He studied her, a barely perceptible narrowing of his eyes a possible sign of him calling her bluff. He took a step back and shifted his weight to the opposite foot. "I'm good. I'd just as soon stick around if it's okay with you."

She took a measured breath and released it slowly, attempting to suppress her relief. "I don't have a problem with that." Cori waited for it, wasn't disappointed at its appearance—that one-sided lift of his mouth—just enough to show he approved. Something about his action had her wondering if he was holding back as much as she was. Another soft rapping on the door tore her away from that train of thought.

Luke went to the door, pulled it open a crack to check out her visitors. A few muffled comments later, he pulled the door open and turned to her, a grin covering his face. "You'll definitely want to see these visitors."

Cori sucked in her breath at the sight of the middle-aged couple entering the room, her eyes misting at the sight of the woman's blackened eyed, courtesy of Shawn Jackson. She extended both hands. "You're Simone Davis! How are you?"

The tall, strikingly beautiful woman took two steps forward and grabbed her hands, her bright smile lighting up her entire face. "Hello, Corrine. I'm fine, and I hear it's thanks to you."

"I don't know about all that, but I'm glad you're okay. I was terrified for you." She leaned over to see the man standing behind her. "You're Deputy Davis, her husband. I nearly had a heart attack when you arrived at the store when you did. In my mind, I could see everything spinning out of control. I kept thinking that if those two had just taken the money and got out quicker, none of that would have happened."

Simone squeezed her hands. "You don't know how

many times I've told Shemar that very thing."

Her husband approached, carrying a flower arrangement. "These are for you, Mrs. Ritter."

"Oh, they're beautiful. Thank you so much, but please call me Cori."

He nodded. "Only if you call me Shemar." He placed the flowers on the table next to the bed and shifted his weight to one leg. He rested one hand on the buckle of his uniform belt, draped his opposite arm protectively around his wife's shoulders. "Simone must have said that a dozen times so far. Unfortunately, it didn't happen that way. The store is only open all night a few times a year for its anniversary sale, Black Friday, and Christmas Eve. On the rare occasion Simone was scheduled to work those hours, Mike and I tried to trade shifts with other patrols so I could check up on her a few times during the night."

"Mike—was that your partner—Deputy Lawson?" Cori's chin quivered when Shemar nodded. "I'm so sorry." She extended her hand and he shook it. She accepted a tissue from Luke and wiped her eyes. "Have you met Luke Oliver? He was my lifeline during the entire episode."

"The 911 dispatcher. I recognize you from the news clip," Simone said, as she and her husband shook Luke's hand.

"It's great to meet you both. I'm sorry about your partner, Deputy Davis. I hear he was a good man."

The deputy rubbed his eyes with the thumb and forefinger of his right hand. A veil of silence engulfed the room, broken only by Cori's quiet sniffles. It took several moments before the deputy trusted himself to speak. "Thank you. I'd known Mike for twenty years, and he was my partner for the last five. They don't come any better than him." He shook his head. "When I think of the animal that's still alive…"

Simone took over when her husband couldn't finish. "Sitting in prison, eating food we pay for, getting free legal services and even a free education if he'd want, which he won't, of course…" She waved her hand. "All those cop haters out there have no idea what these men and women in law enforcement go through every minute of every work day. What their families go through. Every time my husband walks out that door in uniform, I pray that God keeps him safe, keeps me from getting that dreaded call, or that knock on my door from the Sheriff telling me I'll never see Shemar—alive again."

She choked on the last words as tears rolled down her face when she tried to finish. "When I saw Mike shot, I knew it was bad. My heart broke for Jaqueline and those poor little boys—" She had to stop and swallow a sob. "I hope the good Lord can forgive me, because my first thought was to thank God it wasn't *my* husband." She turned toward her husband when he pulled her close for a one armed hug.

****

Luke's heart clenched at the sight of Cori's downcast, tear-drenched face. His first instinct was to hold her close, try his best to comfort her. He held himself back, kept from reaching out to her. She wasn't his to comfort, was she? If he attempted, she could possibly misinterpret and think he was taking advantage of a situation.

He grabbed the box of tissue and stepped closer to the bed. "Cori."

She looked up and reached for the tissues he held out for her, clutched his hand instead and sobbed. "Oh, Luke. That poor family—two little boys growing up without a father, their mom having to raise them alone because she lost her husband—they must be devastated."

He perched on the edge of her bed facing her and clasped her hand between both of his. "I know, hon. It's a tragedy, and something we see far too often in the families of law enforcement officers."

Shemar took a step forward, his wife's hand tucked into the crook of his arm. "We'll be there to help Mike's family, along with everyone else at the department," he said, his voice thick with emotion. "We're all more than co-workers. We're family."

Luke met his gaze and nodded. "Brothers in arms just like in the military. You always have their back."

"I know it may seem strange to some people, since they're white and we're black, but they're our best friends," Simone explained.

"Not strange at all," Cori said.

"We do everything together. Shemar and I don't have any children of our own, so those little boys are like our own kids. They call us Aunt Simone and Uncle Shemar."

Shemar's chuckle punctuated the air. "The guys down at the department call us the odd couple. Or they called us that, anyway." He paused to shake his head. "Damn, I'm gonna miss having him around."

Simone cleared her throat, as though to shake off the sadness, and then set her purse on a nearby chair. She held up a gift bag. "I almost forgot. We brought this for your new baby boy."

"Oh, thank you." Cori removed the tissue paper then pulled an adorable blue and yellow checked romper from the bag. "This is precious!"

Luke reached over to lift the matching hat and booties from the bag and laid them alongside the garment. "It comes with some pretty cool accessories, don't you think?"

Cori clasped her hands together. "Oh, my gosh, that is just too cute! Thank you both so much."

"You're welcome." Simone looked around. "We were hoping to see the baby. Is he in the nursery?"

"They should be bringing him in any minute. The pediatrician wanted to check him out today and see if everything was still okay."

Luke interpreted her glance as a silent plea to check on his namesake. He stood, only too happy to get the little guy. He'd barely stepped out the door when he saw one of two pediatric nurses on duty carrying a blue wrapped bundle toward the room. "I was just sent to see if he was coming back soon. He has visitors." He opened the door to the room, held it so she could enter with the baby.

"Here you go, Mom. All cleaned up and ready for showing off."

"Oh, he's beautiful!" Simone exclaimed, gazing at the infant in the nurse's arms. She turned to Cori, her eyes pleading. "Would you mind if I held him?"

"Not at all," Cori said. "He loves being passed around."

Luke sat beside Cori again and watched as Simone and Shemar fawned over the baby.

Shemar's deep chuckle resonated in the air when baby Luke gripped his finger. "Hey, the kid's got a grip, don't he?"

Simone passed a finger lightly over the infant's wrinkled forehead. "His expression is so serious. It's like he's already trying to figure things out." She looked up at Cori then flashed a grin in Luke's direction. "And you named him Luke after this guy, if I heard correctly."

Luke sat a little straighter. "That's right. She made an excellent choice if I do say so." He stood. "I'm feeling the need for a cup of coffee. Can I get anyone anything?"

"I'm good, thanks," Cori said.

"I am too," Simone added. "But I bet my husband needs a cup right about now."

Shemar caught Luke's gaze. "My wife knows me too well. Mind if I go with you?"

"Not at all." Luke walked with him to the door and turned to look back at Cori. "We'll be right down the hall, but I'll keep an eye on the door."

****

Cori's gaze stayed on Luke until the door closed behind him. She looked away and found Simone watching her. "He's been such a help. It's hard to believe I've only known him a little over a day."

Simone lifted the baby to her shoulder. "From a complete stranger's prospective, the two of you look very comfortable together."

"I can't speak for Luke, but it's strange how comfortable I am around him. You know, I'm not sure why he's still here. He even slept here with me last night so my dad wouldn't have to sleep on the couch."

Simone's mouth rounded. "Oh, sounds promising. Maybe this friendship will turn into something more serious?"

Cori placed a hand over her tender belly. "I can't think about anything like that right now."

"Oh, of course not. I'm so sorry, I just remembered that your husband passed away a few months ago, didn't he? I'd forgotten."

"It has nothing to do with that. The truth is, when he died, we weren't exactly on good terms. Our relationship had been under a lot of strain because I'd been told I'd probably never conceive. I didn't discover I was pregnant until after Jim died."

"Your husband?"

"Yes—James Phillip Ritter, but everyone called him Jim." Cori twisted her sheet tightly in both hands. "He'd been having an affair and had asked me for a divorce shortly before he died."

Simone uttered a small gasp. "Oh, I'm so sorry. Your emotions must have been all over the place."

Cori took a deep breath, released it in a puff as she tried to recall the conflict that had torn at her. "That's an accurate description. I didn't know how to feel about losing him. I loved him, but I hated him for hurting me, and worse was the thought that I'd never have a child of my own with him or anyone else."

Simone's expression softened as she looked down at the infant in her arms. "But you did."

Cori smiled. "Yes, I did, and he made all the hell I'd gone through worth it. It's just him and me, now."

Simone spoke through pursed lips. "I don't know how long that will last. You already have a one-man cheering section. I heard the story of course, but you two sure look good together."

"He's a great guy from what I've seen so far. His

family is too. I think we could be friends." She looked up as Simone's low chuckle reached her.

"I think he's interested in more than friendship, if or when you open yourself up to it, that is."

"Luke? No. He's in his over protective Marine mode." She waved off Simone's blatant 'if you say so' look and changed the subject. "I'm glad the two of you showed up when you did. I feel as though I need to apologize to you."

Simone tore her gaze from Little Luke to Cori. "For what?"

"I'm sorry I left you alone to deal with those awful men. I saw—well, mostly I heard what you went through. I know that man attacked you in the office. I felt so useless, knowing what you were going through."

"None of that is your fault. Honey, my husband is a Deputy. He read your statement. He told me what you heard that animal say earlier. As a mother, it was your responsibility to keep your child safe." She released a shaky breath. "Besides, nothing happened. I regret not being able to thank Jefferson for stopping Jackson when he did. I can't help but feel God took the wrong one that night. Jackson…" She shivered and shook her head. "That man is evil and no amount of jail time is going to change him."

"You don't think he can be rehabilitated?"

"I think animals like him are here to prey on people. He takes from those who are physically weak and he spreads his evilness to those who are mentally weak. Our prison systems are full of people who are susceptible to his manipulation. Unfortunately, he'll thrive in prison."

A frisson of dread shimmied up Cori's spine. She

met Simone's gaze briefly before looking away.

The other woman reached up to place a comforting touch on her arm. "You've got a beautiful baby, and if my gut is correct, a man out there who cares for you. Stop worrying. Things will turn out just fine."

Cori swallowed her trepidation, her own gut telling her she wasn't quite out of the woods.

Chapter 14
A Dish Served Not So Cold

December 26ᵗʰ, 8:30 a.m.

Cori shuffled around her room, slowly getting her things together for her eventual release. She'd finally talked Luke into staying at his own place the previous night, thank goodness. Guilt at keeping him from his family had been eating away at her. The sudden loss at his absence had been a shock she hadn't expected. Now she craved company, or more specifically, Luke's company. She answered her room phone on the first ring, hoping to hear his voice.

"Cori, it's Simone Davis. I'm at the desk downstairs and I have someone with me who'd like to meet you."

"Come on up. I'm waiting on the doctor to release me this morning, but she hasn't come around yet."

"Be there in a few."

Cori pulled open the door at Simone's light knock, and stepped aside to let the two women enter her room. "Good morning, Simone."

"Good morning. Did you have a good night?"

"I did, thanks." Cori tipped her head to study the pretty woman who walked in behind her new friend.

"I'd like you to meet my dearest friend, Jacqueline Lawson."

The tiny redhead reached out a hand. "I hope you don't mind me barging in like this, Cori. Shemar and Simone are accompanying me to the funeral home this morning, and I wanted to stop and tell you how happy I am that you and your baby are doing so well."

Cori clasped the woman's hand, touched at her show of concern, especially in light of the heartbreaking loss of her husband. "Thank you so much, but I can't believe you'd even think about me at a time like this. I'm so sorry for your loss."

Jacqueline lowered her gaze to the floor and nodded. "Thank you. That means a lot to me." As though bolstered suddenly, she lifted her chin. "I've got my boys, thank goodness. I can't let myself wallow in misery for too long. They keep me going."

Cori nodded, amazed at her strength, but no less heartbroken for her. "I imagine they do, at their ages. They're five and three years old, aren't they?"

"Yes, and they're a handful. I don't know how they're going to deal with this. I still can't believe Mike is gone. I keep waiting for him to call me or to walk through the door."

Cori clutched tighter at Jacqueline's hand. "I went through that not too long ago. It doesn't seem real at first. The situation was slightly different for me, but I experienced a bad four months until I discovered my pregnancy. I'll keep you and your boys in my prayers."

Jacqueline blinked back her tears and smiled. "Thank you, also, for mentioning us during your interview. I watched it and I thought it was very gracious of you. I just wanted you to know that gifts and monetary donations have been pouring in since you did that, and I'm truly grateful. The gifts have been a real distraction for my boys. The money will be a tremendous help."

"I was glad to do it. How are your boys since all this happened?"

"They've been preoccupied by the Christmas activity, of course. I doubt…" She paused to swallow, maybe to hold back a sob. "I don't think they realize yet they'll never see their father again. I even let them get involved in sorting most of the donated toys to bring to the local women and children's shelter. My husband had a soft spot for that place because he brought so many battered and abused victims to them over the years."

"That's right," Simone added. "Mike and Shemar both participated in fund raisers for the shelter the past five years." She placed an arm around Jacqueline's shoulder. "They got us involved, and now Jacqui's helping her kids to get involved, also."

"I can tell you both have generous spirits," Cori said.

Jacqueline's soft laughter brought a smile to Cori's face as she explained. "Simone and I usually end up as clowns during the big top event every year. But at least we weren't assigned to the dunking booth, right Simone?"

"Girl, you got that right! Thankfully, people aren't that interested in dunking a cop's wife in a vat of cold water."

Jacqueline pointed a finger at Cori. "But they will stand in line to dunk a cop." Her smile faded followed by a weighty sigh. She turned and faced Simone. "I guess we should be on our way now. My parents are bringing my boys to the funeral home later. I didn't want them with me when I view Michael for the first time." She paused again to dab a tissue to her eyes. "I'm dreading it."

Cori nodded, remembering the initial shock of seeing her husband that first time in the morgue, his face too messed up for anything but a closed coffin. She'd been flooded with emotions, despite the circumstances of Jim's death. How much worse would it be for this poor woman?

She pulled Jacqueline close for a hug. "Thank you for taking the time to stop by. I'll be praying for God to give you the strength you'll need to get through this."

"Thank you, Cori. I'll be praying for you and your beautiful little boy as well. Simone pointed him out to me in the nursery. God bless you both."

Cori nodded. "You and your boys, as well. Thank you so much for coming. You ladies take care, and please keep in touch."

She walked them to the door, watched until they disappeared into the elevator at the opposite end of the corridor. Her ringing phone pulled her back to the moment. Closing her door, she cleared the tears clogging her throat before answering.

"Hey, it's Luke. I wanted to see if you needed anything."

Cori sniffed and wiped under her eyes with a tissue. "Not that I can think of."

"What's wrong? You sound like you've been crying."

She stuffed her slippers into the side pocket of her bag. "I had some interesting visitors, and they walked out of here seconds before your call. Simone came by and she brought Jacqueline Lawson with her."

"Lawson—the dead deputy's wife?"

She fanned her eyes with her free hand. "Yes, and she's a very sweet lady—came to thank me for what I said during the interview. She said the donations have been pouring in for her and her two boys since then and she's very grateful. They stopped by on their way to the funeral home—her first viewing."

"Oh, God. Well, I understand your tears. I'm sure you can relate to what she's feeling. Even if—"

"My dead husband was a cheating dog?"

"I wouldn't have said that...exactly."

"That's because you're a nice man."

His pause was the kind that sounded as if he didn't quite know whether to take her comment as a compliment, even though it was meant to be. Change of subject needed. "Anyway, I'm waiting on my dad to pick me up this morning. I should be released soon."

"I'll be there in a few minutes to collect you and the baby. I offered because everyone else is busy getting things ready for you at my parents' place."

She sucked in her breath at the chance to be alone with him again. "Okay. I'll see you then." Cori ended the call too abruptly, deciding she needed to get a grip on her emotions. She busied herself the next several minutes, loading her bag and zipping it shut.

Nurse Sherrill Ardoin entered, carrying Little Luke. Cori's hackles rose at the woman's tight facial expression, and rigid body language. "Oh, God. What's wrong?"

Sherrill pointed at the muted television hanging on the wall. "You need to put the sound on...now."

****

Luke knocked before he walked into Cori's

hospital room; found her dressed and fidgeting, arms crossed tightly against her chest. Her day nurse, Sherrill, stood close, one hand placed on Cori's shoulder, as though offering comfort.

The look they sent his direction put him into instantaneous protective mode. He searched the room for clues. The baby lay sound asleep in his bassinet beside the bed. Cori's bags were on the couch, packed and ready to go. "What's wrong? Has the doctor decided not to release you today?"

"The local news just said something about an escaped prisoner." Sherrill's tone held an ominous note.

He approached, placed a hand on Cori's shoulder. "It could be any prisoner—"

She turned on him. "A prisoner involved in a recent local hostage situation resulting in a dead law enforcement officer?"

He managed to speak even though his stomach muscles clenched with dread and nausea. "Did they say anything else?"

"Only that they'll tell us more after the commercial break," Sherrill said.

Luke leaned in close to Cori. "Don't borrow trouble before you need to. Maybe it's someone else."

She stopped her fidgeting long enough to stare at him. "Do you really believe that?"

Luke clenched his jaw. No use telling her his earlier suspicions about her situation. "Let's wait and see."

In seconds, the news anchor returned to the screen.

"This just in from the Jefferson County Sheriff's Department. One of two men involved in a hostage situation on Christmas Eve has escaped. The van carrying Shawn Jackson flipped twice when its tire blew out. The prison official driving the van claimed he heard a pop that sounded like a gun shot before losing control of the vehicle. The van flipped, temporarily knocking out both the driver and the accompanying Sheriff's deputy. When they came to, Jackson was missing from the van. Authorities are investigating as to whether a gunshot may have caused the tire to blow. Local and state law enforcement units are all involved in the manhunt. Jackson, responsible for the death of Deputy Michael Lawson, has a long list of drug and gang related priors and is considered dangerous. Jackson had been charged formally with first-degree murder, and was en route to the Jefferson County Courthouse to have his case reviewed before a judge.

The incident involving the shooting death of Deputy Michael Lawson took place at Viv's Toy Emporium in the early morning hours of December twenty-fourth, here in Beaumont. Jackson had taken the clerk, Mrs. Simone Davis, as a hostage, even attempted to rape her before Theodore "T-Bone" Jefferson, his partner in crime, stopped him. Renee Bertrand is standing by for a live news feed at the Sheriff's Department

The camera switched to the same woman who had interviewed them two days earlier.

"I'm here with Simone Davis, the woman taken hostage by Shawn Jackson on Christmas Eve morning. Mrs. Davis, is there anything you'd like to say to our listeners?"

Cori gasped. "It's Simone. She didn't say a word about this."

"Shemar probably got a call on their way to the

funeral home." Luke turned his full attention to the TV screen as the camera focused on the woman he'd met the previous afternoon.

"Shawn Jackson is an animal. If anyone sees him or hears rumors of where he may be hiding out, please call the local police or the Sheriff's Department." She pointed to the still visible bruising on her face. "He did this with no provocation. A few minutes later that monster tried to rape me; I'm convinced he would have had the man he called T-Bone not stopped him when he did. Jackson is psychotic and dangerous. Do not help him. Do not hide him. If you know where he is, please call it in to the police. I heard him say over and over he was prepared to die rather than go back to prison. I heard him threaten Jefferson on several occasions. I'm convinced that if Jefferson hadn't been shot in the crossfire, Shawn Jackson would have killed the man himself. May God forgive me, but Beaumont will be a much safer place when that animal is gone from this earth."

Renee turned back to the camera. "A desperate plea from a brave woman, one of three victims involved in the early morning robbery turned hostage situation. Back to you, Bridget."

Sherrill gave Cori's arm a reassuring pat. "I'm going to alert security."

Cori waited until Sherrill left the room to break down. "Oh, God. He's out, Luke! He's *out*, and he knows who I am, where I am, and that I have a newborn son. He knows everything!" She placed a shaky hand over her heart, her eyes wide with terror.

"Try to stay calm. He'd be crazy to make any attempt to get to you here."

She pointed to the TV again. "Were you listening? She called him psychotic. He's not only crazy, he's evil. How difficult would it be for him to look up my address back home in Louisiana?"

"He's not going to get his hands on you."

"You can't possibly know that!"

"The hell I don't. I'm telling you I won't let him."

Cori's frantic gaze landed on him. "You can't just say things like that to placate me. They're only words, and words won't help a thing in this situation." She placed both palms on her chest. "Oh, God. I can't breathe. I think I'm having a panic attack…"

He turned her to face him and rested his hands on her shoulders. "Stop, Cori. I want you to listen to me. He won't get to you because I'm not letting you out of my sight until he's either back in custody or dead. If there's one thing you should know about me, it's that I'm quite capable of carrying out that second scenario."

"But you can't—"

"I can—and I will." He placed his hands on her cheeks, wrapped his fingers around her skull to pull her closer. "Do you trust me, Cori?"

"Luke…"

"Answer me. Do you trust me?"

"I don't know. Can I?"

"Did you trust me enough to listen to me when you were in that stock room?"

"Yes…"

He nodded. "And I'm asking you to trust me again."

Cori closed her eyes and took a deep breath. She raised her face to his and opened her eyes again. "All right, but before we leave here, I have to know. What's your plan?"

"I think we should both stay with my parents. Jackson and his friends can find your place, and my place without much effort, but he doesn't know who my parents are."

She paled suddenly. "His friends? You think he has friends out there?"

"His priors mentioned gang related activity. I'm thinking they could have ambushed the van—shot the tire to make it flip."

"Oh, God."

"My parents live in a gated community with a security system, and they have plenty of room."

Worry lines marred her forehead. "I don't know."

"Maybe your folks would extend their stay so you'd be more comfortable."

"But your parents—"

"Won't mind a bit, and you've seen them together. They get along fine. Hell, my dad's a *talker* now. Not only that, but he's a retired cop, with friends still employed with the Beaumont P.D. More importantly, I've got my own friends, Marines who'll be glad to step in if I need an extra hand or two."

Cori covered his hands with hers and pulled them from her face. She stepped away from him, turned her gaze on her sleeping son. "Why are you doing this?"

He stared at her back, wondered how to answer. Truth be known, he didn't come up with this plan upon hearing that report. He'd been planning it since Jackson had been taken into custody…just in case that nagging feeling turned out to be more substantial than simple paranoia. He couldn't exactly say why.

"I can't stand the thought of you, either of you,

being in danger. Seeing you afraid makes me crazy."

She turned on him. "But why, Luke?"

He tried to focus on the question, found himself shaking his head. "I don't know why. Not yet, anyway. When I figure it out, I'll let you know."

Her gaze raked over him, from his forehead down to his belt buckle, or somewhere in that area. Cori tore her gaze away, blushed when she found him watching her. She started to turn away from him.

He placed his hands on her arms before she could escape. "Don't."

She looked at the window, at the heating/AC unit below it, anywhere but at him. "Don't what?"

"Don't be embarrassed. Don't pull away from me."

Her blush deepened. "Geeze Louise! How can you expect me not to be embarrassed when you specifically ask me not to be?"

Was it wrong to enjoy her discomfort? Truth was it'd been too damn long since he'd seen a woman blush. That didn't say much for the company he'd kept of late. He lifted a knuckle and brushed one heated cheek. "You look good in that shade of pink."

A knock at the door had them pulling away from each other like a couple of guilty teenagers. He looked up as the doctor entered the room.

"Looks like you're all packed and ready to go. I guess I'm late to the party."

"Yes, Ma'am. We're ready to get out of here."

Dr. Reed looked at Luke. "Did you park yourself, or did you valet?"

"I valet parked. If you're here to release her I'll call them right now." He pulled the ticket from his pocket and made the necessary call to the number listed, while keeping an ear open to hear the doctor's instructions.

"Okay, Ms. Ritter, you've received instructions from your lactation specialist, correct?"

"Yes, she was in here earlier."

"And the pediatrician spoke to you about bringing the baby either here or to your own pediatrician in two weeks for a circumcision if you so choose?"

"Yes, she did. I've already made an appointment with her."

Dr. Reed gave her a quick run-down of what she could and could not do in her condition. Several minutes later, she swiped the electronic pad. "And I see you've already submitted the insurance information with billing and paid the deductible, even. You're way ahead of the game, Ms. Ritter. It looks like all you're waiting on is this release packet." She handed a packet of paper to Cori. "Good luck with everything."

Cori accepted the papers and slipped them into her purse before thanking her.

Luke looped the straps of her bags over his shoulders, and carried the flower arrangements and stuffed bear. He exited to the hallway while Sherrill eased Cori into a wheelchair and placed the baby in her arms. As predicted, by the time the group reached the exit, his parent's car sat waiting for them just outside the sliding electric doors. He pointed to the white Chevy parked in front. "This one."

"What about a car seat for the baby?"

"It's in there. Your mom showed me which one to get online and I picked it up on the way over here. I installed it in the store parking lot."

He stepped into the cold, damp December air and gave the area a once over before opening the rear door.

Luke helped Cori into the back seat of the car while Sherrill buckled the baby into the brand new car seat. She stepped away and waved, wishing them luck.

In under a minute, Luke pulled away from the Hospital entrance's covered awning. He flipped on the wipers to clear the droplets of mist settling over the windshield.

"Is this your car?"

"No, it's my mom's. I figured you'd be more comfortable than in my truck."

"I gave Melissa my car keys. Is my car still parked at the toy store?"

"Roland and Joe picked it up yesterday."

"My car seat is in the trunk. One more thing I put off until the last minute."

Luke chuckled. "Now you have two. You can leave one with Ms. Joan or bring yours back to the store. Consider this one a gift."

"Where's my family?"

"They're all waiting at my mom and dad's place. I hope you don't mind, but the ladies wanted to make sure you got to experience Christmas outside of a hospital room. My folks asked to be a part of it. The plan was for everyone to have lunch at my parents before Charles and Joan brought you and the baby home with them." He checked out her reflection in the mirror. No way in hell would he let that happen now. "I think Roland and Melissa have to go home this evening. I know Joe and Lee do. They all have to work tomorrow."

"What about you? Don't you have to go back to the call center, soon?"

"I'm on vacation, remember?"

"Did you tell me that already? The pain meds mess with my memory."

He grinned. "Don't worry about it."

"How do I do this, Luke? I only brought enough for a couple of days at Mom's. She was supposed to stay with me at my place a few days after the birth. I'm not prepared for any of this."

He caught her reflection in the rearview mirror, worried at the lines of strain on her face. "We have stores here, Cori. Anything you need, we'll get for you. We'll make it work, I promise." He looked again, caught her wiping tears from her eyes. "Try not to worry."

She sniffed and used the back of her sleeve to wipe her face. "I'm just depressed about the way things have turned out, that's all."

"I think that's natural. Mom calls it the 'baby blues' but there's a scientific explanation for it. Your hormones are kind of wacky right now, but they should level off in a week or so." He thought about her situation. "I'm sure you'd planned to stay awake and experience your delivery."

She nodded and sniffled again. "Melissa was supposed to be with me in the delivery room. I remember blood, lots of blood, and then everything went black. I woke up in the hospital with a baby. A single, longshot chance to have a child and I missed everything."

"All that means is that you'll appreciate your next child's birth even more."

"Next child? It's a miracle I got pregnant in the first place. I doubt it'll happen again. Besides, I need a man for that, and my chances narrowed with the birth of my son. There aren't many men out there willing to raise another man's child."

He flipped the turn indicator and took the four-lane leading to his parent's place, taking note of the black SUV with tinted windows two cars behind them. It turned also, remained the same distance behind them. "My dad didn't have a problem with it."

"I know you were adopted but there's a difference. Your parents both adopted you, chose you. It's more complicated because he's my son. It's like the new male lion taking charge of the pride. They don't want anything to do with the previous male lion's cubs."

"Cori…"

"Well, it's true." She wiped at tears that fell too fast to be controlled.

He stopped himself short of calling her silly. No way would that fly in her frame of mind. "This may come as a surprise to you, but some of us men have evolved. We're quite civilized now, even more than lions."

Their gazes clashed in the rearview mirror, her eyes narrowed to angry slits. "Don't make fun of me!"

"I'm not." He wanted to kick his own ass at the way her face crumbled.

"Yes, you are."

"I'm not, but I do think you're worrying needlessly." He turned onto the street, approached the brick entryway with the name of his parents' subdivision on display. He applied his brakes at the second street and waited, relieved when the SUV didn't turn in behind them.

"Says you."

He had to laugh at her pitiful comeback. "That's

right. You need to trust me on that hormone thing, because it'll pass. Now dry those tears. We'll be home in a few minutes and between your family and mine, you are in for a world of pampering for the rest of the day."

She sobered for a moment before seeking out his gaze in the rearview. "Is all your mom's cooking as awesome as those sticky buns?"

He grinned at her reflection in the mirror. "Yeah, it is. I bet you're hungry for something other than hospital food, right?"

"The food wasn't bad, it just wasn't what I craved. Right now I'm craving more sticky buns."

"If she's out, I'm sure she'll be glad to make another batch just for you." He checked the mirror again. At least that brought a smile to her face.

As it happened, their families had been too busy preparing a lavish post-baby/post-Christmas homecoming celebration to watch the news. After another tearful meltdown from Cori, and appropriate fawning over her and her baby boy, Luke sat everyone down to explain the situation.

Charles pulled his chair back, concern for his daughter's welfare etched in the worry lines on his face. "What do we do about this? Have you heard from any law enforcement agencies?"

"No." He threw a hopeful glance in his father's direction. "I was hoping dad could pull a few strings and get us some much needed info?"

Arthur grabbed the phone. "I'll call the department right now to see what's going on and what they can do."

Joan cradled her new grandson protectively in her

arms. "How difficult will it be for that monster to find Cori now that he knows her name, and where she lives?" She clutched the baby tighter. "Things like this aren't supposed to happen to regular ol' people like us."

Melissa gave her mom a one-armed hug. "They do, Mom. Every single day, things like this happen to regular people, just like us—people who don't go out looking for trouble, but just happen to be in the wrong place at the wrong time."

Luke stepped up. "That's right, but most regular ol' people don't happen to have Marine and police vets to look out for them. I don't know if you're aware of it, but Dad happens to have an arsenal at his disposal if we have to scare anyone off."

"And I can assure you, when he's not sleeping in his recliner, he's cleaning his guns, so they should be ready to fire," Dolores added. "You know, we pay good money for a security system we've never had to use. Maybe it's time they earn their keep around here. As soon as Arthur's off the phone I'm going to call them to explain the situation and make sure everything's in working order."

Joan hugged her grandson close. "Well, I admit I've never been one in favor of keeping firearms in a home. But, it's looking better, as long as they're locked up and away from children."

"They're always locked up and I don't even know the combination," Dolores added.

Luke gave Cori's arm a reassuring squeeze. "We've got this covered, don't you worry," he whispered into her ear. His gaze landed on his mother's. "Hey, Mom. Cori wants to know if there are any more sticky buns left."

Dolores headed to the kitchen. "I made a fresh batch this morning; how about one with a cup of coffee, Cori?"

Luke laughed at Cori's reaction. Despite the recent bout with tears, her eyes lit up at the prospect. He walked away and pulled out his phone, shot one quick text out to two different Marine buddies.

—*Need your assistance to protect a lady and her newborn infant from some gangbangers looking to get their butts kicked, or worse. Real scum of the earth type...no lie. Need someone posted outside my folks' home around the clock. Who's in? Glad to reimburse for any expenses incurred throughout operation.*—

The first response was immediate, and from "Cowboy", living in nearby Orange, Texas.

—*If by "posted" you mean hiding so they'll never see what hit them until they're dragging broken limbs and choking on their own teeth, then I'm in. I'm bored as hell with civie life. Sounds like fun to me. Negative on the reimbursement issue. Hell, I should pay you!*—

It took a while longer for "Gator" from Jennings, Louisiana to reply—an entire two minutes.

—*I'm in. Tell the new mom we got her back. I'm assuming it's the looker in the interview with you? A mutual friend of ours sent me the YouTube link. Tex heard about it all the way from his ranch in Blanco, man. Good job, bro. We gonna meet somewhere for recon assignments?*—

Luke scratched at his chin, thinking they couldn't be too careful at this point.

—*That's a negative. I don't want you seen until this is over. I'll send you both my location and coordinates. Check with Cowboy and you two work out a schedule amongst yourselves. We're in my folks' gated subdivision. Get back to me when someone is in position or if I need to find replacements. Status is critical. The scumbag escaped today with help from his gang, no doubt. Assistance needed ASAP.—*

He waited as his mom sat Cori in the most comfortable chair in the living room with a lap tray. She placed a saucer holding a thick caramel-coated bun on one side of the tray, and a steaming cup of coffee on the other.

Cori took a bite and groaned. "Oh, Ms. Dolores, this is heavenly. When things settle down, I definitely want this recipe. That is, as long as you don't mind someone outside of the family getting their hands on it."

"I'm okay with that," Dolores said. "I bet you can do a sight better than this one at your first attempt, too." She thumbed at her son, accusingly.

Cori licked a glob of gooey sweet goodness from her fingertips. "Even if I don't, I won't lay the blame on you or your recipe. I don't expect to get really good at it unless I've had at least a couple of practice runs. I promise I won't stop trying, though. I'll strive for greatness, just like these."

Dolores nudged Joan with her elbow while giving Luke a visual dress-down. "You did a good job with her, Joan. Obviously better than I did with my son, who accused me of purposely screwing up the recipe when his first attempt didn't pan out."

"I was joking." Luke's gaze bounced from his mom, to Cori, then back to his mom. "It was a joke."

Dolores sniffed. "It didn't sound like a joke at the time."

He pulled her close in a one-armed hug, hoping she'd drop the subject. "It was, and I'm sorry if I upset you." Thankfully, she accepted the apology and retreated to the kitchen, followed by Joan. Temporarily relieved, he collapsed into a chair nearest Cori. "I wasn't sure she'd let that one go. It was golden until somebody went and mentioned the *recipe*." Cori's soft snicker had him looking over at her. "Thanks for hanging me out to dry."

"You sound like those old spinster ladies on that TV series, *The Waltons,* and the way they talked about their papa's moonshine recipe. I used to watch it with my grandparents. You probably don't know what I'm talking about."

"Oh, yes, I do. I spent lots of time with my own grandparents growing up, and they lived for that show—well, that and *The Price is Right*. I've always been tempted to make my own moonshine. With my luck I'd probably blow something up, take half the forest with it." He smiled at her sudden burst of laughter, made a face when she winced and placed one hand on her belly. "You okay?"

She took a deep breath and relaxed against the cushion. "Yeah, I am. Thank you, Luke."

He smiled, tipped his head in a slight nod. She certainly seemed better since their arrival here. The presence of family members and newfound friends made all the difference in lifting the new mom's spirit.

Within a few short minutes, the buzz of his phone had him checking to find a reply from Cowboy.

It's a go! None of us can get there until tomorrow. Soon enough?

He frowned, realizing his hope for back-up by that

night had been far-fetched. On the other hand, seeing as Jackson had just broken out that morning, there probably wasn't a rush. If the asshole was going to make a move, he'd probably need time to get organized. He shot back a message saying tomorrow was fine and thanked them both.

"What's that look about?"

He glanced up to find her gaze locked onto him. "It's a message from a friend of mine and you've got nothing to worry about." No use making her think he was overly concerned about her safety, enough to see about organizing an extra security detail. She didn't need any more reasons to freak out.

His dad entered the room and pulled him aside. "The department will have someone here by this evening, Luke. One parked out front and one patrolling."

"Thanks, Pop. I've got my own reinforcements coming in but they won't be here until tomorrow."

Arthur looked from Luke to Cori and back. "Son, is there something going on with you two?"

"Nothing, other than friendship." His sudden urge for more had nothing to do with anything.

"Are you sure? She named her kid after you."

"That was gratefulness, Pop, pure and simple. She said she didn't have a name picked out for him yet. She'd been waiting for a sign, and wanted it to mean something."

Arthur stared at him then gave his head a slow nod. "I think I understand." He slapped him on the shoulder and threw a wink back at him. "Good luck."

"Just friends!" he called out to the man already walking away from him. All he needed was for his Pop to go to Cori with insinuations. She'd run like hell for damn sure.

****

Luke's gaze flicked suspiciously from one pair of eyes to another, until he'd scanned the faces of everyone seated around the table. "Melissa..." Luke dragged out her name in a slow drawl. "Give me your queens."

"Ha!" she cried triumphantly. "Go Fish!"

He growled and reached for the deck, his mouth spreading in a wide grin as he showed them the card he'd pulled from the top. "Picked a queen."

"Dammit!" Roland muttered.

Joe followed with a groan and a less than flattering comment. "I know. He's got more luck than sense."

Luke reached his hand out toward Joe. "Hand over *your* queens, buddy."

Joe threw his pair of queens on the table. "You suck."

Luke placed his four queens on the table, making the fourth of his evenly spaced stacks. "How did I not know you were such a sore loser at cards?"

Lee snorted from her spot across the round dinette set. "At cards, checkers, video games, so called 'friendly' games of pool..."

Joe leaned back in his chair and arranged his cards. "I can't help it if I have a competitive nature."

Lee reached over to place a hand on her husband's knee. "Your competitive nature isn't the problem, sweetness. The issue is you pouting like a big ol' baby when you lose."

"Yeah, bro. You need to man up," Luke added, more than happy to throw a little fuel on the fire to annoy his brother-in-law. The dude hadn't let up on him since he'd arrived with Cori and the baby. It had been a continuous stream of "big daddy" comments and joking insinuations about the end of his manhood.

Joe leaned forward, one elbow resting on the table. "How about we finish this game?"

"Are you that much in a hurry to lose again?"

"Who says I'll lose?" Joe straightened in his chair and lowered his voice to an ominous grumble. "And even if I do, I am not a sore loser."

"You got any sevens, Joe?"

Joe threw a seven of clubs on the table so that it landed face up. Luke fanned his three remaining cards, all sevens, and laid them out next to the club. "I win."

"Dude!" Joe threw his cards on the table and folded his arms across his chest as the other five people in the game howled with laughter.

Cori caught her breath before gasping at a painful hiccup. "Oh, shoot, that hurt!"

"Serves you right for laughing at me," Joe huffed.

Dolores approached him from behind and swatted his head with a rolled up magazine. "Four other people at that table lost besides you, but you're the only one we can hear all the way into the living room belly aching about it. And unless someone cuts a baby out of your lower abdomen and leaves you with a belly full of stitches so you can empathize with her, I'd better not hear you picking on Cori again."

Cori waved off her concern. "It's okay, Ms. Dolores. It'd take a lot more than that to bother me."

"I'm sure it would but I know his mother raised him not to be rude." She tugged gently at Joe's hair. "You hear what I'm saying, Joseph?"

Joe lowered his head, avoiding eye contact with her. "Yes ma'am."

Roland nodded as a chuckle escaped. "Ah, there's nothing quite like being brought to heel by the mom-in-law. It has the same effect as slow-roasting a guy's cojones over an open flame. Been there, definitely done that, and I'm sure I completely deserved it," he added as Joan entered the room.

Joan smiled, obviously having overheard the previous comments. "You have, and you did, but you've been a good boy since then."

"Thank you, ma'am."

Melissa fixed her gaze on her husband. "Okay, Roland, you can stop sucking up now."

"Not as long as it's working, sweetness." He looked up at Joan. "Is it still working?"

Joan lifted her shoulders in a shrug. "I'm not mad at you for anything, so I guess it is."

Melissa walked away with a shake of her head and still grumbling under her breath.

Luke approached Cori after she attempted to hide a huge yawn. "You look like you're done for the day. You ready to hit the bed?" Her reply, a droopy-eyed nod—a good indicator of just how much the day had taken out of her. He helped her from her chair, taking her elbow in one hand and placing his other on the small of her back.

Joan appeared by his side. "You need my help, Cori?"

"No, mom, I just need to get to bed." She paused, glancing at her son, sound asleep in the cradle. "If you could bring him to me when he wakes for his feeding?"

"That shouldn't be for another couple of hours, but

why don't you let me bottle feed him with the milk you pumped earlier today? You'll feel better after a good six to eight hours of sleep."

****

Cori glanced from her mom to her baby, then back to her mom. "I guess so, but only one feeding. If it looks like I'm going to sleep through a second, wake me up."

"I will," Joan promised. "Luke, come get me if she needs me for anything."

"I'll be fine, Mom. I had my shower earlier, and I'm in my gown already. Just relax and visit with everyone for a bit." She continued the slow walk to the back of the house to the guest room where the Oliver family had set her up and made her feel as welcome as any family member.

They entered the room and Luke moved around her to flip back the quilt and sheets on the bed.

"Thanks." She settled herself slowly into the bed, and with his help and a few pillows used for support, found a comfortable position where nothing hurt.

Luke smoothed the quilt and straightened. "Okay. Well, if you need anything—"

"Could you stay for a while?" His mouth spread in a grin that could have passed for relief, if she didn't know better.

"Sure, I'll stay. Want me to read to you or something until you fall asleep?"

"How about if you sit here and tell me everything will be okay, even if you have to stretch the truth?"

He sat on the bed beside her. "I don't have to stretch any truths. It *will* be okay. I'm not going to let anything happen to you, or your son, or your family."

"Tell me the truth, Luke. Do you think he'll come looking for me?"

"I honestly don't know." He cocked his head slightly. "But if he does, he'll find a little more than he or his band of thugs bargained for."

"What do you mean?" He waved his hand to dismiss her, as though that would deter her.

It didn't.

"I know you heard me, Luke. Don't make me call your mother in here."

He frowned, his eyebrows drawn until the skin between them puckered. "Look at you, calling in the big guns already." He tucked the quilt in around her and sat back. "I've called some friends to help. I doubt if we'll need it but just in case, we're covered. Now, that's all I'm going to say, so try to get some sleep." He reached for a book on the nightstand. "What's this?"

"I'm a fan of James Lee Burke's series about the Dave Robicheaux character. Have you read any of them?"

"No, but why does that name sound familiar? Did they make a movie from one of these?"

"Yes." She yawned again and covered her mouth. "Tommy Lee Jones played the main character in a movie called *In the Electric Mist*. They did a pretty good job of bringing his story to the big screen, from what I can remember."

"Yeah, Tommy Lee Jones—I remember now. I liked that movie." He pulled the rocker close to her bed and settled himself in it. "Do you have a page dog-eared already?" He leafed through the book's front matter.

"No. My bookmark is in it, but I haven't had a

chance to start it yet." She huffed. "I would never dog-ear the page of any book."

"Oh." He grinned. "You're one of *those*, are you?"

"If you mean someone who's passionate about never purposely disfiguring a book, I guess I am. Would you?" She asked out of curiosity, even though nothing this man would say could possibly raise or lower her opinion of him at this point.

"Calm down, missy. I've used sections of broken bootlaces, box labels, gum wrappers, or anything I could get my hands on to mark my place in the hundreds of books I've read during my downtime." He lifted the pretty marker covered with inspirational quotes and biblical passages. "These were difficult to come by in the multitude of Afghan provinces I spent most of my time."

Way to prove her wrong. She bit her lip to keep from smiling. Could she be so lucky as to have him read to her?

He sat back and flipped to the first page, beginning to read in a strong, steady voice.

Cori tried to keep her eyes closed, determined to listen to the flow of his words. She failed miserably, called to watch as his perfect lips formed each word that poured forth from his perfectly shaped mouth. After a while, she quit trying to concentrate on the story and just watched his mouth, sucking in her breath at every pause for effect, or swallow, or swipe of his tongue to moisten his lips. God, she'd like to be those lips, if only for a short while. She lost all concept of time as she listened and stared, her breath coming evenly through slightly parted lips.

She jumped as fingers snapped in front of her face.

"Earth to Cori—are you in there?"

She blinked, coming back to the present. "I'm sorry. I must have zoned out for a minute."

"I've been reading for twenty minutes. Have you had enough?"

Had it really been twenty minutes? Her glance at the clock verified his statement. She passed a hand over her face, stopping long enough to rub her eyes. "I think I can fall asleep now. But thanks, and anytime you feel like reading to me, you're welcome to."

His smile lit up her one room world. "Tomorrow evening, same time, same place?"

"I'll tell you what. If you don't find anything better to do with your time by tomorrow, give me a holler, Mr. Oliver. I'll be right here." He stood, laying the book on the nightstand and flexed his shoulders. Cori clamped down on her jaw to keep from asking him to stay.

He walked to the door and turned. "You sure you're okay? You don't need anything?"

"Nope. I'm good. Thanks, Oliver."

One side of his mouth lifted in a half-grin. "Anytime, lady." He touched two fingers to his forehead and backed slowly out of the room. "Anytime at all." One last wink and he was gone, the door pulled closed behind him.

"Holy moly," she groaned, releasing her breath slowly. She picked up the book, saw he'd read to page twenty. She sighed, flipping back to the beginning of chapter one to start reading. It wouldn't be fair to ask him to read any further if she had no idea what in hell was going on, would it?

Cori read until her eyelids grew heavy and she

couldn't hold off any longer. Two pages shy of the bookmarked page she gave it up and closed her eyes. Sleep came quickly, wrapping her in its velvet arms, and blessing her with sweet dreams filled with images of Luke, bare-chested, bronze, and basking on a sandy beach. In the dream, she found herself wishing it was a nude beach, and voila…so it was.

He lay there in a lounge chair, looking like Adonis himself, all sun-kissed golden, completely nude, and extremely well equipped. She'd been watching him from several feet away, had just won the debate with herself over whether or not to approach the Greek god. A few steps away from him, something drew her attention. Some sound that didn't belong on the otherwise deserted tropical beach.

He's right there. Don't look away. As hard as she tried not to, she couldn't resist turning toward the sound. A loud *pop* made her flinch. Something whizzed by her head, so close that her hair moved in the path of air it created. She turned and saw him then, his eyes filled with hatred for her, his hand carrying a black pistol.

Shawn Jackson raised the gun and pointed it at her. "You. It's all your fault."

To her horror he lowered the gun, pointed it directly at her belly, still big and bulging with the life she'd not yet delivered in this nightmare. She wrapped her arms over her abdomen in order to protect her unborn child, her mouth opened wide with a silent scream.

The bedroom door opened, pulling her immediately from the wonderful dream turned awful nightmare. She waited, her eyes squeezed tightly shut, until the edge of her bed sagged with the weight of someone sitting beside her.

"Cori? Are you okay?"

She opened her eyes, and it took a few seconds to adjust to the low visibility, thanks to the room's single nightlight. Finally, he came into focus, wearing flannel lounge pants and a white T-shirt. "How long have I been out?"

Luke brushed the hair from her face and smiled. "A couple of hours. You moaned in your sleep. Are you hurting?"

She took a deep breath, and released it, buying a few seconds. Had she moaned from the earlier beach scene, or cried out from the later episode with the gun? "No, I had a bad dream." She lifted her head at the sound of a muffled cry. "Is the baby crying for his feeding?"

"Your mom's changing his diaper first then was planning to give him his bottle."

She lifted herself on one elbow. "Tell her to bring him to me."

"Are you sure you don't want to go back to sleep?"

"I'm okay. Get him in here." She positioned herself on her right side with a pillow in the crook of her arm.

A minute later, Luke entered, carrying an armful of snorting, snuffling infant. "This kid's carrying on like he's about to starve to death."

"Right now, it's at the top of his 'to do' list for newborns. Eat. Pee. Poop. That's it. That's all he knows how to do. Put him here for me, please." She made a few adjustments after Luke had positioned the baby on the pillow. She draped the blanket over her shoulder so she could bare her breast to her son, and sucked in her breath at his immediate, but somewhat painful latch. "Dang, son, you really were hungry."

With one minor adjustment to his latch, he settled into his meal. She looked up, caught Luke looking the opposite direction and pretending to examine items on the wall. "You can turn around now." How sad was it that it thrilled her because he didn't even ask if he should leave the room anymore?

She closed her eyes, picturing him sprawled out in that dream-conjured beach lounger, wearing trunks one second, and absolutely nothing the next. Had her subconscious mind somehow imagined him larger—more endowed—than he really was? Or was her dreamy guesstimate right on the money? She opened her eyes, discovering he'd pulled the rocker right next to the bed. He sat there, with a half-cocked grin on his face, staring at her.

She grabbed one corner of the blanket covering to keep it from sliding down, never pulling her gaze from his face. "What are you grinning about?"

He shrugged. "Life. Just when I think I have everything all figured out, it throws me something I'd never have expected."

"Like having some strange crazy woman name her kid after you?"

"Among other things."

She didn't dare to hope he'd want to be a part of their lives after this. That would be stupid, wouldn't it? "I wouldn't worry about it too much. You'll be back to your regularly scheduled programming soon enough, chasing some hot beach babes around a tropical island paradise. Hopefully, you'll come home with a pocket full of phone numbers and memories that'll last a lifetime, and not a raging case of the clap—or worse."

He clucked his tongue. "What must you think of me? I was going there to rest and revive, not meet women. My life is hectic enough. I just needed the time away from text books and computer monitors."

"So you traded up by hiding out at your folks with a new mom and her baby, not to mention her entire family. As grateful as I am, I still can't help but feel bad for you."

"Stop it. You're all worth it."

She lifted Little Luke's head with one hand and with a few practiced movements, switched him to the opposite breast before he had a chance to put up a fuss.

"You don't need to burp him in between?" Luke seemed genuinely interested.

"Not on the breast. He doesn't take in any air like he does with a bottle."

"Ah, God's perfect design."

She made a face. "Yeah. Remind me of that when my nipples are raw and my boobs are sagging down to my belly button. Oh…sorry. I forgot who I was talking to for a second, there."

"I don't mind."

"You should. It's not exactly fit conversation with someone who isn't…"

"Isn't what?"

"The other half of a couple, I guess."

"A couple of what?"

"Stop it. You know what I mean. A couple. As in exclusive."

"As in boyfriend and girlfriend?" he said, in perfect imitation of a gawky pre-teen.

She pursed her lips to hide her smile and nodded.

He leaned forward, resting his forearms on his thighs. "Well, who's to say we couldn't be one day? It's not out of the realm of possibility."

"I suppose, but it's well out of the range of probability."

He leaned back in his chair, crossing his arms slowly over his chest. "How about we agree to keep it open for now?"

Rather than shame herself by looking too hopeful, she clamped down on her lips and kept her silence. Minutes later, when Little Luke stopped feeding, she struggled to cover herself while moving him away from her breast. "Could you get my mom for me?"

He stood and approached her. "I'll take him back to Joan for you."

"Thanks," she said, allowing him to take her son.

Luke stood staring at the baby in his arms, rocking gently from side to side. "Maybe you can work on your mom for me, huh kid? Convince her to let me stick around a while?"

Still, she kept her silence. Her life was far from uncomplicated as it was. She had a home to sell in Louisiana, and another to buy in Texas. Eventually, she'd need to find a job here as well. All while raising a child on her own. Relationships could get messy. He could very well break her heart, creating a huge obstacle for her to overcome—one more added complication.

Frankly, she didn't know if she was up to it.

Chapter 15
The Marines Have Landed

December 27th, 11:45 a.m.

Luke's phone pinged. He raised it to check the incoming text from Cowboy.

—*Expect confirmation of placement by 18:45. Have coordinated efforts for maximum protection. Expect zero allowance of any suspicious activity. With your permission, would like to bring in back-up—a friend who happens to be visiting the area, equally bored and eager to kick some gangbanger ass.*—

He responded with an immediate answer.

—*I trust your judgment. Thanks man. Oorah!*—

He slipped his phone in his pocket, his mouth stretched in a tight smile.

Joe nudged his wife. "Look out. He's grinning again."

"I know. It's kinda creepy." Lee looked up from placing the fresh baked rolls in a breadbasket.

Luke swiveled to face Cori, already seated at the dining room table. "Don't listen to her. I have tons of frequent smiler miles built up, whether my sister cares to admit it or not."

Cori looked up at him. "I've only known you a few days but I've seen you smile plenty of times." She jutted her chin toward his phone. "Did you get some good news? Maybe a text from one of your beach bunnies?"

"Hardly. Jealous?"

"Hardly," she returned.

He held up his thumb and forefinger. "Not even a little?"

She shook her head. "I already said you were half nuts for passing up Cozumel to babysit us."

He gave her an exaggerated hang-dog expression then sighed and raised one flexed arm. "Just so you know, this is free for the taking now, but it won't be available forever."

Lee's burst of laughter filled the room. "Does someone need to remind you that the girl just had a baby? And what the heck kind of line is that, anyway?"

He clucked his tongue at his sister. "Honestly, you and mom need to work on your abilities to recognize a joke when you hear one."

"Still—you need to work on that, brother dear."

He leaned in close to whisper in her ear. "Should I schedule a session with your other half for lessons in 'line delivery'?"

Joe's head popped up. "What lessons? Who needs lessons?"

Lee threw a panicked look at Luke before facing her husband. "Babe, I just heard Mom say lunch is ready."

Joe's eyes glazed over in anticipation of pure taste bud delight. He spun on his heels and headed for the dining room.

Lee waited until he'd left before slapping Luke on the arm. "Idiot."

He gave her a playful shove. "Brat."

"Play pretty, you two," Cori insisted. "Don't make me call in the reinforcements—AKA, Ms. Dolores." The siblings capitulated with a pout and a grumble about somebody "...playing hardball". Cori accompanied their comebacks with a headshake and snicker from her spot at the table.

Lunch was a riotous affair, with Little Luke taking center stage as the adults passed him from one eager set of hands to another. Cori was barely able to finish her meal before he started squalling for his. She eased herself onto the sofa, accepted the pillow for her lap from Luke first, and then her baby.

"Here you go. He should be exhausted from being passed around with all this chattering going on during lunch."

She pulled the child close, covered her left breast and his face with a blanket before baring herself to his hungry mouth. In a few short seconds, he'd latched on like a champ.

Luke leaned back on one heel and met her gaze. "You want me to go in the other room?" He asked, more often than not, just to be polite...always praying she'd say no. Something about being in the same room while she nursed her son brought him an inner peace he'd never experienced before. He was beginning to crave the feeling, as well as the sight.

"Please stay. I don't care to be alone right now. Being around people makes me feel better." She pointed to the opposite end of the sofa. "Sit."

"Yes, ma'am." He made himself comfortable, separated from her by a good four feet of empty sofa. Not exactly porn, but today, for some reason, the sight, along with the soft baby-suckling sounds, had a somewhat unexpected and semi-erotic effect on him.

Just when he thought he'd corralled his lascivious thoughts, he imagined that Little Luke was *his* son. The thought and subsequent tightening of his groin area had him reaching for one of his mom's many throw pillows to cover his lap. Confident in his coverage, he turned to face her. "So, what were your plans for the rest of the week had you not gone into labor when you did?"

"I'd planned to..." She lowered her gaze and any remaining comment disintegrated into a snort of laughter.

"What?" He looked down, turned his head to read the stitching on the pillow. "Sassy, Classy, and a Bit Smart Assy?" He shook his head. "What the hell, Mom?" He flipped it over as quickly as he could. "You were saying?" She only laughed harder. He looked down again and read the opposite side of the pillow. "Real feminism is the radical notion that women are more than their..." He paused, squinted to make out the stitching, "hoo-hoos?" He looked up. "What the hell is a hoo-hoo?"

Cori shattered, laughing so hard the women ventured in from the dining room to check on her.

"What's going on?" Melissa asked.

He held up the pillow. "What the hell is a hoo-hoo?"

Melissa joined her sister in laughter. Lee managed to hold it down to a chuckle. Head cocked, she grinned at her brother. "Seriously, Luke, do you need to ask?"

"Well, I'm sorry but I've never heard of a hoo-hoo."

Cori snorted again. "Quit saying it!"

"What—"

"Oh for heaven's sake, son! A hoo-hoo's a vagina," Dolores interjected.

"Would you have preferred va-jay-jay?" Melissa asked, sending Cori into another round of tear inducing laughter.

Lee stood there shaking her head at her brother. "What's *wrong* with you that you don't know that?"

He looked at the pillow, threw it across the room before pointing at his mother. "What's wrong with *her* for having that pillow on display?"

"Hey now, that was a Christmas gift from my Secret Pal at the Red Hat Christmas party."

He frowned at her. "What kind of crazy person would give you such a thing?"

Dolores placed her hands on her hips. "Well if I knew that, it wouldn't be a secret, would it, genius?"

Arthur entered the room, harrumphing. "It could have been any one of those gals." He nudged Charles with is elbow. "Those Red Hat ladies are a bunch of twisted sisters, if you ask me."

"Sweet Jesus!" Luke wiped his face. "The other side wasn't much better."

Melissa gasped, trying to catch her breath. "Well, I've gotta see it, now!" She reached for the pillow and laughed as she read it. "Whoever your Secret Pal is, she's got a fabulous sense of humor, Dolores."

Luke stood from the couch. "I think Pop's right. That's a twisted sense of humor if you ask me."

Dolores grabbed her pillow and held it to her chest. "Well, nobody did, and since when are you such a prude?"

Arthur's hearty chuckle rumbled in the air. "That happened when he was still in high school. Lee showed

Luke's girlfriend his naked baby pictures."

Luke groaned. "It took me seventeen years to forget the trauma of that night and here you go dredging it up again."

"Oh stop being so dramatic." Dolores lowered her voice to a whisper. "I heard Maggie Daniels called him teeny weeny for years after that."

Luke waited for the laughter to die out before shaking his head. "You people need help."

"Sounds like you're the one who needs help, big brother—it can't be healthy to be that repressed," Lee said, choking on her laughter.

Luke wrapped his arm playfully around her neck. "I don't see it as repressed, as much as—oh, I don't know—normal?"

Lee chuckled. "Whatever you say...Teeny Weeny."

Cori wiped the tears of laughter from her eyes. "Okay, everybody. Let's stop teasing Luke now. We wouldn't want to embarrass him."

"We wouldn't?" Lee twisted her head so she could grin at her brother.

Luke released his sister and turned on Cori. "It's a little late for that, don't you think?"

"Oh come on, it was all in good fun," she said, choking back another round of laughter.

Luke wiped his face, feeling the heat of embarrassment, knowing he would never live this one down. "Hell, just shoot me now. Those Red Hat ladies have got nothing on you gals." He turned his back on her and the flash of black SUV in his peripheral vision had his senses prickling. He turned to face the living room's picture window, all his senses morphing into full-blown hyper-alert mode. He stared as the SUV came to a near-stop on the street. Time slowed to a crawl when the blacked out glass of its front passenger window began to lower. "Oh shit! Hit the deck everybody! Now!" He threw himself in front of Cori and the baby.

The following shot, sudden and explosive, shattered the picture window's glass.

"Take cover!" He wiped everything from the surface of the heavy square cocktail table, and lifted it, resting it on its edge as a shield. Another shot rang out, jarring the table in his hands. Revving motor and the squeal of tires followed the third shot, prompting a low string of curses from Luke. He swung around to check Cori, hunched over the baby. "Are you hit?"

She looked up, eyes wide with terror.

He released the table, and it dropped to the floor with a clamorous thud. Luke grabbed her shoulders. "Cori, are you shot?"

"No."

He moved the blanket, had to pry her right hand and arm away to check the baby's condition. Little Luke was half-asleep, still latched onto his mother's nipple, still suckling, as though drive by shootings were a common occurrence in his newborn existence, certainly nothing worthy of interrupting his meal-time.

Luke paused a moment, soaking in the flood of relief, before straightening. "Is anyone else hurt?"

"We're okay," Arthur said, after checking Dolores.

"We are, too," Charles added.

Luke assumed the two younger couples were as well, considering how fast they ran out of the room to check on their children.

Melissa came in first, carrying her toddler. "They're fine, still watching cartoons in the spare room."

"Son of a bitch!" Luke pulled out his phone and called his place of employment.

"Nine-one-one. What's your emergency?"

"Is that you, Sadia?"

"Yes. What's your emergency?"

"It's me, Luke Oliver, and we've got a problem here at my parent's place. Dispatch units to 1955 Halsworth Lane in Beaumont. It's the Buxton Estates subdivision. We've just had a drive-by shooting."

"All right Luke, the dispatch is on its way, and I've got one confirmation, make that two confirmations already. That's not exactly drive-by territory."

"You've got that right. I brought Corrine Ritter here after Shawn Jackson's escape. Tell all units to watch for a black Cadillac SUV, late model, with dark tinted windows. I saw it earlier today. I suspect they followed us here from the hospital yesterday. They fired three shots into my parents' living room windows. In other words," he paused to take a deep breath. "This wasn't random."

Within five minutes, two local police officers arrived at the door. Two minutes later, three deputies joined them. Someone from ballistics recovered the remains of three bullets, all hi-point 9 mm's.

Luke had just given the officers in charge the complete story when Cori joined them, looking shaken, though not nearly as terrified as she had every right to be. He pulled her close for a one-armed hug. Having his arm around her felt so good, he transitioned to a full hug, careful to keep it gentle. "Are you hurting?" he whispered. "Is it time for pain medication?"

****

She laid her head on his chest and returned the hug. "It's getting there. I wanted to make sure nobody needed anything else from me before I took something. I'm so burned out right now I could fall asleep at any time."

The deputy shook his head. "No ma'am. We've got everything we need from you."

An investigator with the Beaumont P.D. gave her a grim look. "There's nothing quite like a drive-by shooting to dampen the Christmas spirit, is there?"

She looked up, focused on the gathering of her family alongside Luke's. The beautifully decorated tree took up an entire corner of the living room. The oak logs sizzled and snapped in the wood-burning fireplace, adding to the room's ambiance, its woodsy scent combining with the fresh cut tree for a delectable aroma. She looked at her son, sleeping peacefully in the Oliver family's antique cradle brought down from the attic, dusted off and polished to a shine. The closed drapes hid the already boarded up window. Despite that and the three bullet holes in the wall and cocktail table, this place still felt more like home than her house back in Louisiana. "For some people, maybe."

Luke saw the officers to the door and turned to face her. "They're posting patrolmen, one in the front and another circling the block."

"Will that be enough?"

"They'll have help." He took her hand in his. "Come with me and I'll explain."

She followed him, stopping long enough to take her meds, then continued to her guest bedroom.

"Sit." He pointed to the bed as he shut the door.

She lowered herself gingerly onto the bed, winced when she tried to nudge her shoes from her feet.

He knelt before her and pulled them from her feet before helping her to lie back on the quilt. "Are you cold?" Her nod had him grabbing a knitted afghan from the back of a rocker. He tucked it around her and sat beside her on the bed.

"I've got reinforcements coming in this evening, and they'll be here for however long we need them. I can promise nobody will get a second chance to get to anyone in this house."

She coughed, winced, and grabbed her belly. "Oh Lord, that one hurt."

"You waited too long. Your medication wore off."

"I know, but it couldn't be helped. Tell me about these reinforcements of yours."

His head tilted to one side. "Let's just say the U.S. Marines have landed—or they will at 18:45 this evening. That translates to—"

"Six forty-five, I know military time. Are these Marines friends of yours, or part of some program—kind of a 'Marines in need' type of thing?"

"They're friends, guys I've served with off and on during my twelve years as an active Marine. I know I can always count on 'em, though."

"Once a Marine, always a Marine…Semper Fidelis and all that…" she suggested.

He made a fist. "Oorah." One corner of his mouth lifted in a sexy semi-grin.

Cori returned the grin, finally relaxing as the pain med's initial wave of relief took hold.

"Feel better?"

She released a long, slow breath. "I'm beginning to." She yawned, succumbing to the emotional drain from all the excitement. "Thank you for going the extra mile for us, Luke. I still don't know why you're doing this. We're not your responsibility."

"I don't see you or your son as a responsibility. I see you as blessings."

She stared at him. "It's not necessary to say things like that if you don't mean them. I'm not a child."

He leaned over her, placed his hand on her face. "But I do mean it. And I've been meaning to ask you something."

She yawned again. "What?"

He smiled. "Maybe I should wait until you're more rested."

She grabbed his arm when he started to get up. "Oh, hell no. What did you want to ask me?"

"Two things."

"Mm hmm?"

He leaned over her again, drew his finger in a gentle motion down one side of her face. "When all this is over, and everything is back to normal, could I see you again?"

"As friends?"

"And more if we're feeling it."

"I'd like that. What's the second thing?" She yawned a third time, rubbed her eyes with the palms of her hands. His rumble of laughter reached clear down to her toes.

"I'm definitely saving that one for another day. The shape you're in now, I doubt you'd remember it."

"But I will." She stopped fighting and let her lids drop. "Remember what?" Somewhere in the fogginess of her mind, she heard him laugh, just before sinking into a deep slumber.

Chapter 16
Semper Fidelis

December 27th, 6:45 p.m.

—The US Marines have landed.—

Luke grinned at the incoming text, pleased with the punctuality of his Marine brother. He sent an immediate reply.

—Any issue with the cop parked out front?—

—Negative. He never saw me. Reaper 1 on the lookout.—

—You flying solo?—

—Until 2000 and arrival of Reaper 2.—

—R1 Location?—

—Roaming. On his arrival, R2 will take the rear. I'll take the front. Tell your lady she can sleep easy from here on out. Reinforcements on the way. SOB's gonna regret taking those shots.—

Luke nodded, remembering both Cowboy's and Gator's reactions earlier today when he'd informed them of the drive-by. No further motivation had been necessary.

He got another text a few minutes before 8:00 p.m. saying Reaper 2 was in position, as was Reaper 3, identity unknown to Luke. He made another round of the house again, checking windows to make sure there had been no tampering. Kept checking the landline to make sure the security system was still operational.

Melissa and Roland had gone home with their two children, and Lee and Joe had gone home with Christopher. They'd all considered postponing their returns to work to stay another night, but Luke had shut them down.

"The fewer people we have to worry about protecting, the better. The remainder of us here will all rest easier knowing you're home, safe and sound."

The two sisters had left under protest but their husbands had finally managed to guide them both away with gentle but insistent hands upon their shoulders.

By midnight, the house was quiet, with Luke keeping watch inside. Joan and Charles bunked down in one guest bedroom, with Cori and the baby tucked safely away in the second. The third time Luke cracked open the door to check on her, she called softly to him.

He approached her as she flipped the switch on the bedside lamp. "What's wrong? Do you need something?" She struggled to rise from the bed and he reached forward to help her up.

She crossed both hands over her top. "Ugh...I'm leaking all over the place. It seems my son slept through his feeding."

"What do you need?"

"I'd like to get up and change my pajama top, only I don't have any extras here."

"Hang on. I can help you out with that." He went to the closet, pulled out a long-sleeve, flannel shirt and offered it to her. "Will this do?"

"Perfect." She grabbed the shirt and went into the room's connected bath.

The second the door closed behind her, the baby

started his snuffling and fussing. Luke reached into the blanket-lined cradle and lifted the child. "Hey little man, what's the malfunction here?" Checking the soggy diaper, Luke placed him on the bed and executed a suitable diaper change. By the time Cori exited the bathroom a few minutes later, she looked more comfortable.

"I feel much better." She finished rolling up the too-long sleeves and passed a hand over the soft material. "I adore flannel. I'll have to thank your dad in the morning."

"It's mine, not Dad's, and you're welcome." He pointed to the rocker he'd dragged to the corner of the room away from the window. "Sit and I'll hand him to you. How's your pain level?"

She lowered herself gingerly onto the rocker. "I'm good for now. I may need another one when he's finished. Hand me that pillow first, please."

Cori adjusted the pillow on her lap then positioned the baby. She unbuttoned the top two buttons of the flannel shirt.

Luke turned away, checking the window latch and then stared outside at the street. The police car wasn't out front, but it wasn't an issue, considering the source of his back-up. He spotted the police cruiser heading along the street, its spotlight beam shining between the houses. A good sign they'd taken this situation as seriously as he did.

Cori spoke from her spot in the chair. "It's safe to turn around."

He did. As always, the sight of her holding Little Luke to her breast kicked him into caveman overdrive. *Protect at all costs.* Ensure the two of them would have plenty of time to work out the details of any future relationship. At least she'd agreed to see him afterwards. Did she remember, or had she been too far gone?

"Do you remember our conversation earlier, by any chance?"

Her wide-eyed gaze clashed with his. "What conversation?"

"About seeing each other after this is over?"

"Did we talk about that?"

Disappointment coursed through him, right up until he saw the slightest tell-tale lift of one side of her mouth, a crack in her sober façade. "You remember, don't you?"

She chuckled. "Of course I do. My entire family spent the holidays with you and your family. I think that has something to do with how comfortable I am with you. Not to mention that you did kind of save my life. I figure I owe you something."

"And I'll keep telling you, I'm one member of an entire team. Any one of us at the call center could have taken that call, with the same results."

"I'm talking about lifting that table in front of us to use as a shield."

"Oh…that."

"Yeah, that. I think I should buy your parents a replacement."

"You're joking, right? They're going to use that as a conversation piece for the rest of their lives."

"No. They won't."

His chest rumbled with laughter. "Oh, hell yeah, they will. Anytime the conversation with their guests takes a turn for the boring, mom will move whatever's covering those bullet holes in that three inch thick slab of oak and repeat the story in detail."

The air filled with her light laughter. "I guess so, but wasn't there a second item you wanted to discuss earlier?"

Luke nodded and approached her. "There was." He leaned forward, placing both hands on the arms of the rocker. He lowered his face to hers, the soft suckling of the baby at her breast sounding more and more like the sound of family to him. "Are you sure you'll remember it?"

She swallowed, her gaze lowered to his lips. "Fairly certain."

He cocked his head. "Corinne…"

Her gaze moved to his eyes again. "I'm positive."

He moved slowly, covering her mouth with his, teasing her, then savoring the taste of her lips. Their tongues melded in a hot, sweet connection. He cupped her face with his right hand, his fingers wrapping around the back of her skull to pull her closer. A soft "pop" signaled Little Luke's reluctant release of his mother's nipple. That sound, along with the following frustrated squall jerked Luke back to reality.

Cori smiled, and with no sign of shyness, pulled back the blanket covering her son's head. She made a simple adjustment before placing him back on her nipple.

Luke stared at the sight, entranced at the gentle movement of the infant's mouth and cheeks on his meal source.

"He's amazing, isn't he?"

Her question had him nodding, unwilling to tear his gaze from the sight just yet. "You're both amazing."

"We think you are, too."

He caught her staring at him through tear-filled eyes. "What's wrong?" He reached up, used his thumb to brush an escapee from the corner of her eye.

"Just emotional—these damn hormones—but also thankful." She sniffed, wiped her eyes with the back of her hand. "Even after everything that's happened, I'm so grateful we met."

He kissed her again, and then rested his forehead on hers. "I am too." He reached for his buzzing phone, read the text on his screen, a frown pulling at the corners of his mouth.

"What is it?"

He turned the screen to show her the text.

"Heads up from Reaper 3?" she said. "Who's Reaper 3?"

"Don't know his identity yet, but he's a friend. If my guess is right, he's posted near the subdivision's entrance. That way he can see if anyone suspicious enters, and he can provide back-up. They'll never know what hit 'em." Her face tightened with fear. "Don't worry. We've got this, but I'll need to turn off this lamp. Are you good with just the night light?"

She nodded. "Should we wake the others?"

He shook his head and reached for the lamp's toggle switch. "Naw. Let 'em sleep. If I were to make an educated guess, I'd say this will all be over before these guys even know what's happening to them."

He sent out a text, squatted next to Cori so she could read the results as they came in.

—*How many vehicles?*—

—*Reaper 3: 1 black caddie suv. This is too easy.*—

—*Reaper 2: They saw cruiser, stopped a block*

down. Two exited the caddie. Driver is still inside. Hold on.—

Barely thirty seconds passed before he sent the next text.

—Driver incapacitated, as is vehicle.—

Cori gasped. "That quickly? I never heard a thing."

Luke chuckled. "That's the idea, hon...quick execution with as little noise as possible. Besides, he's a block away."

In less than five minutes, there was a knock at the front door. The same time, a text came through.

—Special delivery. Three gangbangers, two of them trussed up like Christmas turkeys.—

Cori shook her head as Luke chuckled. "Already?"

"You stay here. I'll go check it out." He walked into the living room, opened the door a crack, and threw it open.

Cowboy stepped forward, dressed in black and his face painted the same. He pointed to two men on the ground behind him, all tied up. "What'd I tell you? Trussed up like Christmas turkeys."

Luke leaned over the two men. "Where were they when you caught them?"

Cowboy touched one of the men. "This one tried to get into your phone box, I assume to cut the wires and disable the alarm system." He pointed to the second. "And Gator caught this gentleman circling around the south side of the house, attempting to gain entrance to the garage."

Luke turned on the porch light to illuminate the captive's faces. "Where's the third?"

"Right here." A big man walked up, pushing a third captive in front of him. "How ya doing, Luke?"

Luke grinned. "Glad you could make it to the party, Tex." He removed the gag from the man's face and frowned. "Great work, guys. Only problem is, none of these guys are Jackson."

"Luke?"

He turned at the sound of Cori's voice behind him. "Hey, hon. I need you to get back in the room until I know it's safe, please." His heart froze at the all too familiar rev of engine and sickening squeal of tires. He barely had time to throw himself in front of her before the blast of a weapon exploded from the street.

****

Cori froze as Luke threw himself in front of her. The instant after the gun blast, his eyes widened and he fell forward onto the floor. Her scream pierced the air, overriding the crash on the street, the grind of metal on pavement, and imploding windshields.

She stood over him, panting and praying for some sign of life.

He rolled over onto his back, and stared at her. "Shit!"

A huge man, dressed in dark clothes, his face painted black, stepped forward. "Are you hit, man?"

"I don't think so. I tripped over something." He sat up, reached for the same 'hoo-hoo' throw pillow from earlier. "This!" he growled. "I hate this damn pillow."

She covered her face with both hands. "Oh God. I thought they shot you!"

He snorted. "Not one of my more graceful moments, I admit, but no." He reached for the man's arm to pull himself up. "Thanks Tex. What was that shot we heard?"

A third 'man in black' approached. "A cop shot a

tire out from under the caddie, man. It hit something and flipped, end over end."

"Gator! Glad you could join the party, man." Luke shook his hand. "We should go check it out."

Cori grabbed at his hand when he took a step toward the door. "Please don't go!"

He turned to her, just then seemed to notice how upset she was. "I'm fine."

"I know, but just for a few seconds, I thought you weren't fine. I thought you were…" She dissolved into a puddle of messy tears. She felt his arms go around her and he hugged her tight.

"We're both okay, Cori. Where's the baby?"

She sniffed. "He's asleep in the cradle." A touch to her shoulder made her turn to see their parents standing in the hallway, their faces masked with stunned horror.

Her dad pointed to the doorway. "What the hell happened out there?"

"A cop shot a tire out and it flipped," Luke said.

"Is that Jackson inside the car?"

"If it's not him it's one of his buddies."

A female officer approached the house, a tall, middle-aged woman with strawberry blonde hair and freckles. "Who's responsible for this?" She pointed to the bound and gagged men on the porch.

Luke pointed to the three Marines. "That would be these gentlemen, right here—all friends of mine. I'm Luke Oliver, and my parents are the owners of this home." He looked at her again. "Who shot the tire out from under that SUV?"

"That would be me," she said.

"What kind of condition are the occupants in?"

"The kind you don't recuperate from." She made a

face. "Looks like the gun went off when it flipped. From what I can tell, that's what took out the driver. The other one's neck is broken."

Cori pulled away from her mother and stepped forward. "Is one of those men Shawn Jackson?"

The cop nodded. "Yes, ma'am, it is. I'd just come around the side of the house on foot when they sped up. Jackson's window was down and he had a gun aimed at this place, no doubt trying to finish what he started earlier today. So I shot at his tire." She offered her hand to Cori. "I'm Officer Margaret Viator, ma'am. Deputy Shemar Davis and his wife, Simone, are good friends of my husband's and mine. I volunteered for this watch out of sheer gratitude. I'm convinced if you hadn't been in that toy store on Christmas Eve, things would have gone much worse."

Cori shook the woman's hand. She stared from her to the wreckage in the street. "I think we're even, Officer Viator. Thank you."

****

By the time the last vehicle left, the sun threatened to crest in the eastern sky. Cori stood over Little Luke's cradle, dead on her feet and hurting. As though he'd read her mind, Luke walked in, carrying a glass of water and her meds.

"Take this, and then you've gotta get some rest."

She gave her son's freshly diapered bottom a couple of more pats and placed him in the cradle. "He's got a full belly, so I'm hoping he'll be down for a while." She straightened and winced. "Thank you." She swallowed the pill and half the water. "Sleep sounds so good, but you know what would make it better?"

He reached out to brush a lock of hair away from

her face. "What's that?"

"You, next to me in this bed."

"If that's what you want." He helped her out of her robe and into bed before walking around to climb in from the other side. He'd just showered and changed into a pair of comfortable flannel bottoms and a T-shirt. "I could use a nap, myself."

When it looked like he'd stay on his side of the bed, she grabbed his arm and urged him closer. "I want you here, not way over there."

"Yes, ma'am. Remember, I left the door open so no funny business. I'd hate to have Charles pull a shotgun on me."

She adjusted her position, winced with the effort. "I can assure you that nothing could be farther from my mind right now than funny business. Besides, I'm exhausted." She yawned.

He inched closer to her and reached his arm around her shoulders.

She laid her head on his chest, releasing a long, satisfied sigh. "Mm, this feels good."

He adjusted his hold on her until they were both comfortable. "I could sure as hell get used to this."

Cori splayed the fingers of her left hand over Luke's belly. She started to speak, but stopped herself.

He kissed the top of her head. "What is it?"

"I'm just wondering if it's really over."

"I'm thinking the bad part is. But something tells me the really good stuff is just beginning."

Chapter 17
Will She or Won't She?

May 24th

"Luke, I've got something!"

"You need any help reeling it in?"

Cori jerked back on the rod to make sure the fish was good and hooked. "Nope. I have him. Just have the net ready to bring this big boy home." She grinned at Luke. "Looks like you'll be cleaning today's catch after all, plus cooking this one for our supper."

Luke quirked his right brow curiously. "You think it can beat my small-mouth four-pounder?"

She gauged the strong pull of the line and chuckled. "I sure do." After a few more minutes of struggling, she finally got the fish near enough to the bank for Luke to scoop him up with the net. "What do you think?" Luke was still hunched over what she knew would be the biggest catch of the day.

"I think he's a keeper!" He stood and faced her, his grin stretching from ear to ear. He lifted the stringer of still living fish from the water and compared the latest to his first catch of the day, the one she'd been trying to beat since this morning. He held them side by side, pooching out his lower lip. "Damn—I think you're right."

She nodded, satisfied that her fish surpassed his by

a good three inches with an obvious advantage in weight. "Heck yeah! No fish guts for me tonight." She looked at her watch. "Unless you want to keep trying? We still have fifteen minutes left to the end of our bet deadline."

"Nah. I'm good. I'm man enough to admit when I've been bested." He raised the winning fish and kissed its belly before turning to give Cori a kiss. "Now it's your turn."

She shoved her hands against his chest. "Ew! Not until you wash that mouth."

"Oh come on, Cori. I kiss you after eating sushi…what's the difference?"

"The shrimp in my Super Crunch Roll is not raw." She pointed to the fish. "Kissing that thing is a deal breaker."

"I think you should kiss the fish, too. Then we'll both have fish lips."

She rested both hands on her hips. "Have you lost your mind?"

He dropped the stringer in the cooler and spun around still holding her fish. "It makes all the sense in the world, babe. Look how cute he is. Don't you want to kiss him?"

Cori lifted one finger. "Luke Harrison Oliver, don't you come near me with that thing."

Luke inserted his fingers into the mouth of the fish and spoke in what he must have thought sounded like an acceptable imitation of a bass. "Kiss me Cori! I love you! Kiiiisss meeee!"

"You are certifiable, you know that?" She started to slap his hand away but stopped when something inside the gaping fish mouth caught her eye. "What the…Wait a minute. That fish has something in its mouth."

Luke grinned. "I'm sure it's just his tiny little fish teeth."

"No, look."

"I already kissed him so it wouldn't feel right. You look."

"Oh, that's just ridiculous! Open his mouth wider so I can see."

Luke pried the still wiggling fish mouth open a little wider. "Is this wide enough?"

She curled her forefinger into the cavity and scooped out a spherical object made of clear plastic.

He leaned forward to peer at the object. "What is that?"

"It's one of those plastic capsule things you get in gumball machines. You know; the ones with prizes in them."

"Or in Cracker Jacks before they stopped giving them out. What's inside?"

"It looks like a ring." She popped the small plastic ball open and dumped its contents into the palm of her hand. "It's just one of those cheap plastic rings." She clutched the ring and reared back to throw it into the lake.

"No! Don't!"

She pitched the object as far as she could, heard it land with a *plunk* into the water. Luke's groan had her spinning around to face him. "What's the matter? You look awfully pale."

"That was…" He paused, swallowed, paled even more.

"That was what?" she asked.

"N-n-nothing. Never mind." He turned away from her, his shoulders slumped, his posture utterly defeated.

"Hey Luke!"

"What..." He sounded as though he'd just discovered he'd washed the winning lottery ticket in a heavy duty cycle of laundry.

"It's not too bad for a gumball machine ring, is it?" He stopped, turned slowly to face her. She held out her hand, palm up, with the diamond solitaire sitting in the center of it. "Gotcha."

Luke fell to his knees, one hand clutched to his chest, his face awash with relief. "Hell's bells, woman!"

She grinned and tapped her sandaled foot impatiently. "You got something to say to me, Mr. Oliver?"

He wiped the sweat from his forehead, an unusually plentiful amount of it, especially since the temperature had barely cleared eighty degrees that day. "Yes, and I will—just as soon as the nausea passes."

"Serves you right for making me stick my hand in that stinky old fish mouth."

"It was only the tip of one finger."

"Semantics."

He shook his head. "I almost had a heart attack when I heard it hit the water."

"But you didn't say anything."

"I didn't want you to feel bad. I figured I'd just buy you another ring and try it again. Definitely would have come up with a different scenario; something not so prone to disastrous consequences."

She smiled. "And that's why I love you so much. You're such a nice guy."

He reached up and took the ring from her hand. "But it would have been a smaller diamond," he added. "A much, *much* smaller diamond."

Cori smiled and crossed her arms, waiting.

Luke cleared his throat, planted one foot on the lake's bank while keeping his opposite knee down. He lifted the ring and met her gaze. "Corinne, you threw my world into a tailspin from the first moment I heard your voice. I didn't know why at the time, but something told me we were destined to meet. Once we did, I knew I wanted to be a part of your life. Since then, you and Little Luke have become my world. I love you, Cori, and I want to spend the rest of my life proving that no one will ever love you or take care of you and your son, the way I can. Will you marry me?"

"Aw Luke, that was so beautiful. Now I feel bad for making you think I threw the ring in the lake."

"As you damned well should. Did I hear an answer?"

"Of course I will."

He slipped the ring into place on her left hand and stared at it a moment before placing a soft kiss on her finger. Luke stood, taking hold of both her hands. "I hope you know how much I love you."

"I certainly do, and I love you right back." Cori slipped her right hand around his neck and edged him closer for a kiss. Several seconds of melded tongues and whisper soft kisses later, he pulled back and grinned at her.

"You kissed lips that kissed a fish."

"And I'm still alive. More importantly, you're still alive," she said, giving him a wink. "Let's go back to the cabin now, please."

"That sounds good to me." He added the latest fish to the stringer and put them back into a small Styrofoam cooler filled with lake water, as Cori gathered the rest of their fishing gear. She clutched the rods in one hand while he grabbed the cooler and draped his opposite arm around her shoulder. "I was about to give up on this plan, you know. None of the previous fish had mouths big enough to hold that plastic container. I was so damn happy when you finally hauled in that big boy."

She chuckled, pulling him closer with the arm she had wrapped around his waist. "What was the back-up plan?"

"I would have had to take the ring from the plastic bubble and put it in one of the fish to have you find it while you were cleaning them."

She made a face. "You really would have made me gut those fish?"

"Just the one…it was vital to my plan."

"A flawed plan."

"Slightly, but it's a moot point since you upped your game and brought in the winner."

She carried the fishing rods up the stairs and held the door open so Luke could carry the cooler inside. "I love this place."

"Me too," he said. "It's got a beautiful view, and primo fishing. What more could you ask for?"

"What can we do to thank Tex for letting us have it for the weekend?"

"That's taken care of already. He called dibs as Best Man for the wedding."

"Did he know you were planning this?"

"Yeah. I'd told him. And asking him to be Best

Man isn't a stretch. I'd been wondering how to choose between him, Gator, and Cowboy. He pretty much eliminated the stress factor for me."

She leaned the rods against one wall of the screened-in porch and kicked off her shoes just outside the door. Cori entered the cabin Tex had practically rebuilt from floor to ceiling, adding modern amenities while still managing to keep the feel of its rustic beginnings. Its interior purred coziness, even as huge windows provided panoramic views of the lake nestled into the beauty of Texas hill country. Decorated in masculine but comfy leather furniture and accented by handmade, rustic looking end tables, the open living area boasted a huge flat screen mounted high on the wall for perfect viewing from every corner of the room. Built on piers to elevate the place far out of the occasional flood range of the nearby Blanco River, she could well appreciate the care the previous owner had taken in the camp's original construction.

"Tex was lucky to have found this place when he did."

"It's all part of the cattle ranch he purchased last year. The previous owners only used this as a fishing cabin once they built their permanent home."

"Is that the one just inside the main gate? It doesn't look lived in."

"It's part of the ranch also, but Tex told the previous owners, an old couple, they could stay in the house as long as they wanted to. I think they moved to a retirement village after the old man got sick last month. Tex could move into the main house if he wanted, but he says it's too big just for him. He says this place is more his style."

She leaned against the counter to get a better look at him. "Except that there's no wifi signal at all and the cell phone service is sketchy at best. But, it is beautiful out here."

"It is. I guess we're lucky to know Tex as well as we do, aren't we?"

"We are. Where'd he go this weekend anyway, so that we could play house in his primitive bachelor pad?"

"He went to Louisiana. He gave me some kind of cryptic message about bad choices and lost chances, and putting things right for a change."

"Ooh, sounds like he's got a girl on his mind. Anyone specific?"

"I've only ever heard him mention one name. I think it was a Riki...no...Niki...somebody. I can't remember her last name. He called her his one regret. I hope he uses this weekend to straighten things out. He's a good guy."

"I don't know him as well as you do, but he seems to be." Cori faced the deep farmhouse-style sink to wash her hands. As an afterthought, she wet a paper towel and wiped her mouth. She approached Luke, giving him a sexy grin.

He leaned in, obviously thinking she wanted a kiss. She took the opportunity to scrub the fish from his lips.

"Gah! You totally psyched me out with that move—and here I was, thinking you found me so irresistible you didn't mind getting sloppy seconds from a fish belly."

She brushed her fingers along his inner thigh. "I do find you irresistible, so much so that rather than have you cleaning fish for an hour, I'm kinda hoping you give those guys a reprieve and throw them all back in the lake to live another day."

He swallowed. "And why would I want to do that?"

She started a slow unbuttoning of her shirt and turned away from him. "I'm feeling the need to shower, and…I don't know…I was kind of hoping you'd join me?" She walked to the hall entrance and turned to face him, delighting in the slow burn of his heated gaze.

"Does this mean…you…we…" He swallowed, his voice failing him.

"I'm thinking a consummation of our engagement is in order—unless you want to wait until the wedding night?"

Luke was out the door in two seconds flat, foam cooler in hand.

"I'll be in the shower!" she called after him, to no answer. She ran to the bathroom and flipped the taps to the newly renovated shower. In seconds, she was out of her clothes and under the spray, lathering herself with her favorite perfumed body wash she'd brought from home, hoping to rid herself of all traces of eau de fish.

"I'm back, Cori. You still okay with—"

"Come on in, Oliver. The water's just right." Her patience wore thin as he seemed to take his time undressing. Finally, the door slid open, reaffirming her belief that some things were indeed worth the wait. An appreciative sigh slipped from her mouth before she could stop it. For a moment, she lost all speech capabilities at the sight of him, all six foot one inch of him, gloriously naked and—she lowered her gaze to below his waist. "Oh…" She grinned and licked her lips at the full-on erection. "Hello there. I've been waiting a long, *long* time to meet *you*."

"Hey!" He snapped his fingers in front of her face to get her attention. "My eyes are up *here*, lady."

Her laughter echoed in the tiled shower stall as she reached out for him while meeting his amused gaze. "I'd apologize, but I totally meant to ogle and objectify you sexually."

He answered with a deep chuckle as he allowed her to use his hardened appendage as a pull handle. "The woman has no shame."

"Not where you're concerned," she admitted. "I'm sorry if you got impatient with me making you wait. I didn't want to bring any leftover baggage from my previous relationship. I wanted to make sure it was only about us." She lifted to her tip toes to kiss him once. *My body and mind have both fully healed from past physical trauma.* "I'm ready for phase two, if you are." She smiled when his rock hard member pulsed in her hand. "Is that an affirmative?"

He pushed her back against the wall. "Hell, I was just waiting on you."

"Yet you never pressured me. Another reason I love you so much." She closed her eyes as his hands cupped her breasts, released a low groan when the pads of his thumbs circled her nipples.

He nipped at her earlobe. "You wash my…back…and I'll wash yours," he whispered.

She smiled at his implication. "With pleasure—lots and lots of pleasure."

He turned, baring his back to her. "Me first."

She filled her cloth with his men's body wash and within seconds, had him lathered up, her fingers slick with the rich, silky foam. "Mm…this stuff smells delicious." She ran her fingers over his corded back muscles, delighting in the shiver that ran through his rock-hard torso. He turned slowly to face her, groaning as her fingers and hands continued their journey over his body. She cupped his pectorals, rubbing the palms of her hands in slow circles over the smooth skin, marred only by the dusting of silky dark hair.

"I'm so glad you don't wax your chest hair," she murmured. "I could never trust a man who spent more time shaving or waxing his body than I do."

"That's good to know because I've sure as hell got better things to do with my time." He sucked in his breath as her fingers skimmed his belly, then lower to his upper thighs. "Ah, Cori?"

"Uh huh?" Eyes lowered, she was just debating whether or not to dip farther south when he took a step back.

"Don't go there, or this will be over before it's started." He reached out to spin her gently around. "Your turn, now."

Her eyelids fluttered closed as his large hands caressed her shoulders, her back, her butt, and down the backs of both legs. When he slipped his hands between her thighs she bit her bottom lip to keep the groan building low in her throat from escaping. He stepped closer, pressing his hardness against her lower back. Her phone rang, vibrating against the tiles of the bathroom counter.

He leaned forward to murmur in her ear. "You want to get that?"

"Whoever it is, I'll call them back later." It rang several times and finally stopped, only to start back up a few seconds later. She ignored it again, but a third round of ringing had her turning to stare at the phone. "Something tells me that's not a good sign."

"I agree. Hang on and I'll get it for you." She shut off the water and reached for the phone when he handed it to her. "It's your mom."

"Oh, crap, this can't be good." Cori answered with a swipe of her finger and put the phone to her ear. "Hey Mom, what's wrong?" Her mouth went dry as she met Luke's gaze and listened to her mother's frantic explanation for the call. She opened the shower door and reached for the nearby towel. "We'll be there as soon as possible."

Chapter 18

One More Emergency

Luke drove like a bat out of hell to shave forty-five minutes off of a three hour drive. He credited making the entire trip without incident to a combination of Cori's prayers and a splash of good luck. He pushed open the door of the pediatric ICU waiting room and let Cori enter first. She headed straight for her mother and sister, both seated next to each other on one end of a long couch.

"Mom!" Joan and Melissa both rose from the couch to hug her. "How is he? I want to see him. Who do we speak to in order to see him?"

Melissa led the two of them to the nurse's station at the center of the corridor. She got the attention of a tall, dark-haired man wearing a white lab coat.

The man stepped around the desk. "Are these your nephew's parents?"

There was no hesitation in Cori's adamant comeback. "Yes, we are."

"I'm Doctor Williams, your son's physician. Come with me, please."

They entered a room with a crib, the mattress raised for easier access to the infant inside. Cori approached the crib, reached out a shaking hand, appalled at the array of tubes and wires attached to her baby boy. She caressed his cheek, took his tiny hand in hers. "He's so still. Will he be okay?"

Dr. Williams checked the fluids attached to the infant by an intravenous drip. "He was a very sick little boy when the ambulance brought him in. Are the grandparents who came in with him your parents?"

Cori nodded. "Yes, they are. My mom told me this came on so quickly. She checked on him in his crib and he was wheezing and turning blue."

"Some infants don't show the signs until they're really ill. You'd taken him to his primary pediatrician for the sniffles only two days ago, correct?"

"Yes, I did, and Dr. Babineaux said he just had a common cold. I *never* would have left him if I'd thought it was anything more serious."

The doctor gave her shoulder a comforting pat. "That's probably all it was at the time. You can't always detect bronchiolitis. That's when the bronchial passages in the lungs narrow, blocking off the normal supply of oxygen to the lungs. Lots of things can bring it on, and sometimes the symptoms appear quite suddenly. Your parents did the right thing by calling 911 as quickly as they did."

Cori was a mess by this time. Her face streaked with tears, her nose running, and her chin quivering with emotion. "Will there be..." She stopped, swallowed hard but failed at holding back a sob.

Luke stepped forward and placed his arm around her waist. "I think she wants to know if our son was deprived of oxygen long enough to cause any permanent complications."

Dr. Williams grew somber, obviously trying not to give too much away. "Honestly, I can't be one hundred percent positive until he wakes up. It's true he was hypoxic when he came in, but once we got him on oxygen, the cyanosis—that blue-tinged skin—disappeared. He was slightly dehydrated, but after connecting him to an IV drip for fluids, he stabilized immediately. The good news is he tested negative for Respiratory Syncytial Virus antibodies in his blood—you may have heard it called RSV, for short."

"Then how did he get this? What causes bronchiol—whatever this is?" Luke asked.

"Bronchiolitis—and it's usually found in infants during the winter months. Neither of you smoke, right?"

"No. Never," Luke answered for both of them. "Is this contagious?"

"Yes it is. If he was anywhere near another infant who exhibited cold symptoms recently, he could have contracted it that way."

"He goes to a daycare once or twice a week," Luke said.

"That's probably where he caught it. You should let the proprietor of the facility know about this, so they can take proper precautions."

"Great…" Cori shook her head.

Luke took hold of her arms and gently turned her until she faced him. "I know what you're doing, and you need to stop. You are not to blame for this. This is nothing you could have prevented."

She shrugged out of his grasp. "Uh, yeah, it is. I could have not brought my son to *Mommie's Day Off* for a half-day, twice a week to run errands. I was selfish, and now look at him."

Doctor Williams stepped forward. "He could just

as easily come into contact with this if you'd been carting him around with you to grocery stores, malls, the post office—more likely, in fact. No one is to blame here."

"But, he looks so pitiful."

Luke caught the doctor's gaze, silently pleading for assistance. It worked.

"The fact is infants are exhausted easily when they've had to struggle for breath. He's been sleeping since he's been under our care."

"Is it just sleep, or is he…" Cori covered her mouth to stifle another sob.

The physician at last gave her a reassuring smile. "Oh, he's not comatose, if that's what you're worried about. Your son is only sleeping very hard. I promise."

Luke pulled her close for a hug. "He's a strong little boy and he's gonna be fine, sweetie. You'll see."

****

Cori stepped toward the bed and reached for her son again. She ran her hands down the child's leg, and cupped his feet in both hands. She pressed the pads of her thumb lightly on the bottom of Little Luke's foot—an action that usually had him pulling away from her in a ticklish fit of belly laughter, or at least eliciting an adorable grin. Now, he remained in a deep sleep. "Wake up, baby boy. Please wake up."

Luke leaned in close to whisper soft encouragements into her ear. "He will, hon, when he's good and rested."

"I want him to wake up now."

"Sleep heals, mom. Try to remember that," Dr. Williams murmured. "The human body performs miraculous feats of healing every day of our lives, replenishing antibodies, renewing cell growth, and other things you had no idea were going on inside each and every one of us."

Cori nodded and wiped her eyes. "I know, but I still can't help but wish I hadn't left him."

"As quickly as these symptoms appeared, no matter who your son had been with, the outcome would have been the same," Dr. Williams said.

Luke squeezed her shoulder. "So stop blaming yourself."

Cori fought the nearly irresistible urge to shake off Luke's touch, no matter how well-meaning. "I can't think about that until my baby boy wakes up." She leaned over the crib to place a kiss on her son's forehead. A single message looped continuously through her mind. *I should have been here.*

She straightened, and faced the doctor. "How much longer do you think he'll sleep?" Her jaw clenched when the man lifted one shoulder, a non-committal gesture that had anything but a reassuring effect on Cori.

"He's been sleeping soundly for a couple of hours already. If I were to take an educated guess I'd say he could be like this for several more hours."

"Is that the best you can do?"

"Cori…"

She crossed her arms tightly against her chest, choosing to ignore the disapproving tone of Luke's comment. "Well, I'm sorry, but I wasn't aware that the colleges of pediatric medicine specialized in educated guesses." Something about the way Luke lowered his head, bringing his hand up to cover his mouth, had her regretting her words. She turned, stiff-backed and faced the doctor. "I'm sorry, Dr. Williams. It's just that…"

"You're terrified seeing your baby that way, and it's understandable." The doctor's reply exuded sympathetic acceptance.

Thankful he didn't hold her rudeness against her, Cori couldn't manage anything more than a nod.

"Listen, your son is breathing easier and he's resting now. Give him a few more hours to sleep before driving yourself crazy, okay? Everything looks good. I really believe he'll be fine."

Cori accepted the tissues Luke handed her. "Can I stay in this room with him?"

"Of course you can. We ask not to have more than two people at a time back here, please."

Luke nodded his thanks before the doctor left them alone.

Cori walked into Luke's embrace. "I'm so sorry if I embarrassed you."

He hugged her tightly. "I was more shocked than embarrassed, but it's totally understandable. Now, do you want me to go out there and update your family?"

"I'm pretty sure they've heard it already. I just want to stand here with you for a few minutes and watch over him."

"You've got it." Luke kept one arm around her waist and the two of them faced the crib, and stared at their son. He reached into the crib and folded the baby's tiny hand into his much larger one. "Hey!"

Cori searched his face for clues. "What?"

"Look, he's holding my finger."

Cori's gaze landed on her son's chubby hand clutching Luke's finger. She reached out to grab her son's feet, placing her thumb pads on his soles.

Immediately, he pulled his feet out of her hands. In the next instant, his opposite fist was rubbing at his nose and eyes. A big yawn followed, and then he opened his beautiful eyes. He stared up at her, seeming to study her facial features before turning his gaze upon Luke.

"Hey, little man. Are you back?"

Little Luke answered him with a toothless grin.

Swallowing the lump in her throat, Cori managed to speak. "Did you have a good rest, baby boy?"

The baby turned his gaze back on his mommy, and released a delighted squeal, holding his arms out to her.

"Oh, I want to hold you, sweetie, I just don't know if I can." Cori turned a helpless look in Luke's direction. He ran out of the room, returning seconds later with the doctor.

"Well, look who decided to join us. Just in time to keep your folks from worrying," Dr. Williams said, laughing at his patient's excited kicks. "I tell you what, mom and dad. He seems fine to me, but why don't the two of you step out so I can run a few more tests on him? This shouldn't take longer than ten minutes."

****

Cori entered the waiting room, hand in hand with Luke. Melissa and Joan rose to approach them.

"How is he? Is there any change?" The tightness of Joan's voice matched the worry lining her face.

Cori approached her mother to hug her. "He's fine, Mom. He just woke up, and he's smiling and kicking away, like normal. The doctor thinks he's fine but asked us to give them a few minutes to run some tests."

In seconds, her mom had Cori wrapped up in a tight hug. "Oh, thank God!"

Melissa approached from the side. "I never

doubted it for a minute."

Cori hugged her sister and stepped away to wipe tears of relief from her eyes.

Melissa grabbed at Cori's left hand. "Well, *this* is new."

Her mother's gasp was followed by a rapid-fire sequence of questioning.

"When did this happen?"

"When's the wedding?"

"Have you set a date yet?"

"Am I the maid of honor?"

"How'd he ask you?"

"Were you surprised? I want details, Sis!"

Cori grinned and raised her hand. "It happened not long before we got your phone call, so no, we have not discussed a date." She threw a glance at Melissa. "Or any other details about a wedding, but I think since you're already married, you'd be a *matron* of honor."

Melissa's face scrunched. "But I'm younger than you. Matron makes me sound so *old*. Besides,"—she aimed her next question at Luke—"they don't call married groomsmen anything but groomsmen, do they?"

"Not to my knowledge," he admitted.

Melissa frowned. "See? That's just sexist."

Luke threw up his hands. "Don't blame me! I didn't come up with the terminology."

"It doesn't matter, because I'm not going through all that hoopla. I did it for the first one and look what that got me. I'd really prefer a private ceremony with close family and a handful of friends." She faced Melissa. "Luke's friend, Tex, will be the best man and you, little sister, can call yourself whatever you like, as long as you're standing beside me."

"But this will be Luke's first wedding. He might want a big hoopla!" Joan insisted.

Cori faced her fiancé. "Do you want a big hoopla, Luke?"

He shrugged. "I wouldn't mind a ceremony. Maybe a half-a-hoopla?"

Cori poked his rock hard abs with her finger. "See, now you're just making fun of me, Oliver."

He gave her a sexy half-grin. "A little, but seriously, I'll go along with whatever kind of wedding you want. Small, medium, or half-the-town large…it's all fine with me."

She pulled him off to the side. "You do realize that the size of the wedding is in proportion to the length of time you're willing to wait before saying 'I do' and moving in together."

His eyes narrowed as he seemed to contemplate her words. "I admit I hadn't thought about that."

"Yeah, I figured as much." She looped her arms around his neck and reached up to kiss him gently on the mouth. "So, how long are you willing to wait to start our life together?"

"Hmm…" He nibbled at her lower lip. "This entire incident has made me see that I don't want to spend a second longer away from you and Little Luke than I have to. Can you throw something together between now and next Saturday?"

She caught his face between her two palms and smiled. "No, but I can in one month. Think you can wait that long?"

He grinned. "It'll be rough, but I'm pretty sure I can manage."

Chapter 19
A Little PB & R Never Hurt Anyone

June 22

"I think I'm gonna be sick." Luke took a deep breath, winced, and adjusted his necktie.

Tex slapped him on the back. "You getting cold feet, bro?"

Joe stepped forward. "There's still time. I'll distract everyone while you make a run for it. You know I've objected to this marriage from the beginning."

Luke turned on his brother-in-law. "You have not."

"I admit I kept it to myself, but I realize my mistake now. I should have been more vocal about my opinion. Dude, you had it all. Babes, beaches, fun in the sun, a life of freedom. You know I lived vicariously through your tales of conquering all that big-busted booty."

Luke lowered his voice and looked around to make sure the priest was nowhere near. "You do realize we're in a church, right?"

"I know where we are. I'm just saying. Why would you want to give it all up? Man, you're throwing away all that beautiful freedom for a mortgage, a never-ending honey-do list, and a wife and kid."

"I'm not throwing away anything. I'm trading up."

Joe snickered. "Says you."

"Does my sister know you feel this way?" He took Joe's silence as a distinct no. "Maybe she should be told."

Joe lifted his finger and opened his mouth. He seemed to think better of saying whatever had been on his mind and snapped his mouth shut again. "I adore your sister as much today as the day I married her."

Tex slapped Joe on the back. "Good answer, man. Take it from me, Joe. Being single when your heart is somewhere else is no walk in the park. I only wish I'd got my head out of my…behind…and realized that a little sooner." He shook his head and sighed, his entire persona oozing with a reserved sadness. "Maybe we'd be having a double wedding right now."

Luke rested his hands on Tex's shoulder. "I've just had a revelation. I think a trip to Louisiana is what's called for at this juncture of your life."

Tex shrugged. "Your revelation comes even later than mine, but with the same sad results. I made that trip, but by the time I got to her apartment, she was gone. Her old roommate told me she'd just moved back home with her mom."

Joe gave him a sympathetic nudge. "Just go talk to her at her mom's place, Dude. What's the problem?"

"Her mom lives in St. Louis, Missouri."

"Oh."

"Yeah." Tex shrugged. "I guess she'll always be my 'what if' girl. As in, 'what if I hadn't been such a dumbass and chased her off?'"

Luke placed a hand on his shoulder. "How about 'what if she's the one for you, and you're too stupid to move heaven and earth to get her to see that?'"

"I honestly think it's too late, man."

Luke gave a single grunt before sharing his opinion. "I don't think it's ever too late if you really care about someone. Missouri ain't China, Tex. It's what, twelve or thirteen hours away? That's a half-day and a few tanks of fuel in that gas guzzler of yours. What's a half-day compared to the rest of your life?"

Tex grabbed both sides of his tuxedo jacket's lapel and stared down at his boot-clad feet. "Maybe you're right."

Joe stepped forward. "He is right. I think you should go for it, before you have us all boo-hooing in our cheerios." He tapped his watch. "Now come on, guys. We have a wedding to get through before we can crack open that keg of beer."

Luke grinned at his brother-in-law. "It's truly astounding how you prioritize what's important in life, Joseph. Let's make our way to the front of the church. Everybody got everything we need?" He gave a final pat to the single red rosebud Lee had pinned to his tuxedo earlier. "We have our boutonnieres..." He pulled a folded piece of paper from his pocket. "I have my vows..." He pointed to Tex. "You've got the ring, right?"

Tex raised both hands. "I don't have any ring, yet."

"Oh, that's me!" Joe said. "Lee gave them to me earlier." He tapped his suit's outer pockets, then the inner pockets, then his pant pockets, his smile slowly fading with each unsuccessful search. "They're here somewhere."

Luke gave him an impatient sigh. "Okay Joe, this isn't funny. Give the rings to Tex, please."

"I just had 'em. Hang on..." Joe started searching

the area. "They're here, I swear they are." He glanced up at Tex. "Are you sure I didn't give them to you already?"

Tex crossed his massive arms across his chest. "No, and don't even think about trying to blame this on me."

"No, I just…" Joe started looking on the floor. "The box must have fallen out of my pocket when I took my jacket off earlier." He got on his knees to look under chairs, tables, every item of furniture in the small enclosure on the side of the church's altar. When that search failed he stood, his face a study of serious concern. "Where the heck could it be?"

Luke got up in his face. "Okay Joe, I've had enough of your playing around. I want to see those rings. Now."

When another search of every pocket in his suit proved fruitless, Joe's look of concern took a turn for full-blown panic mode. He pulled out his phone and shot a text to his wife's number, asking if she had the rings. Luke waited with him for an answer, watching over his shoulder. In seconds she called him. He lifted the phone so Luke could hear as well.

"You lost the rings?" she said. "How could you possibly lose them in the fifteen minutes you've had them in your possession? I just gave them to you, and you walked straight over to meet Luke, didn't you?"

"Yes, I came back here. I didn't make any pit stops."

"Then search every cubic inch of that place until you find them. They have to be in there."

"You're right, they are. No worries." Joe shut off his phone and slipped it into his pocket. He turned to find Tex and Luke both glaring at him. "You, uh...you didn't find them by any chance, did you, Tex?"

Tex crossed his arms, chin lowered to his chest, looking formidable. "Does it look like I found them?"

Joe's head sank. "No, man. It doesn't look like you did." He raised his hands and let them fall to his sides, totally defeated. "Luke...I'm sorry, man. I'm so sorry. I don't know what happened to them. I just don't know."

Luke shook his head. "We'll have to go through with the ceremony without the rings. I'll explain to Cori. I'm sure they'll turn up somewhere."

A knock at the door had the three men turning to face the priest.

"Are you gentlemen ready?"

Luke placed a hand on Joe's shoulder and gave Father Pete a nod. "Yes, we are." He leaned closer to Joe. "It's all right. Don't sweat it."

"Don't sweat it? Man, I'm completely sick about this. How can you be so calm?"

Luke shrugged. "I'm marrying the woman of my dreams and adopting a child. Life couldn't be better."

"Well..." Tex drawled. "It could be a little better...if you had wedding rings to commemorate the ceremony."

Joe's face turned from pale to a shade of puce green, and then back to pale.

The three men exited the tiny room and made their way to the front of the church, flanking the altar on one side. Luke couldn't help but feel a little sorry for his brother-in-law. Joe looked more like a nervous groom than a groomsman/keeper of the rings, still fidgeting and checking his pockets.

Luke waited until the two bridesmaids lined up to

make the walk up to meet them before leaning over to touch Joe's arm. "Hey, Joe."

Joe turned his miserable face toward him. "Man, I'm sorry. I'm stumped."

"It's okay, man. Really."

Joe's hand landed on his stomach, as though he was trying not to hurl. "No, it isn't."

"Yeah. It really is. Do you, by any chance, remember that incident at Christmas? You know, that Santa you paid to lay one on me?" The slightest narrowing of Joe's eyes had Luke struggling to keep a straight face. Very slowly, he nodded at Tex, who pulled the rings from his pocket to show Joe he'd had them all along.

Joe's face turned three shades of pale before settling on a nice red blush. "Dude!" he hissed. "Please tell me we're even." He slapped his hand over his heart. "I don't think my ticker can take another scare like that."

Luke reached around to slap Joe lightly on the back. "Don't worry man. *Now* we're even."

Chapter 20
A Fitting End

June 24, Belize, Central America

"Well, hello there, beautiful. Could I interest you in a drink?"

Cori lifted her head from the beach chair, adjusted her sunglasses to peer up at the tall hunk of man before her. "What kind of drink do you have in mind?"

"Oh, something garnished with a juicy slice of pineapple and topped with a little umbrella, maybe— preferably with double shots of coconut rum so you'll lose all your inhibitions." He stared at her over the top of his expensive aviator style shades. "I'm dying to get you into my bed."

She repositioned her sunglasses and let her head fall back against the canvas lounger. "I think my husband may have something to say about that. He's a big guy, too—a real stud—ex-Marine and all. He can kill a man with his bare hands if he has to."

"I've always heard there's no such thing as an ex-Marine."

"I've heard that somewhere before, too. The thing is he wears so many hats these days it sometimes gets difficult to think of him as a tough Marine. He literally saved my life on two separate occasions as a 911 dispatcher. Now, he's a loving husband, an adoring father to our son, a college graduate, and about to start up his own contracting company."

"Wow—all that, huh? The guy sounds whipped, if you ask me."

She sucked in her breath. "Ooh, I wouldn't let him hear you say that if I were you. He gets real testy if anyone questions his manhood."

The man snorted. "I can handle that jerk. Call him over here so I can tell him what an idiot he is for leaving his beautiful wife alone on a beach around a horny stud like me. I still say he's whipped."

She laughed. "Let's ask him, shall we?" She lifted her glasses and looked up at the man. "Hey babe, are you whipped?"

He gave her that sexy as hell one-sided smile again. "Why, yes. Yes, I believe I am, and proud of it, too." He leaned over her chair and gave her a kiss. "Here's your beer, you relentless little ball-buster."

"Whipped and a ball-buster…we're a perfect pair."

"Mmm, a match made in heaven." He settled down in the lounger beside her. "So, what are your plans for the rest of the evening, Mrs. Oliver?"

She sipped her beer and pursed her lips. "Oh, I'm thinking a quick shower first, then a walk over to the dining room for another fabulous meal and a couple of those inhibition destroying drinks you suggested a minute ago. We can do some mingling with the other couples, and maybe a little dirty dancing before heading back to our lovely, private, ocean front cabana for a live video chat with our beautiful little boy. After that I believe I'd like to make love to my new husband all night long." Cori gave him an adoring grin. "How does that sound?"

"It sounds a hell of a lot better than what I would have been doing in Cozumel back in December had I not postponed my reservations."

"But you may have met the woman of your dreams there if you'd kept them. You never know."

"I knew back then I'd made the right decision, and every time I see you and our son, it's confirmed."

She reached over to place a gentle touch to his face. "Good answer."

"You like that?"

"I certainly do." Cori winked at him before allowing him to help her up from her chair.

Hand in hand, they crossed their private stretch of beach to their temporary home away from home provided in the Honeymoon package. Luke pointed at the sun dipping slowly into the Caribbean, painting the sky with fiery reds and golds. "Look at that sunset. Is this place fantastic, or what?"

"It's gorgeous here," she agreed. "I went to Cancun on my senior trip after high school graduation. Belize has that place beat by a thousand times. I love it here." She looped her arm around her husband's waist as they approached the steps to their private cabana painted in a cheery red with bright white trim. "Maybe we could play a little game later tonight."

He frowned. "I think I should warn you. I get easily bored with board games."

She quirked one eyebrow. "Are you up for a little role-playing?"

Luke slapped his hand over his heart. "Did you pack a French maid's costume, by any chance?"

Cori's laughter rang out. "Sorry to disappoint you, but no. I was thinking I could play the part of a woman in serious need of some sexual attention." She stopped on the covered porch, the ever constant ocean breeze whipping at her hair. She swung toward him and looked up, tracing his lips with her index finger. "And you could be a dispatcher at an emergency call center. Think you could get into that?"

Luke tunneled his fingers into her windblown hair and lowered his mouth to her ear. "I could give it a damn good try." He moved his mouth to hover over hers. "Nine." He kissed her. "One." He kissed her again. "One." And one more that had her shivering from head to toe before he pulled back to let her catch her breath. "What's your emergency, beautiful?"

A word about the author…

Lori Leger is an award-winning author of southern-based contemporary women's fiction and romance, both sweet and mildly spicy. She hails from a large family in south Louisiana, where good Cajun cooking, helping your neighbors, and saying "y'all" is as normal as hurricanes, heat, and humidity.

http://lorilegerauthor.com

www.ingramcontent.com/pod-product-compliance
Lightning Source LLC
Chambersburg PA
CBHW070331260626
47160CB00003B/1014